The
Kingdom

By

H.G.Hussein

ISBN:
978-1-78926-372-5

Dedication

First and foremost I want to dedicate this novel to the One who has All-Power over everything. The One who continues to Bless His creation with every heartbeat and every breath, My Lord, Allah, Most High. The One who Blessed us by sending the best and master of creation, His Beloved, the Prophet Muhammed, peace and blessings be upon him, his family and those that continued his teachings after him.

Content

No.	Chapter	Page
1	From the east	1
2	Sleepless nights	4
3	Surprise on the mountain	12
4	Returning stranger	19
5	What lay ahead	32
6	To the Damascus	57
7	Eyes in the dark	65
8	Benghazi	85
9	The White Mountains	96
10	Through the darkness	113
11	Chief Akbar	127
12	A friend in the woods	144
13	A hidden treasure	156
14	Invasion	173
15	The fall	190
16	We are Bani Hakeem	202
17	Battle of Abu Rashid	217
18	Attack	232
19	Secrets on the wall	248
20	Alsam	260

ACKNOWLEDMENTS

To Adam and Safiya, both my inspirations and reasons for writing this book.

To Nihad my constant support and rock from day one.

Love you all.

1.
From the east

The sun was setting over the old forest, the creatures both in
the sky and on the ground could always be heard clearly
during this time. But not now, instead all that could be heard
was the panicking footsteps of soldiers running in fear.

Earlier this same day, just after the dawn, these same
soldiers walked into the forest from the east. They were
attired in their traditional battle gear, covered in steel and
leather. Each with a long spear in his right hand and a large
shield on the left tucked up against their chest. At the top of
each of their spears was red banner tied on to it. Lastly their
swords that had been handed down from their elders, with the
handles refurbished and sheathed were hanging on their
adorned belts. Thirty soldiers came marching into the forest
under the rising sun. The stories told to them by their fathers,
regarding their ancestors had made them feel proud, mighty
and unbeatable.

Many hours had passed since then and now the sun was
setting, the soldiers were now returning, entering the forest

from the west but this time they were fewer in number. Only five and the pride and arrogance had faded as had most of their armour and all of their weaponry, with the exception of a few shields. No longer were they walking in an organised fashion, instead there was panic and confusion. They heard their heartbeats pounding, so much so, that they felt the vibration travel all the way up their chests and into their throats. The one beneficial thing from all of this was that they no longer heard the terrifying sounds that they were running away from.

As the soldiers ran through the old forest they saw streams of sunlight coming through in front of them, the hope began to grow in their hearts; they believed if they could just make it out of this forest then they might have a chance of escape. But a few moments later the familiar shaking of the ground started again and the trees began to shake almost as if the fear has engulfed them too. The soldier in front, who believed he would be leading his troops in victory back to their city, wanted to turn round and check his few remaining men but the fear would not allow him to. He had been struck by nearly every branch and rock in his path as his sprinted through. With the lack of armour the tree branches and wild thorny bushes tore at his garments and then eventually his flesh, but the blood and pain were completely phased out of his mind as the tremors grew under his feet. Now the full force was beginning to appear from above the treeline, with only a few steps before he was out of the forest a tremendous crash occurred ahead of him, just outside the forest. Both the ground and the trees in front of him exploded towards him, the force carried him back a large distance. He was temporarily unconscious when he hit the ground; the remaining pieces of armour broke away from him. He turned his head to the right and left slowly to see what happened to his men but they were nowhere to be seen, he then realised

2

that his final few men, his friends, had been taken without him realising.

The ground shook violently.

2.
Sleepless nights

The cool crisp morning air began to warm as the first light of the sun appeared on the border of the mountains. The Muezzin began to perform wudu, before slowly walking up the spiral stairs to the top of the minaret. Once at the top he stared out into the open, looking down at the various villages, government buildings, empty markets and then finally just in front of the glowing mountains the palace of the Sultan. Every time the Muezzin began the call of prayer, in his mind he felt he was calling to just one person, the Sultan; it was the Sultan who brought him from southern Egypt during the Mamluk wars. During those harsh times the Sultan came and brought peace and stability to the land.

The Muezzin cleared his throat and praised Allah, he was of medium height and slender build, his arms and fingers were long, his feet rough and his eyes as focused as a falcon's. His skin was dark and smooth like black ivory; he was attired in his traditional red and yellow Egyptian robe, which the Sultan encouraged him to wear and to never forget his ancestry, even at the doorstep of the Sultan.

"Allahu Akbar! Allahu Akbar!" the Muezzin's voice echoed across the land, his sweet voice that attracted the Sultan's attention many years ago.

The Sultan stood at the balcony of his bedroom looking out towards the Grand Mosque, attired in his white suit, dark brown long coat and black turban. His beard was dark brown with streaks of grey, his eyes hazel and his skin light brown. He gently repeated the words of the adhan as they came from the Muezzin's lips. The Sultan tried to focus on the words strongly to reinforce belief that Allah was indeed the Greatest and that there was no limit to His Greatness. He also reminded himself that he, as the Sultan, was placed on this earth to ensure that his Lord's laws were spread across the lands and that the teachings and examples of the Holy Prophet, PBUH, and his followers were conducted both in the palace and in every government building to ensure the rights of everyone was delivered. "Ash Hadu Anna Muhammed Rasulallah," both the Sultan and the Muezzin had tears in their eyes as the Holy Prophet's, PBUH, name was mentioned, it was that love and reverence that brought such a strong connection between the two of them. As the Muezzin completed the adhan the Sultan prayed his Sunnah prayers in the palace and then began to make his way to the Grand Mosque.

He gently walked through the royal garden, his feet crunching on the white pebbles that made the pathway between the various beautiful flowers of tulips, roses and jasmines. The Sultan would admire the smell each time he walked through the garden to the Grand Mosque, he heard the sound of the water fountain coming from the far end of the garden to his right. The white marble fountain was engraved with various ayahs of the Quran that circled the fountain, as well as the beautiful names of Allah, Most High, and His Beloved Messenger, PBUH.

The large stone dome started to appear along with the four large minarets, the incredible detailed blue, white and gold geometric tiles and paintings could be seen around the arch, doorways and walls. The Sultan began walking up the stairs and was greeted by various governors, scholars, sheikhs and elders at the archway. One-by-one they came forward and kissed the hand of Sultan.

"Salam Alaikum my Sultan," they all said, the Sultan returned their greeting in full and smiled. As he headed to the entrance he took off his shoes and began making his way to the front of the prayer hall. He saw the Muezzin coming down from the minaret, the Sultan smiled, he went over and embraced the Muezzin strongly.

"Your voice always makes my prayers seem sweeter oh brother Umar," said the Sultan, he released his embrace and saw that Umar was smiling.

"Thank you for your kind words Sultan, may Allah, Most High, protect you and your kingdom."

"Ameen," replied the Sultan.

The Sultan led the people in the Fajr prayer on the red and gold carpet of the mosque, each prayer segment of the floor was adorned with red images of flowers and various shapes surrounded by a golden border. Once the prayer had finished the Sultan remained at his spot doing zikr till the sun appeared, then the Sultan turned around and sat on his knees facing those in the Mosque.

"Oh my people please remember that I am here to deliver your rights, which come from Allah, Glory Be to Him. So long as I deliver those rights obey me and support this kingdom, for it is through unity and love for our brothers and sisters in Islam that we receive mercy, guidance and knowledge from our Lord." The Sultan raised his hands and made dua for his people.

Later on the Sultan made his way back to the royal garden and stared at the flowers gently swaying in the breeze, it was then that he heard the familiar steps coming from behind. With a slight limp he heard his Sheikh making his way to him, the Sultan quickly fetched a stool by the fountain and aided his teacher to his seat. His Sheikh, Abdullah Mahmoud, was dressed in a very modest grey suit, with a large white turban. His beard was long and white, with the strong scent of amber emanating from it. His skin was old and wrinkled representing the amount of knowledge from within. His Sheikh began to wipe his face with his hand while praising Allah, Most High and sending salawats on the Prophet, PBUH.

"Is there anything I can get for you my Sheikh?" asked the Sultan.

"Yes my Sultan…"

"Please my Sheikh, you do not have to call me 'Sultan', call me by my name…"

"No!" interrupted the Sheikh forcefully, "You are Allah's representative on earth; you are the one chosen to ensure justice prevails in this world, the Sultan and the Caliph of this Ummah! It is not a task that I would entrust upon my enemy due to the magnitude of it. Because of this you must be respected and obeyed, by everyone." The Sultan nodded humbly, appreciating the teachings from his Sheikh, which he had been taught ever since he was a child.

"Now my Sultan, you asked me before if there was anything you can get for me, well there is something."

"Of course my Sheikh, tell me and I will fetch it personally."

"You can start by fetching me the problem that has been circling around in your head since this morning." The Sultan was shocked, indeed there had been something praying on his mind since he woke up, in fact it was this problem that had caused him to wake up in the middle of the night. The Sheikh could see both the shock and curiousness in the Sultan's face.

"My dear Sultan, I have known you since before you could walk, I can tell when there is something wrong from simply your tone or posture. Tell me what is bothering you and Inshallah I will try to help." The Sultan smiled and looked upon his teacher, for many years he had listened to the words of his Sheikh, sometimes soothing and sometimes harsh. But whatever the tone and whatever the message he knew that there was always good in it and vast knowledge, the Sultan exhaled gently before speaking.

"Oh Sheikh Abdullah, I am fearful that my Lord is angry with me," Sheikh Abdullah studied his demeanour for a moment before gesturing with his hand for the Sultan to continue, "for the past two weeks I have been having the same occurring dream. I am walking in the desert and there is nothing around me, after a while of walking I come across a city. It is empty and the buildings are old and decrepit. As I look around the city I see that it has been many years since there has been life there. As I peer through the windows of houses and other buildings I see that everything is empty, no furniture or any other items. I look up and see a large black round object that starts to hover above the city, it blocks out the light from the sun then a loud crashing noise comes from above and the huge object starts to fall from the sky towards the city." The Sultan stops for a moment to see if his Sheikh has anything to say but he doesn't, he simply waits silently.

"That has been the same dream for the past week," continues the Sultan, "except last night, I saw the same dream but from a different position." Sheikh Abdullah becomes more curious and leans in slightly as the Sultan continues.

"I was on top of a mountain and saw the old city, as I had in previous dreams. But now I can see what the object is above it. It is another city, hovering, but when I look closely I see that it is the same city but it looks different. I see there are people living in it, markets, houses and official buildings are filled with people going-on with their daily lives, they do not

seem worried that they are floating in the sky. Then
something large and golden crashes into the flying city at
high speed."
"Can you see what the object is?" asks Sheikh Abdullah, the
Sultan shakes his head.
"No, it moves too fast, quicker than a cannonball being fired,
then the flying city begins to fall and the people start to
scream as they plummet to the earth."
"Is that everything?" asks Sheikh Abdullah.
"Yes my Sheikh".
"Bismillahir Rahmanir Raheem," responds the Sheikh, "do
not worry my Sultan; your Lord is not angry with you rather
you are being given a task. A task that only the Sultan can
fulfil, through the Will of Allah," the Sultan listens
attentively to his teacher, "there is a city that will end in utter
destruction, unless you intervene and help them. This dream
is telling you that they are suffering now and will continue to
suffer unless they are sent help, from you."
"But where is this city my Sheikh?"
"Do you accept this task that has come to you oh Sultan?"
"Of course my teacher," immediately replied the Sultan. The
Sheikh slowly stood up, quickly supported by the Sultan. As
he rose up the Sheikh placed one hand on the Sultan's right
shoulder.
"At the last part of the night go to the Grand Mosque and
perform your Tahajud prayers, once you have completed
raise your hands and cry to your Lord for the answers you
need," the Sultan nodded.
"Yes my Sheikh," the Sheikh began to make his way out of
the royal garden. The Sultan aided him to the exit and then
ordered two of his men to escort Sheikh Abdullah to his
home. The Sultan would have preferred to escort his Sheikh
himself but he needed to meet with various governors and
generals concerning both domestic and international matters.

The moon shone down onto the Grand Mosque, the Sultan completed his final set of prayers. He was dressed in a black robe, with a hood. Not wanting to be disturbed he kept his identity hidden so the other worshippers would not come to him during this time. He raised his hands and lowered his head and begged Allah, Most High, to show him where the city was and to help him complete his task. The Sultan wept silently until his beard was soaked, it was at this time that the Sultan heard someone approaching him, the man sat beside him and began to perform zikr. The Sultan did not want to be distracted and so continued asking Allah for help.

"Salam Alaikum Leader of the believers," whispered the man beside him.

"Walaikum Salam my brother, please do not let people know I am here," replied the Sultan, slightly shocked that he had been recognised.

"I know my Sultan; I have come with a message from Sheikh Abdullah Mahmoud."

The Sultan quickly wiped his tears away and faced the man; he was young, no more than twenty years old, fair skinned with light brown eyes and hair. He was adorned with the same type of suit as his Sheikh so the Sultan ascertained that this was a new student of Sheikh Abdullah.

"What is your name?" asked the Sultan.

"My name is Tarek your majesty."

"May Allah reward you Tarek, what is the message you have for me?"

"My Sheikh, our Sheikh, has asked for you to meet him at his quarters, after you have completed your prayers." The Sultan nodded silently, the young man got up to leave but the Sultan held on to the bottom of his trousers. The young man quickly sat back down not wanting to look down at the Sultan.

"Yes your majesty?"

"How long have you been following Sheikh Abdullah?"

"Only one year my Sultan, my father sent me to him just before he died, he was ill and wanted to make sure that I was under the guide of someone before he passed."

"I see, do you have other family?"

"Yes I live with my mother and two younger siblings," the Sultan nodded and reached into his inner pocket and handed the young man a bag of gold coins. The young man looked shocked and embarrassed.

"Your majesty I completed this task for my Sheikh, not for any material gain," the Sultan smiled at him.

"I would never have doubted you for a moment, but this gold is not for the task. You have chosen to follow a true servant of Allah at a young age, which can be difficult, yet you still pursue to do so. Please take the gold and every first day of every month go to the royal office and you will collect the same amount," the young man was speechless.

"Tha…Thank you Sultan," the Sultan smiled.

"Please keep me in your duas Tarek," the Sultan quickly got up and made his way to Sheikh Abdullah, not wanting to keep him waiting a moment longer.

3.
Surprise on the mountain

The hot sun blazed down on a small rural village on the
outskirts of the city capital, most of the villagers were locked
away in their homes to escape the heat. On the top of a small
building was a man working away in the blistering heat,
dressed in an old white vest and plain beige trousers. He was
bare foot as he was able to keep his balance better when
walking on his roof, the heat that came off the roof into his
feet was immense but he ignored it. Due to the many years of
fighting in the battle field both in extreme hot and cold
conditions he had been able to train himself both mentally
and physically to endure discomfort and certain levels of
pain. He had a small white turban wrapped round his head to
protect him from the heat but he could still feel the sweat
drops pouring down his light skinned face into his grey and
dark blond beard. His strong blue eyes stared down at the
bricks that had been damaged several months ago during a
small earthquake. Adam was holding the chisel firmly as he
used the small hammer to remove the old mud cement

holding the broken brick in place. He had mixed fresh mud cement with his bare hands and started to apply it onto the new bricks when he heard the sound of galloping horses approaching.

Adam slowly stood to his feet and turned to see the horses and more particularly the riders. Rarely did the villagers see or even hear the sounds of animals galloping with such aggression, in this village things had always moved in a far gentler pace. Adam could see three horses coming towards him between the rows of small houses and huts. The ground was covered in patchy grass and stone gravel, the huge mountains were in the background behind the riders, from which they came from.

Adam began to make his way to the ground climbing down the western wall facing the riders, he stood directly in front of his house towards the riders, his turban soaked in sweat, his vest stained with dust as well as mud cement covering his hands and most of his forearms. His was still bare foot as the riders came within eye shot, Adam could tell from the rider's uniform as well as their dark-brown horses that they were from the royal guard of the Sultan. There were two riders, their speed beginning to slow; they were dressed in smart military suits made up of blue, white and gold tops, white trousers, black boots and green turbans. They had brass buttons and golden décor on their shoulders and sleeves. One of the riders was also holding the reigns of a third horse which had no rider. The riders came within three meters of Adam before they finally halted, one of the riders dismounted and walked with great strides towards Adam before stopping in front of him. He had a large broad frame, tall in height and dark olive skin. His beard was thick but short, and apart from the grey patch on his chin and side burns the rest of his beard was jet black. He had large brown eyes and thick eye brows. "Salam Alaikum Hasan, it has been a while my brother," said Adam. Hasan smiled, it had been nearly five years since he last cast eyes on Adam, they had spent many years out in the battlefield spreading the empire and religion of Islam. The countless years they ate, slept, prayed and witness the world side by side as brothers together.

"Walaikum Salam Adam," he looked Adam up and down "you are looking…busy I see." Adam smiled and looked at himself and then back at the roof he had just descended, he realised how comical he must of have appeared in front of the royal guard at that moment. He wiped the sweat from his face with the upper part of his right forearm which wasn't covered in mud.

"Yes, my life is a lot different since we last met, many changes," Hasan walked passed Adam and inspected the outside of his home briefly before once again looking Adam up and down again.

"I don't understand Adam, you were given a large sum of money for your sacrifice, how comes you are living like this?" Adam lowered his head to the ground briefly before turning towards Hasan.

"There have been a few setbacks, which have used up a lot of the money that I was given," Hasan walked back to Adam.

"What has happened?" asked Hasan, Adam smiled.

"Always the concerned Captain, Hasan do not worry my life is how I want it, quiet and simple." Hasan stared at Adam for a moment before looking over to his fellow rider, apart from having the same colour eyes and skin he was starkly different to Hasan. His frame was thin and his beard patchy and light-brown, his face had a softer appearance than the stern look of his colleague. Hasan looked back at Adam.

"The Sultan has asked us to come and collect you. We are to bring you to him as a matter of urgency," Adam was shocked at his words, "he has informed us not to leave this area until you have mounted this horse." Hasan motioned to the third horse with his head that had no rider.

"I don't understand," responded Adam "I have been away from the army for many years, has something happened?" "The Sultan did not go into details, in fact he was quite tight lipped on the whole matter, can you please get your things in order and come with us?" Adam looked down at his state and back at the roof.

"Of course, I will need some time to clean myself up and get changed if that's ok?" Hasan nodded his head and made his way back to his horse; he mounted it and looked up at the sun.

"We will go to the local Mosque and pray Asr, when you have finished come meet us there and we will make our way to the Sultan, Inshallah." Adam nodded and made his way back into his house; he heard the horses galloping away towards the Mosque.

The moon shone brightly on the mountain as the three men sat around a small fire, Adam had quickly washed and dressed himself in a white shirt and loose black trousers earlier. He had also covered himself with a thick olive green robe that his father had once owned before his passing and finally a black cap on his head. Hasan slowly poked at the fire with a long twig to allow more oxygen into the flames, the cracking sounds of the fire became louder and the heat more intense. Hasan sat back down again and crossed his legs, Adam sat towards his right in a similar position and the third rider who at this moment had not uttered a single word up until now began to recite Surah Yasin. Adam was completely taken aback at the beautiful tone that emanated from his lips. For the whole duration neither Adam nor Hasan uttered a word until he had finished.

"You recite with such beauty," said Adam, the man briefly looked at Adam and then towards the fire.

"What is your name?" asked Adam.

"Ali," responded the man, never looking away from the fire as he did so. Adam continued to look at him but could see that he was not a man that enjoyed conversation.

"His father was the same," said Hasan "most of his family have this gift, so the Sultan's father told them not to waste it on idle conversation but rather preserve it to glorify your Lord." Adam looked at Ali with a new found respect. Ali got up and walked away from the camp fire.

"Don't venture too far Ali," said Hasan, Ali raised his hand in acknowledgment of his orders as he walked off into the shadows.

"Did I offend him with my words?" asked Adam in concern, Hasan shook his head.

"No, Ali has always found it difficult to socialise, he just prefers silence and open space. Anyway we should be getting some rest before dawn. I think Ali's strolling off was his way of saying that he will take the first watch." Both men got up and retrieved small blankets from their horses and settled around the fire to sleep.

"It's good travelling with you again General," said Hasan, Adam smiled.

"That was many moons ago Captain," replied Adam, "Salam Alaikum."

"Walaikum Salam, General," said Hasan.

It was now close to Zuhr time and the three riders were now making their way down the mountain towards the city centre. Due to the steepness of the mountain they had to walk with their horses, each holding the reigns of the animal. The lower half of the mountain was covered in trees predominantly scott and black pine.

After several hours of walking the horses started to get annoyed and began pulling away from their masters.

"What's wrong with them?!" shouted Adam, while struggling to hold on to the horse. The three men kept looking around to see if any danger was around them. A huge roar bellowed lower down the mountain and they immediately saw the danger that was terrifying the horses. A large brown bear was heading towards them at great speed

"Let go of the horses and arm yourselves!" ordered Adam, each horse had a sword attached close to the satchel, they tried to retrieve them before the beast got close but they didn't have enough time, apart from Ali who managed to grab a large knife. They quickly released the horses and they galloped west-wards away from the beast. The bear charged at Ali first who was able to hit the bear over the shoulder with his knife, both Adam and Hasan ran towards the bear and attacked it from both sides using large rocks and sticks they found on the ground. They both knew from experience that a full on attack was the only way to force the bear to retreat, running away was not an option as the bear would easily chase them down. The bear continued to charge towards Ali on all four paws, it growled and exposed its teeth, Ali could see the large tensed muscles in its shoulders and arms.

The others attempted to wound the animal from the sides, neither soldier wanted to kill the bear but they felt they didn't have a choice as the animal seemed set on slaying Ali. Ali kept backing away while defending the bear's attacks, both Hasan and Adam realised that the bear was trying to push Ali to the large set of boulders further down the mountain to pin him down, they increased their attack on the bear to halt it. The bear swung his paws wildly at the pair, knocking Hasan off his feet and wounding his side. Only Adam remained to save Ali, he jumped on the bear's back and tried stabbing it with a large piece of wood but the bear stood up immediately. Adam fell off and he hit his head on a rock and started to fall unconscious. The bear quickly turned round to pounce on him.

Adam could just about see the bear looming over him as everything was getting dark; he then heard a faint sound

17

that came from behind the bear before blacking out completely.

4.
The returning stranger

Adam's vision slowly started to come back to him; although everything was dark and misty he was aware of the sounds in the background. He could hear birds singing, the conversations of people and the wind blowing calmly. He felt heat on his right arm and most of his chest; he was now able to see the ceiling above him which was magnolia in colour. There was gold leafing squares that had red and black calligraphy depicting the different names of Allah and various short ayahs in the Quran. He looked around and realised he was lying in bed, the room was large with a big beige, green and red Egyptian rug on the floor with various quadrilateral shapes. There was a small dark pine desk beside the bed and a glass of water on top which was covered by a small saucer. The window was beside his right side, it was open and the sunlight was shining in, he was able to raise himself just high enough to see the clouds and the tips of tall buildings before falling back to the bed. He was still very fatigued as well as sore and light headed from the head wound. He felt tightness around his head and touched it with his hand; it was wrapped with a cloth. He must have cut himself during the fall, he thought, he also wondered how long he had been unconscious. Adam looked down at himself and saw he was wearing a long white robe under the red bed sheets. He reached over and took a sip of water; he then heard the sound of footsteps coming towards the closed door of the bedroom.

There were three knocks at the door; Adam told them to enter in a low tone as his head was still hurting. Ali wandered in through the door and smiled upon seeing Adam awake. It was the first time Adam has seen such an expression on his face, he tried to sit up but Ali rushed over to stop him by placing his hand gently on his shoulder. "Major please do not sit up, reserve your strength so you can reach full health," Adam nodded and slowly laid back down. Ali reached over to a small stool and brought it to the side of bed and sat down. He was dressed in the same military uniform as he was the day they met.

"Salam Alaikum Major, it's good to see you awake," Adam was confused at being called Major.

"Walaikum Salam, Ali I'm not a Major."

"You are now Sir, it was the Sultan's final instruction, before he left, that you be both reinstated and promoted from your previous position as General along with a higher salary and new residency within the city centre. He wanted me to ask you what belongings you wished to have brought over from your home in the east when you awoke?" Adam was trying to digest all the information that Ali was throwing at him, along with the dull pain in his head and the dizziness.

"Ali...I've been reinstated? When did this happen and what have I been reinstated for?" Ali could see that the conversation was taking its toll on Adam and he was starting to get frustrated.

"Sir you need to rest and not get worked up, otherwise your recuperation will take longer. But I will address your questions so you have some peace of mind. The Sultan reinstated you two days ago, on the actual day you were brought to the palace..."

"The palace?!" said Adam in both a shocked and bewildered tone. Ali nodded allowing the news to sink in.

"You are staying in one of the guest rooms in the Sultan's palace; he wanted you to remain here until he returned. You've been unconscious for two days and this morning, Sir." Adam remained silent looking up at the calligraphy on the ceiling.

"With regards to the reason of you being reinstated I'm afraid that I have limited information, I know that a trip is being arranged, which you will be heading. There was no mention of any battle or major incident that needed addressing so it could be an ambassadorial meeting, but that is just a guess Sir." Adam started to feel a little calmer as the picture was now starting to appear clear, it made sense for a seasoned officer to act as an ambassador for more delicate or potentially volatile situations. He still remained looking up at the ceiling.

"How is Captain Hasan doing, I saw him take a bad knock from that bear?" asked Adam, Ali remained silent at the question; Adam looked over and could see the pain and sadness on his face

"Ali?" Ali closed his eyes for a short period and then looked at Adam.

"He passed away didn't he?" asked Adam, Ali nodded regretfully, "But how? It didn't appear to be that hard of hit he took?"

"The doctor said there was some kind of internal bleeding that couldn't be stopped, he died the day you were both brought in. The Sultan led his funeral prayer before he left the city." Adam could see the difficulty Ali was having telling him this.

"Ali, to Allah we belong and to Him we return."

"Ameen," replied Ali softly, who still visibly looked distraught.

"Captain Hasan is, was, very close to my family, particularly my father," said Ali, "he helped me when I was growing up; especially when I joined the army and fought overseas. I could have done...I should have done more." Adam stared at him for a moment and then sat up, the pain and dizziness was excruciating but he still persisted. Ali tried to stop him but he waved him off. Once seated he turned his whole body directly to Ali and pointed his finger towards him.

"Brother Ali, we have not known each other for that long a time but given our dramatic past and the losing of a close brother I feel I can speak freely to you as I would to a relative. There was nothing more either one of us could have done. Everything happened in an instant all we had was a small knife, a few sticks and stones." He leaned in closer to Ali.

"This world is not Paradise, so we shouldn't expect not to suffer or have difficulties. Embrace the difficulties and the pain, for these times clean us," Adam placed his hand on Ali's chest, "they wipe away the darkness in our heart and the sins we have committed," he then pointed to Ali's forehead "they also increase our knowledge for with every calamity there is knowledge but most people simply focus on the difficulty and nothing else. Don't make the same mistakes I have made." Ali was shocked at this admission from him.

"Learn from this pain," continued Adam, "and become better." Adam slowly laid back down on the bed.

"I can see why the Sultan wanted you Major, rest well I will see you in the morning. I will have someone come up with food and fresh clothes for you," Ali got up and headed towards the door

"Salam Alaikum Sir."

"Walaikum Salam Ali, thank you for visiting me, please pass my condolences to Hasan's family," Ali nodded and left.

Adam was awoken by the sound of a plate being placed on the cabinet by the bed; he turned his head slowly and saw a man dressed in a green and white uniform with a red cap. He recognised the uniform as the personal staff of the Sultan who operated within the palace walls; he had blue eyes and a blonde beard with a fair complexion.

"Salam Alaikum Major, apologies for waking you."

"No apologies necessary brother, thank for bringing me food, what is your name?"

"Ahmed, Major," Adam nodded and slowly sat up, Ahmed helped him to sit up and placed an extra cushion behind him to support his back and neck. He then placed a wooden tray on his lap and put the plate of food on top, there was white cheese, black olives, tomatoes, a boiled egg and a piece of bread.

"Would you like some food Major?"

"In a bit, but the water will be fine for now and please Ahmed call me Adam, if you're not in the army then you do not need to refer to me by my rank."

"As you wish Adam, is there anything else that you wish from me while I'm here?"

"Actually I do have a few questions, has the Sultan given you any information as to my reason for being here, apart from the recuperating?" Ahmed sat on the stool next to the bed.

"I'm happy to answer the question providing you eat while I do so; the doctor said you need to eat as soon as you're awake to ensure full recovery." Adam nodded and began eating the bread; Ahmed passed the water over to him and placed it on the tray. Ahmed cleared his throat and thought for a second before speaking.

23

"The Sultan has been having many discussions with his Sheikh and brothers regarding some kind of disruption or problem within a particular city, they had agreed to send someone over there to help resolve the situation. Shortly after that the order was given by the Sultan that you were to be fetched immediately, I can only assume that you are the one chosen for this task." Adam thought silently while sipping the water.

"But I'm sure the Sultan and his Sheikh will explain everything to you when he returns in two days."

"Returns?" asked Adam.

"Yes, he had to sail to Cyprus as one of his relatives was very ill," Adam looked out towards the window.

"Did the Doctor say how long I had to stay here, can I go out?" Ahmed shook his head.

"No, the doctor said you must rest for at least one day after you woke up."

"Understood, would it be possible to have my clothes ready for tomorrow morning?"

"Of course, we will have your uniform sent to your room after Fajr."

"Thank you Ahmed, you have been very helpful," Ahmed smiled and said goodbye before leaving.

Adam began to climb the steps of the Grand Mosque; he was dressed in the same blue and white uniform as worn by Hasan and Ali previously. He adorned a solid black turban which only Majors in the Sultan's army bore, along with a sheathed sword on his black leather belt. As he approached the entrance he took off his boots and sword which he left just under the archway. Immediately familiar memories and emotions began to stir within him, the amount of times he prayed within the Grand Mosque both behind the Sultan and before that the Sultan's father. He followed the Imam in the Zuhr prayer; he recognised the voice of the Sultan's brother,

Prince Saleh, whom he had acted as his personal guard during several trips across Asia for Hajj and Umrah.

Once the prayer was finished Adam remained seated and went through past memories when he was both in this mosque and in the city centre. His daydreaming was interrupted by a friendly voice.

"Salam Alaikum old friend," Prince Saleh seated himself in front of him; he was almost the mirror image of the Sultan with the exception of his height and size which were both bigger. He was adorned with a dark olive suit and a long white coat, his turban was white with a red cloth wrapped round it. He looked at Adam with eyes of affection due to their strong history together, more than he had with the Sultan himself.

"The Sultan told me that he had sent for you but I told myself I wouldn't believe it till I saw you with my own eyes," he lent forward and embraced Adam in the sitting position, he patted his back firmly as he held him before releasing.

"Walaikum Salam Prince Saleh, it's good to see you again Sir," the Prince waved his hand away at Adam.

"Oh come now Adam, we grew up as children together playing in my father's garden, forget the formalities," Adam shook his head.

"Throughout the whole time we were growing up together my father, who was your father's shadow, always reminded me to never forget the royal family's position as they have a burden that we couldn't imagine, so to honour my father's words I cannot do that your majesty." Prince Saleh patted Adam on the shoulder.

"Far be it from me to go against the words of such a wise man, will you join me for dinner this evening after the Isha prayer?"

"Of course Sir, it would be both an honour and a pleasure," Prince Saleh smiled at his remarks.

"For the both of us," added Prince Saleh, "sadly I have a few official obligations that I must attend to but I will meet you after the Isha prayer. We will adjourn to the royal garden for a light dinner and a chance to catch up properly." Adam smiled and agreed with a nod, they both stood up and embraced before Prince Saleh left the prayer hall.

As Adam looked down the prayer hall he saw the sixteen stone pillars, eight on either side, covered in sculptured flowers, spheres, stars and crescent moons. Above each pair of pillars was a dark blue arch with golden lines travelling along each side and various Quranic verses, written between the lines in gold also. By each pillar stood a sheikh or scholar delivering lessons on various Islamic sciences relating to belief, jurisprudence and spirituality. Adam walked passed the teachers, who were surrounded by seated students and listeners. He saw the different types of teachers from various lands some from here and others from Asia and Africa. They all spoke with different ascents, but taught the same source of knowledge from the Prophet Muhammed, PBUH.

As Adam was reaching down to pick up his boot he felt a poke in his back, he turned round and saw an older gentlemen poking him with his cane, dressed in a basic white suit with a matching white turban. It was Sheikh Abdullah the beloved teacher of the Sultan and his family, even Adam's own father was his student. Adam immediately bent down and kissed his hand, the Sheikh smiled.

"Salam Alaikum Adam, my how you look so much like your father," Adam returned the greeting and walked with the Sheikh to the nearby corner on the right of the mosque. He sat on the floor as the Sheikh rested himself on a stool brought to him by one of his students.

"It has been many years since I saw you in this mosque Adam, how have things been?"

"Things have been good Sheikh Abdullah, Alhamdullilah."
Sheikh Abdullah stared at Adam for moment and then closed
his eyes and exhaled slowly. He then poked Adam in the
stomach gently with his cane.

"You disappeared for a long time Adam, never contacted
anyone or attended any gatherings or festivals, are you sure
that everything is ok?" Adam remained silent, understanding
that Sheikh Abdullah already knew the answers to these
questions. He was not asking for an update rather he was
educating him; still Adam remained silent not knowing how
to start the sentence.

"Speak up, you may be the Major but right now I see the
same young man that I taught with the princes of this
kingdom, speak up and tell me why you vanished?" again
Sheikh Abdullah poked at Adam stomachs but more firmly.

"My wife passed away from an illness several years ago, she
was pregnant with our first child and…and I was angry and
upset." Sheikh Abdullah lowered his stick and stood it on
floor resting both his hands on the handle.

"I didn't want to be with anyone or have anything; I gave
away my home because of the memories and gave away most
of my money. I inherited a small house in the east and
decided to live there away from everything…and everyone".

"And did it help?" asked the Sheikh, Adam shook his head.

"You see Adam, we cannot run away from these events,
ultimately in this world all we do is go through a serious of
events, some easy and some hard. All that matters is how we
conduct ourselves in these events." Adam lowered his head,
the Sheikh placed his hand on Adam's shoulder, he looked
back up at the Sheikh.

"The pain you went through, are going through, is difficult
and for some it may be understandable that they retreat like
this. But you are the son of a great soldier who was raised
with the family of the royal family and their teachers. You
understand what you should have done Adam?"

27

"Yes my Sheikh," the Sheikh smiled. "Alhamdullilah, this may seem harsh for some but for the Major of the Sultan's army it is imperative, this baggage cannot be in you when you set off for your task." Adam's focus quickly changed upon hearing those words. "Sheikh Abdullah what is my…" the Sheikh quickly held up his hand to silence him. "All in good time Major, the Sultan will return tomorrow, I suggest you spend that time resting yourself." The Sheikh stood up with the aid of one of his students who was waiting nearby, he said farewell to Adam and headed to one of the pillars to deliver a lesson to his students that were already seated waiting. Adam slowly got up and made his way out of the mosque.

He headed south towards the central market making his way past various official buildings like the Royal Court and the Treasury. He approached the entrance gate of the central market; he began to smell the exotic aromas of different spices such as cumin, turmeric, saffron and cinnamon. The spice stalls were located by the northern entrance of the market; there was a mini stone fortress that surrounded the market place, around seven feet high and two feet in depth. While Adam was serving the empire previously there were two entrances from the north and the east, due to massive expansion of the empire over the past three to four years and increase in both population and trade within the city, the Sultan ordered an extension to the fortress on the western side to allow more space for trades people and housing of stock. To ensure accessibility of both the delivering and picking up of stock, a larger third entrance was introduced on the newly built west side.

Adam wondered through the pathways between sellers and buyers in the spice section of the market. Traders were selling from market stools, small carriages and mats on the ground. Adam was astonished at the variety of both spices and the people that were around; the expansion had meant that more sellers from different parts of the world such as Africa and Asia were now coming to sell in the market place. He saw people from Persia, Egypt, China and Western Europe coming to sell and trade, the vastness in choice for just the herbs and spices was amazing. But this increase in supply was not only limited to spices and herbs, Adam ventured through all the sections of the market including pottery, clothing, perfume, weaponry, art and food to name a few. Adam spent nearly the whole day wondering across the market and engaging with various sellers and buyers to catch up with what he had missed for all these years. By the time he returned back to the palace it was nearly Isha time.

The moon shone down amongst the large rain clouds in the sky, a white tent which was cube in shape with a pyramid shape roof at the top was erected in the royal garden. There were maroon decorative lines going across the top and at the base of the pyramid roof, as well as around the window sections and the bottom of the tent. Within the maroon line was a selection of green squares in three different shades which added to the exotic design. Inside the tent with the doors open sat Prince Saleh and Adam on black leather cushions that were scented with lavender. They had finished their lentil soup with dried bread as well as dried figs and plain yoghurt for dessert. Ahmed was pouring their black tea into glasses.
"Is there anything else you need your majesty?" asked Ahmed as he finished pouring.
"No thank you Ahmed that will be all, please go back into the palace and have something to eat, the soup was wonderful Alhamdullilah, please tell the chef thank you from me."
"Me also," added Adam. Ahmet smiled and said goodbye before leaving them both. The Prince slowly sipped his tea while running his fingers with his other hand through his

beard. Adam stared out at the garden, looking at the rain drops falling to the ground. The sound of the rain landing on the roof of the tent helped him to remember fond memories of when he was growing up here, he smiled at the memories. "I remember our fathers getting angry at us because we would spend too much time playing in the garden," said Adam, the Prince smiled.

"Yes I was thinking about that the other day, your father chased you with a stick once when you spent the whole morning playing in the bushes and ruined your new garments that your mother had made for you." Adam burst out laughing as he remembered the incident.

"Your father was so angry that both I and the Sultan ran to tell our father what was happening."

"What did he do?" asked Adam.

"He chased us with a stick too because we didn't stop you from ruining your clothes!" they both laughed out loud, almost spilling their tea. Soon after they both settled down and just stared out the door at the rain.

"Adam, the Sultan told us about your mission a few weeks ago. At that time he had not decided who he was going to send, the instructions that both myself and the other Princes were given was that we couldn't share details of the mission to anybody, not even our wives and children." Adam looked at the Prince as he spoke, he could tell from his expression that he desperately wished he could share that information with him as they were so close, but he also knew that he would never disobey the orders of the Sultan, not for anything in the world.

"However he did not say we couldn't advise you on the matter," Adam's eyes widened upon that statement.

"Your majesty, how can you advise me on a mission that you cannot tell me about?"

"With great subtlety Major Adam, there is a possibility that I will not see you tomorrow before you leave for your mission, and I want to make sure that I impart some advice to you in case I don't, is that ok?"

"Of course Prince Saleh, whatever advice you give will be most appreciated," said Adam nodding strongly.

"Bismillahir Rahmanir Rahim, there are two pieces of advice that I want to give you. The first I know will come easily to you," holding out his index finger while speaking, "firstly whatever befalls you, trust in your Sultan, whatever orders he gives to you trust it to the letter."

"I always do your majesty."

"I know you do Adam, but this situation will be different, you will be away for a long time and most likely not have contact with the Sultan for most of that period. During those long moments when you are alone and unable to seek advice it will become easy to divert from the orders, but refrain from that at all costs." Adam nodded accepting the first piece of advice. The Prince held up two fingers.

"The second piece of advice is slightly trickier, keep an open mind," Adam did not fully understand what was meant by that and his expression showed it, "what I mean by this is do not refer solely to your past experience on the battlefield. You have gained valuable experience throughout the many years you have served both my father and the Sultan, but you will encounter events that are new to you, in order to fulfil the orders of your Sultan you will need to think in ways that you haven't before. Trust in Allah and you will come up with the ideas needed to complete your task, Inshallah." The Prince sat silently looking at Adam as he soaked up all this information.

"This is all I can say Adam, I hope it helps, Inshallah."

"Thank you for your advice Prince Saleh I have no doubt it will," they both sat and chatted about past events for a while longer before they both retired for the night.

5.

What lay ahead

There were two large doors three meters in height and two meters in width, made from solid wood from the trees of the northern mountains. The wood had been stained with an intense black, so much so, that it shined with a misty dark blue tint when sunlight fell upon it from the large window on the right hand side of the corridor.

Since the Prophet, PBUH, proclaimed the message of Islam, his followers and those that followed them had always pondered and reflected at the many gifts and blessings from their Lord at every moment. They wanted to ensure that this remembrance was constant, both for themselves and for the rest of human kind. Upon the face of both doors were sculpted designs, they were comprised of various celestial bodies such as the sun, planets, single stars, constellations and various depictions of the moon at different stages of its cycle. These beautiful creations offered the gifts of sight, warmth, guidance, direction as well as the incredibly beauty that they cascaded down onto the earth. The precision of the carving was both fine and detailed, the darkness and smoothness of the finish could have almost be mistaken for black marble until one touched it. At the base of the door were carvings of waves, again, a reminder of the gift of life which stems from water. Around the border of the doorway were cream marble tiles from the quarries, south-east from the capital. In each square tile was a blue and red detailed geometric design, which reflected on the gift of mathematics in both it's practically and beauty in this world.

These were the doors that led to the Sultan's personal study, on each side stood a soldier, dressed in his blue uniform and armed with a sword on his belt. They both wore white turbans with a purple cloth wrapped round, the personal guard of the Sultan. Adam stood in front of the doors as the two soldiers slowly opened them, the sunlight flooded into the corridor from the study. With squinted eyes Adam was able to make out a large table in the centre of the room. Adam walked forward at a steady pace, the sunlight began to blare more strongly as he entered the room, he held up his hand to shield the light from his eyes. The doors closed behind him; he walked a few steps more before the sunlight was no longer blocking his vision.

In front of him was a large dark mahogany desk, on the legs were carved tulips and rose petals with the Shahadah carved just under the top of the desk between the two legs. At the desk sat the Sultan all dressed in white, apart from his maroon turban. On his desk were several open documents, to his right, to his left two scrolls wrapped with red silk ribbons. There was a candle burning in front of him, the Sultan had his head down signing a document with a quill, he then reached into a drawer and fetched a piece of red wax. He held it to the candle for a moment before dripping it onto the document that he just signed; he stamped the wax with the royal seal using his ring that his father had passed down onto him before he died. Throughout the entire time Adam waited in front of the Sultan, standing straight with his arms by his side. The Sultan rolled up the document and tied it with a red ribbon, he then looked up at Adam for the first time, his eyes were stern and his face expressionless. He motioned for Adam to sit in the chair in front of him which he did with haste. The Sultan got up and walked over to the window and opened it, a cool breeze came flowing in. On either side of the open window were thick green velvet curtains to protect the room from the artic winds that blew in from the mountains each winter. The Sultan stared out through the open window and cleared his throat.

"Salam Alaikum Major Adam, it is good to see you again after all these years," Adam returned the greeting. The Sultan turned round and faced him.

"I have no doubt you are desperate to know the nature of you being here, but before I do that there are a few things that I need to make clear as well as a few questions that need to be addressed also." The Sultan walked back to his desk and sat down; he placed his arms on the desk with his hands palm down on the table.

"The reason you are here is because both my Sheikh and my brother, Prince Saleh, recommended you in high regards, I have no reason to doubt either of their judgements, especially Sheikh Abdullah. You are held in high regards but that also means that I have high expectations of you." The Sultan paused for a moment as if he was trying to find the best way to say his next sentence.

"Sheikh Abdullah has informed me of your loss, for which I am deeply sorry, to Allah we belong and to Him we return," Adam nodded silently with closed eyes, "I wish you had come to us so we could have aided you in this situation, the Muslim Ummah is one family and as a family we support each other throughout difficult times."

"I'm sorry your majesty…"

The Sultan interrupted him by holding up his hand slightly.

"Do not apologise Major, my words are not meant to punish nor point out flaws, rather they are out of love and concern. Bearing all this in mind, I will ask you this one time and one time only, do you feel you are fit to return to action?" Adam sat silently for a moment; he lent slightly forward towards the Sultan.

"Begging your pardon my Sultan but I don't know how to answer that question with the limited information I have. In fact to be honest I have no information at all and would be both foolish and unprofessional to give you a definitive answer in either case," the Sultan smiled at the response. "It's like I have your father in front of me again, thank you for your honesty. What I need most, for a mission like this, is honesty," the Sultan got up and walked round the desk, "let's go for a little walk," both the Sultan and Adam left the study and headed downstairs to the royal garden.

The Sultan stood by the fountain, with Adam standing close by. They both stared at the gushing water, the Sultan signalled to the two personal guards who had followed them down to leave, which they did. The Sultan turned to Adam. "Major, what I am going to say will seem rather strange and not like anything that I or my father has tasked you with before," the Sultan sat on the edge of the fountain. "I need you to go to a city, there seems to be some issues that need resolving, issues that require tactfulness and diplomacy, otherwise I would simply just send an army to fix the problem."

"Where is this city your majesty and what kind of issues are they facing?" the Sultan stood up and smiled a little.

"This is where things become more complicated."

"How so your majesty?" the Sultan placed a hand on the shoulder of the Adam, he explained the situation with his dreams and the advice given to him by Sheikh Abdullah. Adam stood completely still and did not react to the words.

"Before I left for Cyprus I had spoken with both my brothers and my Sheikh, because of the lack of knowledge on the situation we thought best that we should send a single person rather than a large group otherwise an offering of help could descend to open war."

"But Sultan how can we be sure that this is the right course of action, it may be that an army is what is needed," the Sultan nodded silently and placed his hands behind his back and walked through the garden at a slow pace.

"I thought the same thing myself initially, as I didn't want to risk the lives of my soldiers or anyone for that matter. But over the past weeks a feeling has been growing inside my heart that an army would not be the best option." Adam walked beside the Sultan as he strolled round the fountain.

"But we do not know where this city is?" asked Adam.

"No, but we do know how to find out, after several days of asking Allah, Most High, for help a message was sent to me from the governor of Benghazi. He informed me that several Bedouins from the desert had come to him for help; they had been attacked by a fierce group of people, one they had never come across before. Their language and appearance was unlike anything they had seen before."

"Were there any fatalities?"

"No Alhamdullilah, they managed to escape on camel back but lost everything they owned. I believe that this is connected to the dreams I have been having."

"So you think the city in trouble is Benghazi?"

"No, I would've recognised it in my dreams; Benghazi is a step in the right direction."

"But Leader of the Believers, fights between Bedouins and bandits are not something strange; unfortunately they are quite common in certain areas," the Sultan stopped walking and faced Adam.

"You are right Major, but something was said by one of the Bedouins that convinced me that this situation was different."

"What was that my Sultan?"

"When the governor asked them about the attackers they were unable to speak at first due to fright, bear in mind Bedouins are renowned for their toughness and bravery," Adam nodded in agreement "but when they were finally able to speak they mentioned something peculiar," the Sultan leaned closer to Adam, "they told the governor 'We only knew they were men because we heard them speaking to one another, before that we were convinced they were some kind of wild beast' after that none of the Bedouins would say anything else on the matter."

"Where are the Bedouins now?" asked Adam

"They are still with the governor in Benghazi; they refuse to speak about the matter to anymore and will not show anyone where they were attacked out of fear. The governor asked if he could send soldiers out to search the area, but I thought sending armies to an unknown enemy is risky. I informed him that I would be sending someone to help with the situation based on my orders." Adam realised now what he had to do.

"Do you think these…wild men, are the cause of the problems for this undiscovered city or rather just a means for us to find it?" asked Adam, the Sultan started to walk again, with Adam close behind.

"Who knows Adam, right now we simply act upon the information we have, but it's good that you have an open mind at this moment rather than settling for just one theory," Adam smiled to himself as he remembered the advice from Prince Saleh.

At that moment one of the Sultan's personal guards appeared at the doorway of the palace by the front of the royal garden, the Sultan was surprised as the soldier was aware of this meeting but yet still came.

"Speak," said the Sultan.

"Forgive me Sultan but someone has arrived at the palace asking to see you."

"Did you not tell them that I was having a meeting?" the soldier became nervous at the tone of the Sultan.

"Y..yes your majesty, actually they already knew you were in a meeting with the Major," the Sultan was surprised at these words.

"I only told a few people about this meeting, those that I trust completely."

"Then it must be something important Leader of the Believers, but it is your decision if you wish to see them now," responded Adam. The Sultan told the soldier to bring the guest through. To both the astonishment of the Sultan and Adam it was the Muezzin, Umar. Ever since Umar had arrived from Egypt he had never came to meet the Sultan uninvited, he had solely focused on his role as the caller of the prayer never getting mixed up with anything else. The only time that he offered advice was at the behest of the Sultan or his Sheikh for they knew that Umar was both a very trustworthy and knowledgeable man. He came from a long line of scholars and sheikhs from both his father and mother's side. Both men rushed towards him, he was dressed in a long black robe with a white hooded cloak. He had a white cap on his head and was holding olive stone prayer beads.

"Salam Alaikum Leader of the Believers and to you as well Major," they both returned the greeting to Umar, "I am so sorry to disturb you Sir."

"That is ok Umar, is everything alright?" asked the Sultan. Umar seemed both nervous and tired, he had been deliberating with himself as to whether to come and see the Sultan, and it was only at that moment that he decided to come.

"My Sultan, due to your kindness and support from the first moment we met I have always been too shy to ask you for anything, even though I know you would be all-to-happy to help me."

"Of course Umar, you have always been one of my most trusted companions, you are my brother." The Sultan placed his hand on his shoulder, Umar almost seem to sink slightly due to the heaviness of the request he was about to ask.

"What is it Umar? Please tell me," said the Sultan, the Muezzin let out a long sigh before speaking.

"I wish to accompany the Major on his mission to Benghazi, oh Sultan," both of them were shocked, especially Adam; as he knew Umar quite well and had always seen him to be a man of peace and knowledge, not war.

"Why do you wish to accompany him Umar? You have such a vital role here in this city, your voice and strong intentions have lifted the spirits of many. Why would you wish to leave that gift and responsibility?"

"Your majesty, the Bedouins that were attacked near Benghazi are my kin," Adam tried to speak but the Sultan placed his hand on his chest to silence him, he then signalled for Umar to continue, which he did, "they are connected to me from my mother's side and are a brave people; I want to go with the Major to aid them." Adam looked at the Sultan to see if it was ok for him to speak, the Sultan allowed it.

"My Sultan, although it is indeed noble to protect ones family the main objective of this mission is to both find and save this unknown city, if we end up stopping and focusing on every previous event it may become impossible to fulfil the task that you have been entrusted with." The Sultan turned to Umar to hear his response.

"Your majesty whatever you command me to do I will follow," the Sultan thought for a moment.

"Umar while I do completely empathise with your situation I'm afraid I cannot allow you to go, after weighing everything up, your input here is far too important, I'm sorry Umar." In spite of his emotions Umar accepted the Sultan's orders without hesitation. After a brief period Umar headed back to the Grand Mosque to make preparations before making the adhan for the Zuhr prayer, both the Sultan and Adam remained in the royal garden.

"I have met few people with the integrity and strong spirit as Umar; it pains me deeply to refuse a request from a man of his calibre, especially with such a noble cause." The Sultan began to walk back to the garden entrance of the palace, followed by Adam closely.

Both of them retuned back to the Sultan's study. While the Sultan went through a few documents Adam stared out of the window looking at the beautiful blue sky and the many gulls that glided so gracefully on the gently breeze provided to them by Allah, Most High. He stared at the docks and the various vessels stationed near the pier and docking stations, he saw small fishing ships, coastal trade ships and large naval ships. There were also several empty small ships that were used by government officials or soldiers for boarding naval vessels that were unable to come too close to land. The Sultan came up to Adam and handed him a rolled up scroll.

"This is the document sent to me from Abdul Muiz, the governor of Benghazi. He explains the whole situation in detail with regards to the attack on the Bedouins and their refusal to speak about the event." Adam took the scroll and started to open it, the Sultan placed his hand on the scroll to prevent him from doing so.

"No, go back to your quarters and study it in detail without any distractions, after you have done that visit the armoury next to the royal court and pick up weaponry that you feel would be best for this mission. Once you get to Benghazi the governor will provide you with various necessities for your mission." Adam put the scroll in his inside pocket.

"Thank you Sultan, I will head to the armoury now and study the message upon my return, will I be setting off to Benghazi today?"

"That was my wish earlier but I feel it would be best for you to study the document this evening and then give me your thoughts of the situation, maybe add some input that we have overlooked thus far. After sunrise tomorrow we will head to the docks."

"We?" asked Adam

"Yes Major, I will accompany you by carriage whereby I can give you any late advice that comes to mind from now till sunrise tomorrow."

"Understood, Leader of the Believers."

"Good, I will hopefully see you after the Zuhr prayer," responded the Sultan; he escorted Adam to the entrance of the study before they parted ways.

Adam began to make his way to the armoury; he walked through the grey brick pathway between the government buildings, the entrance to the market and other residences of the people living in the city. He came to two large wooden panel doors that were made of dark timber, there was horizontal panelling going across both doors. Adam knocked and was told to enter by the person inside. Once inside he saw a large office on his immediate right by the front corner, the office was encased by two wooden walls at the front and the left side wall. The right side and the back were merged against the armoury building itself. On the front wall of the office was a window with four metal bars inside, Adam peered through and saw a soldier sitting at a desk going through various books and checklists. He seemed young, dark skinned with a fistful length of beard that was as black as an olive stone. His turban was white and red. He seemed totally engulfed on the checklist that he was reading, Adam assumed that he had been working on these checklists for some time based on his mannerisms.

"Salam Alaikum, how can I help you?" asked the soldier without looking up from the books."

"Walaikum Salam, I was told to come here by the Sultan," the soldier quickly stood up upon the mention of the Sultan, knocking the chair over behind him that he was sitting on. Adam was amused at the reaction but did not show it for fear of embarrassing the young solider.

"The Sultan?" questioned the young solider.

"Yes, I was told to come by and pick various weapons for my mission."

"Yes! Yes! I remember now, you are Major Adam Sir?" Adam nodded and smiled at the nervous soldier.

"That is correct soldier."

"Haris sir, my name is Haris," replied the soldier.

"Would it be ok to go through to the armoury and select a few weapons?"

"Of course Sir! Let me just get the keys and I will let you through." The young soldier quickly rummaged through his desk before pulling out a set of keys from under a pile of books.

"You seem to have a lot of things piling up there Haris?"

"Yes Sir, normally my Captain helps me with certain tasks as I am newly appointed here, but he has been away these past few days."

"I see," replied Adam.

Haris opened the front door of the office and walked further down the stone flooring to the end of the front room, in the centre of the back wall was a metal black gate which Haris unlocked. Once inside Haris picked up a lit torch that was hanging on the wall on the right and handed it to him. He also gave Adam a set of three large brass keys.

"Carry on walking ahead, down the stairs…"

"Thank you Haris but I have been here many times before and am familiar of the layout; you may go back to your office and lock the gate behind me. I will call you through the gate once I come back up."

"Ok Sir, simply put the weapons that you wish to take aside and I will have someone transport them back to the palace tonight." Adam thanked Haris as he started to make his way back to the office. Adam heard his steps echoing down the dark stone stair case, he briefly looked behind him and could just about see remnants of the bright lights shining between the bars of the metal gate he had just came through.

Once Adam reached the bottom he came across a thick wooden door with a large wood beam going across the centre. The beam was padlocked against the door frame from both sides; Adam used the keys to unlock the padlocks and the final key to unlock the door itself. With a large pull Adam was able to open the door, as he stepped in he immediately felt the warmth of the room engulf him like a blanket, there were many torches attached the walls of the armoury to enable soldiers enough light to inspect the weapons in the dark room.

Adam immediately saw row upon row of cannons. They varied in both style and size; he quickly recognised the silver and bronze battering guns that were mostly used within fortresses, as well as attacking them. He placed his hand on the slightly cool cannon, the cannon was supported on two wheels connected by a platform made of thick wood and metal underneath. As Adam touched the cannon he remembered the roaring sounds of the many cannons firing at once during battles in the Asian and African continents. The sound of buildings crumbling and people shouting, war was never something Adam ventured to. Seeing death and destruction around you should never be something that is enjoyed, his father constantly reminded him of that when he was close to death. Adam remembered being at his father's death bed, his father reached over and took his son's hand and spoke words with a gentle tone.

"My son, pray that Allah, Most High, forgives me and grants me mercy, some households are blessed in different areas of their lives…whether riches, skills or the burden of running an empire. We have been blessed with the ability of leading and commanding the minds and bodies of strong men on the battlefield but remember, war is never something we seek out or derive pleasure from. Never take joy in taking a life my son; we fight because we serve our Sultan who protects us under the banner of Islam. The followers of the Prophet, PBUH, fought in many wars, each time outnumbered in every way, but they never fought to satisfy their desire, but rather it was to serve the Prophet, PBUH, and pleasing Allah, Most High. Serve your Sultan my son, the moment you feel joy in war is the moment you only serve yourself and your ego. Promise me you will remember that my son…promise me!" Adam held his father's hand tight and promised he would never forget his last words.

Adam still had his hand on the cannon when he heard the sounds of footsteps behind him.

"Are you planning on taking a cannon for your mission Major?" Adam turned round to face the voice, to his pleasure it was Ali. Adam noticed a changed in the soldier as Ali walked up to him, his stride, posture and general mannerism were different, he almost seemed older and wiser. There was an element of peace to him that he had not seen since he first met him. He smiled at Adam as he shook his hand firmly.

"It's good to see you again Ali, you seem more positive since we last spoke," Ali took a deep breath and exhaled.

"Yes sir, I had time to think and reflect these past few days. The loss of Hasan has forced me to look at myself and my actions; I know there is much I need to focus on with regards to my faith and my position here in the empire. As you said I need to learn from this and not waste it." Adam was pleased to see Ali blossoming before his eyes; he was amazed at the change in him in such a short period of time.

"I noticed that you were looking at this cannon for some time," said Ali, Adam looked back at the cannon briefly. "Yes I was. Seeing it here just brought back a few memories from the past," he tapped the cannon with his knuckles before stepping away from it.

"I spent many years hearing the blasts from these beasts," said Adam, "in Baghdad, Algiers and even Benghazi, in fact the last time I was in Benghazi I came with cannons like these, now I go back there again."

"Did you ever witness the giant cannons Sir?" Adam nodded and gazed back at the cannons.

"The great castle bombards, I remember the shaking of the ground and the deafening sound before the complete silence, until our ears adjusted from the explosions. The fortress would just disappear piece by piece. After each shot we hoped that the leaders would yield as we never wanted to attack but their arrogance wouldn't allow it." Adam's tone began to sound sterner as he walked away from the cannons and rested against the wall with his back.

"It took these great monstrous cannons to break that arrogance." Ali walked over to Adam and leaned against the wall beside him.

"How long has it been since you were on a campaign Sir?"

"Must be about…five years I think, yes five years this winter," Adam stood up away from the wall, "I best stop wasting time and choose what I need."

"Do you know what it is you're looking for Sir?" asked Ali, Adam shook his head.

"Due to the limited knowledge that I have about this mission I keep thinking of different scenarios I may encounter, each encounter would require different tools to deal with."

"If I may ask Sir, if you had to commit to a choice between acting in stealth or open confrontation which would seem the best option?"

"Stealth," replied Adam, almost immediately.

"There we go, follow me Sir," Ali stepped away from the wall and headed left, by the right hand corner was an archway entrance. Ali took hold of one the torches and headed down the entrance, followed by Adam.

At the bottom were two archway entrances, on the left and right, with a dead end wall in front.

"Which would you care to look at first Sir, weapons or armour?"

"Weapons," responded Adam, after a bit of thought. Ali walked through the entrance on the left. The room inside was large, there were nine stone partitions starting from the centre of the room and going on towards the left. Each stone partition was the height of the room, four meters, and came out about three meters. The thickness of each wall was one meter, the stone walls were dark grey and smooth to the touch, as the light of the torch flickered the reflection seemed to dance on the silky surface.

"Remain here for a moment Sir," Ali walked off to the left and disappeared down the third partition. Adam peeked through the first partition and saw hundreds of small daggers on the floor and then the same amount on the four thick wooden shelves that went up the back wall. He bent down and picked up a dagger, the handle was jade in colour and curved at the end. The sheath was golden and engraved with dark sliver lines which intertwined to form a sequence of circular shapes and diamonds; Adam drew the dagger out of its sheath and examined the blade. The dark blade had a slight curve at the tip; at the base of the blade was gold oriental writing and two thin dentures in the centre that travelled up two thirds of the blade before it curved. At that moment Ali appeared holding a small sword in a black sheath. The tip was covered with a thick silver case that had the seal of the empire on it. The handle of the sword was made of polished white bone and wrapped in dark red leather. Ali handed the sheathed sword to Adam, who took it with his right hand, while holding the dagger with his left.

"A yataghan?" asked Adam.

"Yes Sir, it's more mobile and easier to conceal than a large sabre sword," Adam placed the dagger in his belt and then unsheathed the yataghan. The blade was thin and sharp on one side; there was a slight curve in the centre and a fine tip at the end.

"The sword may be smaller than a standard cavalry sabre but it is more useful and discreet in close confrontations which would cater to your stealth strategy Sir." Adam tested the feel of the blade by doing a few practice moves, it felt light and easy to swing in any direction. He sheathed the sword and handed it back to Ali.

"Yes I will take it Ali, along with this dagger".

"I suggest taking two more daggers sir and hiding them on your person, just in case your sword is taken from you and you need to fight your way out of a situation." Adam was impressed with Ali's thinking.

"Will you be taking a bow as well sir?" Adam nodded, he followed Ali to the right hand side of the room through a small opening, again he saw partitions in the same manner but only five. Ali went down the partition furthest away and disappeared for a few minutes; Adam heard the moving of objects and the sound of metal hitting metal. Ali appeared with two bows on his shoulder, he held them both out in front of Adam by the tip of the bow. Both bows were fairly similar, they were both composite bows so they were small; they were also recurve bows so the tips of the bow curved away from the archer. The main difference between the two was there appearance, one being more of a light oak colour and the other a dark pine look.

"Both these bows are smaller and deliver higher impact with less force then our self-bows," Adam took the darker bow and examined the outside; he ran his thumb over the smooth material.

"It's sinew" said Ali.

"Yes I can see," replied Adam, "very good workmanship," Adam then turned the bow round and examined the inside, "I'm guessing that's horn?" Adam asked.

"Yes Sir, with a pine wood core. They are a bit trickier to make with all the various parts needed but the end result is certainly worth it. A bow that delivers more force then most other bows without requiring as much effort from the archer and they are much easier when mobile such as on a horse or a carriage." Adam studied the bow a bit and practiced by pulling the string back.

"What's the difference between the two?" asked Adam.

"Just the colour Major," Adam kept the darker bow.

"I would also suggest using a leather case Sir, the glue in these bows tends to get affected in humid climates".

"I'm surprised at your length of knowledge Ali."

"My family have always been keen archers Sir, both in tournaments and campaigns with the empire, shall we choose the armour now Sir?" Adam agreed and they headed back to the base of the staircase and went in the archway entrance on the right. Ali advised Adam to get thin chain-mail armour that could be worn underneath a thick leather garment so the armour would be hidden. He would still appear as a civilian but at the same time protected for battle.

Ali escorted Adam back up to the ground floor.

"I will have Haris bring your selections to the palace later this evening," Haris was still in his office working away; Adam looked over Ali's shoulder at the young soldier.

"He is very keen, just needs a bit of support to reach his full potential," said Adam.

"Yes, I have been mentoring him for the past few months, but I have been away for two days so he's been maintaining the armoury himself for the first time. Still needs a bit of work but he's getting their slowly."

"Ali, thank you for your support, I feel bad asking but I have one more final request to make and it isn't a small request."

"Anything Major."

"I would like you to accompany me on this mission tomorrow," Ali was stunned.

"Me Sir?"

"Yes, your knowledge and skills would be a valuable asset, think about it and get back to me this evening. I would still need to ask the Sultan if he is willing accept it, but I wanted to ask you first before I did so."

"I will deliver your weapons to you personally this evening after Isha and give you my answer then Sir." Adam left the armoury and headed back to the palace, he wanted to spend enough time studying the note from the governor of Benghazi as he only had one night to prepare for tomorrow.

Asalam Alaikum Leader of the Believers,

I swear by Allah that He is One, and that He alone is deserving of worship.

I also swear by Allah that He sent His most Beloved, the Master of creations our Messenger in this world and the next, the Prophet Muhammad, may peace and blessings be upon him, his family and those that follow his example.

Oh Sultan, I write to inform you of an issue that has arisen in these lands. Two days ago three Bedouins came to our city from the desert on camel back; they are from the Bani Khalid tribe, close by the White Mountains.

They had been attacked by strangers and lost everything; most of their injuries were not severe with the exception of one Bedouin who received a head wound.

The reason I bring this to your attention your majesty is because of the account from the Bedouins. During the night, while two of the Bedouins slept, the Bedouin on guard was attacked by a group of men. The other Bedouins woke up upon hearing their fellow tribesman screaming, but they were over powered easily by the attackers. When I asked them to describe the attackers they simply said 'beasts and bones'. Whenever I asked them again to describe the attackers they just kept saying the same phrase 'beast and bones, beast and bones'. They were, and still are, terrified of speaking on the matter.

The only additional information we have been able to get from them was that the attackers were men, because they heard them communicating in a foreign language, originally they thought they were wild beasts. We also know there were at least five of them and they were armed with weapons. They were very powerful and aggressive, like wild animals.

I am keen to send out a batch of soldiers to search the area to find clues as to what happened and hopefully apprehend these criminals and submit them to you for punishment.

Abdul Ibn Muiz

While sitting alone in his room at the palace, Adam read the letter many times, the lack of description was the area that kept running through his mind. During his time in the army he had encountered similar incidences where both soldiers and civilians were unable to account events due to the fear that engulfed them, but that had always been during times of war, this was different. There was a knock at the door.

"Enter," said Adam, the door opened slowly and the Sultan entered the room, Adam quickly stood to attention.

"Please Adam, sit down and go about your business, I simply popped in to check that you found everything you needed in the armoury?" Adam sat back down on the stool.

"Yes Sir I did, the staff there were most helpful," the Sultan smiled.

"I glad to hear that, well I will leave you to get back to your work," the Sultan turned round to make his way out of the room.

"Your majesty, could I speak to you about one thing?" the Sultan closed the door behind him and walked up to Adam, who quickly stood up.

"Of course, what would you like to speak about?"

"Sir I would like someone to accompany me on the mission tomorrow," the Sultan's eyes widened.

"I see, was there someone specific that you had in mind?"

"Yes Sir there is..."

"Very well," interrupted the Sultan, "tell them to visit the armoury also and get whatever provisions they need." Adam was surprised at the response of the Sultan.

"But my Sultan, do you not want to know who I have chosen?"

"No need I trust your judgement, I wouldn't have sent for you otherwise. I never doubt my Sheikh, when I asked him to put forward names for this mission he said yours without hesitation and no one else's. For that reason I accept your judgement too, was there anything else?" Adam scratched his head and thought for a moment, still slightly stunned.

"No Sir…nothing more, I guess I will speak with Ali and ask him if he will join me."

"Ali ibn Osman? The soldier who escorted you back to the city?"

"Yes sir."

"A good choice Major, inform Captain Ali ibn Osman that he is ordered to get his things in order and be prepared to set off for Benghazi tomorrow at sunrise, I will catch up with you later this evening." The Sultan exited the room and Adam sank back onto his stool. The sound of Umar's voice echoed from the mosque to signal the arrival of the Zuhr prayer. Adam placed the note in his inside pocket before getting up and completing his ablution. He then made his way to the Grand Mosque through the royal garden.

Once the prayers were completed Adam quickly got up and made his way outside the mosque and waited at the top of the stairs, he waited for several minutes before he spotted Ali coming out of the building. He waved for Ali to approach him.

"Salam Alaikum Sir, do you need anything else from the armoury?"

"Walaikum Salam Captain Ali, no thank you I don't but I have been given orders from the Sultan to relay to you."

"He has ordered me to join you for the mission tomorrow hasn't he?" Adam felt bad at the response as he had originally told Ali that he would allow him to make the decision.

"Apologies Ali, I never told the Sultan your name at first but…"

"It's quite alright Sir I had already made up my mind to join you before I even prayed," Adam was relieved at the response.

"Ali, are you free to come with me to the royal garden, I want to show you something regarding the mission."

Ali went with Adam to the royal garden; they sat on two stone stools by the fountain. Adam took out the note from his inside pocket and gave it to Ali. He spent five minutes reading the letter several times before handing it back to Adam. Before he could say anything concerning the note both the Sultan and Prince Saleh entered the royal garden from the Grand Mosque side, Prince Saleh was attired in a long dark grey suit with a white coat on top and a black turban.

"Ah! I'm glad to see you both here preparing," said the Sultan, they walked up to the two soldiers who quickly rose and offered their seats to them, which they declined. All four men stood by the fountain.

"Major, have you had any other thoughts or ideas since we last spoke?" asked the Sultan.

"Yes Sir I have, the one area of concern is regarding the Bedouins and their refusal to speak," the Sultan nodded in acknowledgement, "I am worried that it may prove difficult to gain the information we need in good time, as based on the dream you told me the destruction of the city could be soon."

"Don't stress yourself too much about time limits Adam, the destruction of anything is with Allah alone. You just need to focus on the right course of action, which is how do we get these people to give us the information we need?" said the Sultan.

"Sultan if I may," asked the Prince, the Sultan nodded with approval, "both Adam and Ali are being sent on your behalf, any refusal to comply with their wishes is an act of disobedience to you therefore treason," both Adam and Ali were slightly puzzled as to the direction the Prince was heading in. The Sultan remained clear minded not wanting to make assumptions about his brother till he had finished.

"If they are not willing to give the information then we need to be firm and warn them that they will be punished if they do not comply." The Sultan remained silent and cleared his throat before looking at the two soldiers.

"Do either of you two have anything to say to that, as you will be the ones meeting with these Bedouins?" both of the soldiers looked at each other briefly, Adam could tell from Ali's expression that he didn't agree with the Prince but was not comfortable saying that in front of the Sultan and his brother.

"Your majesties," said Adam, "I completely agree that treason cannot be tolerated. But a man's refusal to speak out of defiance and a man's refusal to speak out of fear cannot be seen as the same and therefore we need to act differently in each circumstance." Both the Sultan and the Prince looked at one another and then back Adam.

"I agree with the Adam," said the Prince "I think I may have been too hasty in my judgement." The Sultan looked back at his brother and patted him on the back.

"That is why we have these discussions my brother; I also agree that we need to be more diplomatic in our approach with the Bani Khalid."

"My Sultan?" asked Ali, the Sultan looked at Ali slightly surprised as he had been quiet for so long.

"Is not Umar from that tribe Sir?"

"Yes he is Captain, I'm not sure if the Major has informed you that Umar asked to be part of this mission but I refused him."

"May I ask why you refused him Sir?" further asked Ali, Adam quickly looked at Ali with a stern look.

"Do not question the Sultan, Captain," said Adam firmly, the Sultan raised his hand at Adam.

"No Major it is fine, without questioning from my troops it would be impossible to succeed anywhere, in answer to your question Captain I felt that Umar's role and responsibilities here were too great for him to leave."

"Your majesty," responded Ali humbly, "I know that the Bani Khalid are a very close community and have their own dialect and customs. I believe Umar is aware of these cultural traits, would not he be the best option we have of getting them to speak with us?" both Adam and the Prince knew what Ali said was right, but they dare not say anything until the Sultan spoke. The Sultan looked at the ground for a moment and then at the Grand Mosque to his right.

"Yes Captain, I believe you are right on this matter," he looked at the Prince, "Saleh?"

"Yes Sultan," the Prince responded.

"Go speak with Umar and inform him that he will be escorting both Major Adam and Captain Ali to Benghazi tomorrow," the Sultan turned his attention to Ali, "Captain?"

"Yes Sir," responded Ali

"Go to the armoury and get the weaponry prepared for all three of you, unless anyone else has anything to add?" all three men remained silent, "Good, I will see you tomorrow after sunrise, Inshallah."

6.

To the Damascus

Four soldiers rode on black horses at a medium pace; they stayed in a two by two formation and were constantly on guard, ensuring nothing out of the ordinary was occurring. Further down the back were another six soldiers also on horseback, in the same formation with an extra row. All ten soldiers had been trained from a very young age to be the bodyguards of the Sultan, the Royal Guard had always very selective in who they choose to guard the royal family. Each of them had been trained in multiple areas of swordsmanship, archery, artilleries and horse-riding. They were the elite of the Sultan's guards. The only time all ten came out together was to protect the Sultan himself whenever he left the capital.

Between the riders was the royal carriage, black in colour with red and gold trims on the four large carriage wheels. On each door was the crescent moon as well as the name of Allah, Most High, and the Prophet Muhammed, PBUH. The carriage was pulled by four black horses and handled by a seasoned soldier, beside him was also another member of the Royal Guard armed and ready with a bow and many arrows in case an ambush occurred.

Inside the carriage sat four men on green leather seats, the Sultan, Adam, Ali and Umar. The Sultan was dressed in a white and green robe with a long cream coat, as well as a large green turban. The other three men were dressed in the standard blue and white uniform, it was the first time that Umar had dressed in the army uniform since coming from Egypt.

The Sultan sat silently drawing back the white curtains and peering outside the carriage. On his left he saw the edge of the stone path that ran alongside the bottom of the mountain, in the distance he saw the coast and three long wooden peers. He cast his eyes on the third peer that seem to have the sun floating just above it and a long gold chain ripple that lead from the peer all the way up the sea from the warm sunlight. He saw the large galleon ship that waited for the members he had selected in the carriage.

"Is there anything that needs to be asked or brought up before you embark to Benghazi?" asked the Sultan. All three soldiers looked at each other for a moment and remained silent.

"Very well, I have a few instructions I want to lay down, firstly, for the entire mission Major Adam is tasked with leading. You must all obey him completely as he represents my orders and therefore represents the Sultan. Any disobedience or refusal to listen will be considered treason, is that understood?"

"Yes Leader of the Believers!" All three men said firmly, the Sultan nodded at their confirmation.

"Secondly, while you are on the ship Commodore Abdul Karim will be the lead officer, I have already advised him to seek your counsel Major during any incidents that may occur on the journey but ultimately the Commodore has the final word, understood?

"Yes Leader of the Believers!" said Adam.

"Thirdly, when you reach Benghazi Governor Abdul Muiz will remain in charge of the city; you will obey him, pray behind and support him in all matters. However he has been instructed that anything concerning the mission is to be led by the Major, and he is to be both obey and support the Major at all times regarding the mission while he is in the city." The Sultan remained silent for a few minutes and occasionally looked out the window to see where they were in their journey. Umar remained still and did not engage in conversation or look to anyone else. Adam studied the Sultan closely, making sure he didn't miss any orders as they came from his lips. The Sultan did not speak again until the carriage had got to its destination.

The Sultan looked out the window and saw the three mask galleon ship close up; the sails were cream in colour and had both red and green crescent moons on them. The ship was three decks high and contained eighty cannons and around three hundred crew members. The ship was dark mahogany in colour and was one of the most advance ships in the fleet.

"I specifically asked for this ship to transport you to Benghazi, it's called the Damascus and was commissioned a year ago," the three men stared at the ship through the open door of the carriage.

"I wanted to ensure that you get to Benghazi swiftly and without any trouble, which is why the Damascus is taking you there." The Sultan remained in the carriage as the three soldiers got out; they all lined up outside facing the Sultan, who raised he hands.

"Oh Allah I ask these three men to witness that I have done everything in my power to help the people of this city. I have no power to keep them safe or to help them achieve their mission that Power is with You alone. You are the Most Merciful, the Most Compassionate, The Just and The All

Powerful; we are unworthy to receive Your Blessings and Support. We are weak and have no power so please help us and send Your Blessings to Your Beloved, the Prophet Muhammed, PBUH, Ameen."

"Ameen," said all the soldiers surrounding the carriage. Several men from the Damascus came and picked up the belongings of the three soldiers. They were dressed in aquamarine colour uniforms and black trousers, which was the uniform for the Royal Navy of the Sultan. As the three soldiers turned to walk towards the ship the Sultan asked for Adam to come to him for one final word, both Umar and Ali continued walking as Adam approached the Sultan in the carriage.

"Yes my Sultan?" the Sultan stared at Adam for a moment. "Adam, while I hope and pray that you complete your mission and return safely, we both know that lies in the Hands of Allah," Adam nodded in agreement, "so I want to know, if anything befalls you, would you advise the leadership role be passed to Ali to continue the mission or should the mission cease and the rest of the party come back to the capital and regroup?" Adam thought for a moment at the Sultan's question before answering.

"My advice would be for both Ali and Umar to return to Benghazi, not the capital, my Sultan."

"Why is that Major?"

"Because your majesty, by that time we will know what the situation is with the city, or at least the area around the city. Once both Ali and Umar return to Benghazi they can then send word to you of the situation and you can then decide if more troops are needed or not. I have no doubt about Ali's resolve and strength…but he is still only one, whereas you have an empire, your majesty." The Sultan looked at Adam with admiration, for years he missed the advice of Adam's father now he seemed to have that support back again with his son.

"Thank you for your words Adam, I agree, that is what we will do. Once you have departed and become settled tell both Ali and Umar what we have agreed."

"Of course Leader of the Believers," the Sultan placed his hand on the top of Adam's turban.

"May Allah protect you and keep you strong...and also keep your head attached to your body", the Sultan smiled as did Adam.

"Ameen," they both said before saying their goodbyes. Adam turned and began making his way to the galleon.

Adam walked all the way down the long peer and gazed at the magnificent Damascus, the ship was around one hundred and eighty feet in length and the beam was forty five feet. There was a plank connected from the peer to the boat which Adam used to board, he dropped himself down on the main deck and looked around at the many sailors working on the various upper decks. He saw roughly one hundred and eighty sailors cleaning the decks, bringing on cargo and adjusting pulleys and ropes. There must have been another one hundred below deck also working hard to prepare he thought.

Adam looked through the sea of busy sailors in search of Umar or Ali until he saw them higher up on the Stern-castle deck. They were both talking to a man who had his back to him; he was resting his right elbow on the ships helm. Adam quickly made his way up to them. Once there he saw the older man, with his long grey beard and dark brown skin and eyes. In his left hand he held a long back cane with a white oval handle made from bone or ivory. The man stopped talking when both Ali's and Umar's attention turn towards Adam.

"Salam Alaikum Major, my name is Abdul Karim and I am the Commodore of the Damascus. I am at your service for as long as you are on this vessel, Major." The Commodore shook Adam's hand firmly.

"Walaikum Salam, thank you for your kind welcome and we all appreciate the support, please call me by my name, given your length of servitude and rank it is I that should address you as such," the Commodore smiled and looked over at Umar and Ali.

"Charming man your Major," he said while pointing his head towards Adam, they both smiled as did Adam, "very well, what may your name be soldier?" asked the Commodore, Adam smiled.

"My name is Adam...Adam ibn Mustafa, Sir." The Commodore looked puzzled and then slightly shocked, his eyes widened as he gazed at Adam.

"Is everything ok Commodore?" asked Adam. The Commodore was still in a daze for a few more moments before coming to.

"Apol...apologies Major, your father, was he Mustafa ibn Ali?" asked Abdul Karim, Adam nodded. The Commodore immediately grabbed Adam and hugged him tight, almost lifting him from his feet. The other two soldiers looked at each other and laughed in both a humorous and confused manner.

"He wasn't that happy when I told him my name." said Ali.

"Nor me," added Umar, they both laughed some more. The Commodore released Adam and looked at his face closely; he placed his hand on Adam's cheek.

"By Allah, I can't believe it is you," he smiled and laughed loudly, "by Allah it is you!" Adam tried to calm the Commodore down, Abdul Karim calmed down and took a few deep breaths.

"Adam...I and your father were virtually brothers, for thirty years we fought and bled together. Don't you remember all the times you came with us on trips around Europe and Asia, you never left your father's side."

"How old was he?" asked Umar.

"Oh he must have been…eight or nine, something like that. I heard you had progressed through the ranks but never got to see you. You look so much like him," Adam looked down embarrassed.

"Well I'm glad our paths crossed again ibn Mustafa," said the Commodore.

"I as well…Uncle," the Commodore patted him hard on the back before walking down to the quarter deck.

"This way gentlemen, I'll show you to your cabins," the Commodore walked down the ladders and through the door on the quarter deck. He went through the passage way and stopped at the two doors on the left.

"The first door is your room Adam, and the next room is for you two soldiers, I will let you settle into your rooms. Your things should have already been brought on board. We will cast off in about an hour, dinner is after Maghrib. You will join me in the great cabin, all of you. Will you be needing anything else?"

"No thank you Commodore," said Adam, the Commodore nodded and smiled before making his way to the upper decks. All three soldiers retreated to their rooms.

A large thick grey matt was rolled out onto the floor of the great cabin, the one room dedicated to whoever was in charge of the vessel. In this cabin stood a large desk by the window, which was positioned at the stern of the ship. On the walls were various maps and calligraphy art.

Abdul Karim sat crossed legged on the floor dishing out pieces of dry meat and fruit to his three guests in front of him. Normally the Commodore would eat with his crew on the main deck or orlop deck, but on this occasion however Abdul Karim wanted privacy when speaking with his three new crew members. All four men began eating in silence, Umar and Ali ate from one plate while Adam and Abdul

Karim shared another. It wasn't long before the silence was broken.

"The Sultan informed me that I would be transporting three men to an important mission that was situated near the city of Benghazi, I was further told not disclose any information to my crew members or anyone else that may come by during this trip." The Commodore took a sip of water; the others had stopped eating once the Commodore initially began speaking. "I was told that I had to ensure, Inshallah, that all three of you, especially the Major, got to Benghazi safe and sound, that is all I have been told." Adam took a sip of water himself before speaking.

"Commodore, unfortunately we are not allowed to divulge any information about the mission without the express permission of the Sultan…"

"You miss understand me Adam," interrupted the Commodore, "I didn't bring this up in order to gain more information, I just wanted you to know the situation in case there were any expectations you had from me."

"Roughly how long will the journey take to Benghazi?" asked Umar.

"Around eight days, with good weather maybe even a week," replied Abdul Karim.

7.
Eyes in the dark

It had been two days and nights since the Damascus had set forth to Benghazi, on the Forecastle desk, positioned towards the bow of the ship, stood Adam staring up at the night sky. He loved watching the stars and different constellations, the cool sea air brought calmness to him that he had not felt for a long time.

Umar climbed up to the deck and stared up at the sky beside Adam.

"It's impossible to stare at those stars and not be amazed with your Lord, how incredible He is and how small and insignificant we are," said Umar, Adam smiled and looked over at his friend who continued to stare at the night sky.

"And yet despite our weakness and disobedience He still blesses us with countless gifts every time our heart beats," added Adam.

"Allahu Akbar…Allahu Akbar," responded Umar, they both stood silent for the next few minutes.

"Do you miss your home Umar, since you came with the Sultan from Egypt?" Umar looked back over towards Adam.

"No, my home is wherever the Sultan wants me to be," Ali also climbed up and joined them on the deck.

"The Commodore said we are making good time and should reach Benghazi in about five days," informed Ali.

"Alhamdullilah," said Adam, he walked over to the right and leant on the wooden barrier.

"Umar can you tell us more about the Bani Khalid tribe, like there history?" asked Adam.

Ali walked up to Adam and leant on the barrier beside him, whereas Umar sat down on his knees in the middle of the deck.

"From what I remember there were three brothers that travelled to the White Mountains, this would have been just before the Prophet, PBUH, received revelation."

"Do you know if they followed any religion during those times?" asked Ali, while he ran his fingers through his beard.

Adam stood silent and still, resting both his hands on the barrier.

"Yes they did, they followed the ancient religions of their region. There were no books or scriptures; the religion was only spoken, never written."

"What did they believe?" further asked Ali.

"I don't know exactly, they did believe in a Supreme Being that governed the universe, but I don't know much else than that. The tribe ended up becoming Christian and then eventually Muslim under the rule of Umar ibn Al Khattab, may Allah be pleased with him," Adam walked closer to Umar.

"Tell us more about the three brothers, who were they and where did they come from?" asked Adam.

"They came from the Kingdom of Macuria close to southern Egypt. My grandfather told me that there was a large battle between the family regarding mining and trading. To ensure that the family didn't destroy themselves the chief banished three of the brothers and their families out of the Kingdom to be sure no more bloodshed occurred. They eventually travelled north-east until they reached the White Mountains where they settled for many generations until now." Umar adjusted his position and sat cross legged, Adam sat down beside him as did Ali.

"So all the brothers remained there for the rest of their lives?" asked Adam.

"No, the brothers ended up fighting one another because each wanted to claim leadership of the tribe, the older brother Khalid forced his two younger brothers to leave the area."

"Do you know where they ended up Umar?" questioned Ali, Umar shook his head.

"No, that is the last we know of them. From then on various other Bedouins came and joined the Bani Khalid with the permission of the chief," Adam looked back up at the stars and thought for a moment.

"Were there any known enemies of the Bani Khalid, any historical battles or ongoing wars?" asked Ali, Adam thought this was a good area to investigate in the part of the Captain.

"Not that I know of, I mean there was the occasional confrontation with other Bedouins or bandits but because they were close to the garrison city of Benghazi it was very rare."

"That's what makes this incident even stranger," added Adam.

"Yes sir," confirmed Umar, they all remained on the upper decks for the next hour before they retired for the night.

On the fifth day of the journey under the hot sun, Commodore Abdul Karim lead the Asr prayer from the poop deck, the whole crew followed behind across the main deck up to the bow of the ship. There were also worshippers below in the orlop deck and cargo hold. Adam, Umar and Ali prayed in the row just behind the Commodore.

The Commodore's first officer was Ibrahim; he was tall, broad and dark skinned. His eyes were brown and his beard black and medium length. He was dressed in the standard Royal Navy uniform and bore a white turban, he had prayed further down on the main deck. Ibrahim shouted out as he rushed over to starboard on the vessel.

"Commodore look! Off the starboard bow!" the Commodore rushed over to the side of the poop deck towards starboard and looked over, he now saw it too as did everyone else on the vessel. A large galleon ship that seemed a drift, the ship seemed similar to the Damascus by design but smaller, There were three masks and what appeared to be three decks, the sails, although were up did not seem secure and there was no crew on the upper decks. The Commodore ordered one of his crew members to fetch him his brass telescope, once they did he checked along the side of the black hull to see if any gun ports were open and cannons pointed out, which there weren't. Every port was closed as far as he could see.

"What do you see Commodore?" asked Ibrahim who came rushing up from the main deck. The Commodore put the telescope down and looked out at the vessel with his naked eye; he looked both confused and concerned.

"Very strange indeed," said the Commodore, he looked over to his first officer "Ibrahim?!"

"Yes Commodore Sir?!"

"Tell them to drop anchor and ready the cannons!" The crew immediately went to work opening all gun ports and preparing every cannon, with at least two men to every cannon. The Helmsman stood by the helm awaiting orders. The Commodore walked down to the main deck to starboard and placed his hands on the side staring at the strange vessel. Adam stood next to the Commodore and looked upon the vessel also.

"What is the range of our cannons Commodore Abdul Karim?" asked Adam, the Commodore remained silent, studying the vessel some more before turning his attention to Adam.

"One thousand meters Major, we're out of range by about one hundred fifty meters."

"As are they?" added Adam, the Commodore nodded.

"There have been cases where pirates have pretended to be in distress and hide their crew," said the Commodore, "once a ship is in range they will then start firing or threaten them to surrender, but rarely do I see pirates in possession of such ships."

After several minutes Abdul Karim made his way to the navigation room, which was under the poop deck. He went through the doors and down the passageway before entering the navigation room on the right. He studied the map and looked at the distance they had left. A few moments later there was a knock on the door.

"Enter," Adam, Umar and Ali entered and closed the door behind them; in the room were two large dark mahogany desks. On the walls and desks were various maps and charts, as well as scrolls, small model ships and figurines of vessels.

"What are your orders Commodore?" asked Adam, Abdul Karim stared at the map and looked at the three men.

"We are roughly three and half days travel from the city; it seems dangerous for pirates to be operating so close to a garrison city, not to mention operating in waters that are in the heart of the biggest empire in the world today."

"So you don't think they are pirates?" asked Umar, the Commodore stared at the map again.

"I don't think so, but I can't be one hundred percent sure of that," the Commodore let out a long sigh of frustration, "this is a dilemma gentlemen."

"What are our choices Commodore?" asked Ali.

"Well we can send some of the crew over in long boats to investigate and keep the vessel out of range or we send the vessel over, armed, and take a closer look."

"Could we not just leave the vessel?" asked Ali, the Commodore looked out the window at the back of the navigation room towards the mystery vessel.

"That is a suggestion, but while I am tasked with transporting you three to Benghazi I am also tasked with protecting these waters and everyone in it. If there are people on that ship who need help I am responsible for that, likewise if there are pirates on that ship I am responsible to take them out of action before they attack anyone else." Adam stepped closer to Abdul Karim.

"Let me go by long boat to check the situation Sir?" the Commodore was shocked at the request.

"Absolutely not Adam, I have been given explicit instructions to transport you safely to Benghazi; you are the last person I would allow to go."

"With all due respect Commodore nobody aboard this ship is more experienced than me when it comes to armed combat, we both know that this ship is more superior in every way to that vessel and if there are pirates on board they will see that too."

"What are you suggesting Major?" enquired Umar.

"I'm suggesting that I go by long boat followed closely behind by the Damascus, if you see any gun ports opening or intentions of firing take them out, your cannons are already prepared to do so."

"But what if you get hit in the cross fire?" asked Ali.

"I won't, Inshallah, as soon as the firing begins I will dive into the waters and wait till the firing stops, it's almost impossible for a cannon to hit a small target like me."

"Ok, let's say you make it on board and are attacked or taken hostage?" questioned the Commodore, Adam shook his head.

"They won't be foolish enough to kill me when they know this vessel could destroy them with ease. If they capture me I will tell them that we do not trade or negotiate with criminals and if I am not returned then you will open fire with me on the ship." The Commodore looked at Adam with a frustrated expression.

"This is a big risk Adam; the Sultan would not allow this…"

"The Sultan has always placed the welfare of his people first, that is what we are doing. I wouldn't do this if I felt it was too risky, do you have better suggestion, anyone?" all three remained silent.

"But why go alone?" added Umar.

"It's quicker and easier if just one person goes, one person is less likely to be seen and escape is easier too. The last thing I want is to have to keep an eye out for the welfare of someone else."

"Very well," said Abdul Karim "you can go, providing that Ibrahim accompanies you…"

"But Commodore…" the Commodore slammed his fist on the desk.

"No buts! He will go with you on the long boat and remain there port side of the vessel, in case you need to escape fast, agreed?" Adam stared at his colleagues.

"Agreed Commodore."

"Ok, I will speak with Ibrahim and get the long boat ready; you get your things in order and then come to the main deck for briefing." The Commodore left the room and made his way to the main deck, the others remained in the room.

"Are you sure about this Sir?" asked Ali

"Do you have a better idea Ali?"

"Yes, let me go instead, I am also experienced in combat and more expendable then you Major."

"Expendable hardly, I spoke with several of the royal guards and members of the royal family about you before we left the city. They said that you are the best archer they have ever seen and that your vision is second to none, is that true Captain?" Ali remained silent out of embarrassment.

"It is true Sir," confirmed Umar.

"Then that settles it, get your bow ready and head to the poop deck, it will have the best visual point on the whole vessel."

"Why Sir?" asked a confused Ali.

"I trust your vision and accuracy over any of these cannons, as the Damascus gets closer you will be able to take out anything that blind sides me, ok Captain?" Ali nodded.

As all three made their way out to the main deck, the long boat had already been lowered to the waters on port side. Ibrahim was sitting in the boat with a sword, a bow and many arrows. Adam peered over the edge and saw the items that he had. He looked over to the Commodore, who was also looking down at the boat.

"I thought you said he was just going to remain by the side of the ship, why the weapons Sir?" the Commodore looked back at Adam.

"I won't be taking any chances with my first officer and yourself. He will remain port side but just in case anything comes at him, that isn't you, he will be able to respond accordingly." Adam thought it made sense and started to climb down the ladder to board the boat. He threw down his weapons first before descending. Ibrahim with his strong arms and shoulders was heading towards the strange vessel with ease; the Damascus was slowly coming behind but stopped once it was fifty meters away. Adam was in front of Ibrahim, looking over him at the ship.

"Not too far now Ibrahim, start easing up."

"Yes Sir," gradually the long boat slowly came into contact with the ship, Ibrahim reached and grabbed the low hanging ladders on the side and pulled the long boat forward till it was side by side with the ship.

"Whenever you are ready Sir, would you like me to board the ship if I don't hear from you after a set time?" Adam pondered for a bit and looked up at the sun, he pointed up towards it.

"If you have not heard from me once the sun starts descending then go back to the Damascus and receive your orders from the Commodore." Ibrahim shook his head. "The Commodore ordered me not to come back to the ship without you." Fair enough Adam thought, he looked up at the ship then at Ibrahim again.

"Ok, once the sun has begun to descend behind the Damascus climb up to the edge of the main deck and look around, don't board entirely unless you are absolutely sure." Ibrahim nodded and then held onto to the ladder to keep the long boat still as Adam climbed up.

Adam leapt over the edge and landed on the main deck, he wore his bow over his chest, with the handle behind his back, along with his arrows. He unsheathed his sword and began to walk slowly across the main deck towards the stern. He stopped once he got to the step that led to the quarter deck; he felt the ship moving unsteadily as the sails were not secure and the anchor had not been dropped. He saw the lever for dropping the anchor by the main mast, Adam knew that pulling the lever would end all hope of remaining undetected so he left it alone, for now. Adam thought the great cabin would be the best place to start. As he walked towards the door he scanned the area and noticed everywhere was clean and bare, probably due to being stranded for a long period and the natural elements such as wind and rain taking everything that was not tied down, he thought.

He walked through the door slowly; the passage way was dark and damp. He just about saw the light that surrounded the door that led to the great cabin. Adam placed the side of his head gently on the door and listened, all he could hear were the creaking noises of the ship moving around in the water. He gently held the round brass door handle and started to turn slowly; to his surprise it was not locked. He opened the door quietly and it began to open inwards but the door stopped after only a few centimetres.

Something was budged up against it; preventing it from it being opened, Adam then knew someone must be inside. He got on the floor and laid on his chest; he peered through the small gap under the door and saw a few table legs, possibly a chest of drawers and a few chairs that seemed to be up against the door. He looked further and saw what seemed to be a white blanket or large piece of cloth in the middle of the room, from the shape there appeared to be something underneath it. Surely if there was someone under it they would have reacted when the door hit the furniture behind it, Adam thought.

Adam ran outside to the quarter deck and then ran up two decks to the poop deck. He climbed over the back and looked down to the window of the great cabin. He slowly eased himself down onto the extension of the great cabin; he looked over and peered through the window upside down. He had difficulty seeing through the window due to the sun light reflecting off the glass but then he saw the white blanket in the middle of the room on top of a burgundy and yellow rug. He also saw there was someone under the blanket; from the person's expression he was either dead or very close to it. Adam knew he had to act quickly so with his sword in its sheath he struck the window several times breaking it; he used the sword to clear any remaining shards on the frame before lowering himself down and swinging into the room.

The room smelt like stale bread and felt humid, he bent over to the man lying on the floor, he was white with a long brown and grey beard. His hair was balding but was long on the back and sides. He eyes were slightly closed as was his mouth; Adam placed his ear close to his mouth and could just about hear the faintest sound of breathing. He looked around for any water but there was nothing in the room apart from a few scraps of food waste. Adam ran to the door and moved away all the furniture that was obstructing the exit, he then gently picked up the man and placed him over his shoulder, the man was dressed in a beige shirt and trousers with a brown waistcoat. His nails were long and his back was cold and clammy. He opened the door and made his way to the decks outside, realising he had no choice he pulled the lever on the quarter deck and dropped the anchor.

The Commodore noticed Adam racing back to Ibrahim with a possible survivor; he ordered the Damascus to get closer. Ibrahim heard Adam approaching, as he looked up he saw Adam with the strange man on his shoulder. He climbed half way up the ladder and was able to catch the man as he was lowered by Adam.

"Get him back to the Damascus and come straight back!"

"Where are you going Sir?"

"To see if there is anyone else on the ship that needs medical assistant, now hurry!" Ibrahim obeyed and quickly set off back to the Damascus.

Adam quickly searched the spaces and rooms in the orlop deck below, with the gun ports closed the light was limited but apart from cannons and several barrels there was not much else, all of a sudden he was hit by a strong smell that almost made him retch. His nostrils burned and his eyes watered, he recognised that smell, it was the smell of death. Something was decaying away but was it human or something else he wondered. As he walked carefully the ground seemed to become sticky but due to the lack of light Adam could not see what it was, he bent down and touched the ground, something had spilt on the floor and appeared to cover a large surface area. He smelt his hand and anticipated the copper like smell; it was blood and lots of it. This must have been the reason that the sailor locked himself in that room but was the danger still on board Adam pondered. Not wanting to take any chances Adam drew his sword and began checking the galleys by the stern of the ship.

Adam walked up to the hatch which was two thirds up along the orlop deck; the hatch had been broken from the inside. Fragments of wood and metal seemed to have exploded outwardly and were scattered on the floor around the hatch frame. There did not seem to be any powder burns or signs that a cannon had been used, what could have done this Adam thought? He looked down at the cargo hold below and saw nothing, it seemed completely dark. Adam knew he couldn't go down without any light and considered opening some of the gun ports to allow light in but then remembered the Commodore would start firing if he did. Adam bent down and peered into the hatch, he was able to make out some barrels and stacks of boxes. After a while his vision began to adjust to the lack of light and he slowly lowered himself down using the ladder to the bottom of the cabin hold.

The Commodore was starting to get inpatient; he looked over to Umar and Ali who were both standing beside him on the main deck.

"I don't like this, if I don't hear anything soon I'm sending a bunch of my men over there."

"Commodore," said Ali, "please trust the Major, he can handle himself". The Commodore pulled out his pocket watch and checked the time.

"I'll give him another fifteen minutes, and then we go in", Ali nodded in agreement.

Adam slowly placed his foot on the floor and stepped away from the ladder, the decaying smell was so strong that Adam had to focus on only breathing through his mouth and not his nose. He walked forward quietly scanning the cargo hold. There were lots of boxes stacked on top of each other and many barrels tied up in large batches. He found it difficult to see what was on the ground due to the lack of light; he bent down and felt the floor which was even stickier then on the upper deck.

As Adam felt the ground he heard the sound of something breathing, he looked ahead of him and saw some kind of movement in front of him about twenty meters ahead.

He saw two glowing dots, almost like orbs floating ahead, after a few moments more the breathing sound transcended into a growl. The mystery figure came closer and then Adam saw what was in front of him but his mind could not comprehend what he was seeing.

Ibrahim had made his way back to the strange vessel and looked over his shoulder at the sun; it had begun to set and was slowly making its way towards to the Damascus.

Adam was staring at a large male lion; he couldn't understand that on a strange deserted ship that had been drifting aimlessly was a huge lion. Its mane seemed black due to the lack of light; its eyes were like sparking jewels. Adam could just make out the front half of the lion's body, it was clawing away at the ground beneath him and its growl was becoming more intense. It started to crouch down slightly and Adam could tell that it was about to attack, before it did Adam quickly reached for his bow and an arrow. The lion had already covered ten meters before Adam was able to aim his arrow, with only five meters remaining Adam launched the arrow and it graced passed the beasts left shoulder, wounding it slightly. The wound stunned the lion and it ran off into the shadows between the boxes and barrels. Adam knew that the injury would not hold it off for long and he was a sitting target on the ground with the lack of light. He quickly ran to his left and climbed up the boxes which were seven rows high; when he got to the top he was five meters above the ground and able to look down at the partially visual dark floor. He looked behind him and saw the ladder in the distance, there was no way he could make it without the lion catching him, he would need to at least injure or trap the lion to stand a chance of escaping.

Ibrahim began climbing the ladder to board the ship. Once on the main deck he scanned the area with his sword in hand, after a few moments he started to make his way to the stern of the ship to search the various cabins for Adam and any other survivors.

Adam could hear the occasional growl and the sound of movement below, he slowly walked forward with his armed bow while checking the ground on both his right and left. At the half way point Adam heard a huge growl behind him, he quickly turned round and saw the injured lion climbing up the last row of boxes. Adam tried to shoot again but the lion's speed was too great, so he jumped of the boxes and hoped not to break anything. Instead of hitting the floor Adam landed on a bunch of barrels that were covered by a thick net to hold them together. The lion started to make his way down the boxes, Adam quickly fired two arrows, each one missing but scaring the lion enough to retreat again into the shadows.

Adam saw there was a brig to his left roughly twenty feet ahead, he immediately started running and heard the lion close behind him. He got to the cell and slammed the door shut, with no way to lock it Adam took three steps to the right so he was no longer in front of the door but instead in front of the cell wall. The lion automatically charged to the cell wall and slammed against it. It stood up on its back paws and tried to grab Adam by putting his front paws through the gaps in the bars. Adam had about six feet of space in the cell and was able to avoid being mauled. Realising that it was only a matter of time before the lion noticed the cell door Adam armed his bow again and fired. The arrow launched deeply into the lion's left shoulder, with a massive roar the lion retreated into the shadows again. Adam took the chance and ran for all his worth to the ladder at the far end of the cabin hold.

Ibrahim was making his way back to the quarter deck, after searching all the cabins, when he saw Adam coming through the hatch on the main deck

"Sir is there anyone else?!" Adam looked back at Ibrahim with a terrified look on his face before he could say anything the roar of the lion came pouring out of the hatch. Ibrahim was both shocked and still when he heard the sound. The sailors on the Damascus also heard it, including the Commodore.

"Bring the ship closer men!" he ordered. The lion leaped onto the main deck and locked his eyes onto Adam; the arrow was still wedged deep into his shoulder. Ibrahim was about to jump down to the main deck to help the Major but Adam signalled to him to keep still, he looked over at the Damascus. He saw the sailors looking on, he couldn't make them out individually but he knew they could see what was happening.

"I hope you're as good as they say you are," he muttered to himself before turning round and running towards the bow of the ship, dropping his bow and pulling out his sword while running. The lion starting running after him, Ibrahim shouted to get the lion's attention but it did not work.

"What is he doing?!" shouted the Commodore, Ali knew very well what he was doing and began running to the forecastle deck. Adam leapt onto the bowstrip that stuck out twenty-five feet in front of the bow. As he climbed up the bowstrip the lion also began climbing up in pursuit. When he got to the end he turned round and saw the lion was only around eight feet away, he held his sword tightly and waited for the lion to get a little closer. The lion leapt forward towards Adam and was about to land on him when an arrow struck it on the side of the head, the lion fell to the sea. Adam quickly looked down and saw the lion floating motionless on the water, it was dead. Adam let out a long breath and stayed there for a few minutes. He looked over at the Damascus that was now a lot closer, he saw Ali standing on the forecastle deck holding his bow.

"You really are that good," Adam said to himself quietly.

He began to make his way back down the bowstrip where Ibrahim was waiting for him.

"A lion? Where did the lion come from?" asked Ibrahim, Adam shook his head.

"I'm not sure, I found him in the cargo hold, maybe the sailor can tell us if he isn't dead already". The Damascus came closer and both Ibrahim and Adam made their way back to the vessel.

Two days had passed since the turmoil on the strange ship. The stranger from the vessel woke up in bed, his vision was blurred and his head was throbbing. His mouth and throat were dry; he tried to swallow but the pain made it difficult. Slowly his vision became clearer and he saw that he was lying in bed; he looked around and noticed the bare room which contained nothing more than a bed, chest of drawers and a small stool. As he looked over to his left he noticed the door was slightly opened, he began to have a panic attack, his breathing became short and he started to sweat profusely. He tried to sit up but his body wouldn't allow him to, at that moment the doctor of the Damascus, Amir, walked in. He was short and broad, with a small beard. His skin was black and his eyes dark brown, he was dressed in the standard aquamarine uniform but had a white scarf folded over his shoulder, which all navy doctors attired themselves in. Amir noticed the panic attack and rushed over to the man.

"The door! Please shut the door!" shouted the man, Amir quickly closed the door.

"No he will get through…you must barricade us in, please Sir!" Amir realised what was happening, he moved the stool beside the bed and sat next to him, he held the man's hand who was now starting to cry.

"It's ok; you are no longer on your ship," said Amir, the words had a massive impact on the man who looked at Amir with confusion which then led to relief. His head collapsed back onto the pillow and he placed both his hands on his face, the crying still continued but they were not tears of pain but rather relief. Amir gave the man time before speaking, after several minutes the man stopped crying and moved his hands away. Amir could see that the man's hands were still shaking slightly, the trauma from the other vessel still affected him greatly he thought.

"How…how long have I been here Sir?"

"You have been aboard the Damascus for two days now."

"The Damascus?" questioned the confused man, Amir nodded.

"It is the naval ship of the Sultan, Caliph of the Islamic Empire; I can assure you that you are safe now." So many questions were flying through the man's head; Amir could see that he was trying to formulate questions in his mind. The doctor placed his hand on the man's shoulder.

"I can see that you have many questions on your mind, maybe if I brought in your rescuers they could help you make sense of everything."

"Who are my rescuers?"

"Major Adam, he was the one who found you and Commodore Abdul Karim who is in charge of this vessel, would it be ok to bring them in?"

"Will you stay here too?"

"If that is your wish?" the man nodded, "Then I will stay also, give me a few moments and I will fetch them for you," Amir left the room and closed the door behind him.

A while later the man woke up to find both Adam and Abdul Karim sitting on stools beside the bed, the doctor was standing behind them with his back against the door.

"Well, well I'm glad to see you awake sailor," said the Commodore. Adam smiled and nodded his head at the man. The stranger slowly raised his head; Adam aided him by placing two pillows under him to support his neck and head.

"Did I fall back to sleep again?"

"Yes," answered the doctor "you were snoring when we entered and we didn't want to wake you."

"How long was I asleep for?"

"That doesn't matter, the only thing that matters is that you're ok," said the Commodore, "now then, perhaps you could tell us your name sailor?"

"My name…yes, my name is Alonso…Alonso Lopez."

"Well then, let me greet you with the greeting of our beloved Prophet, PBUH, Salam Alaikum Alonso, my name is Abdul Karim and I am the Commodore of the Damascus. To my right is Major Adam, who was the one that found you on your ship and behind us is Amir ibn Suleyman, the ships doctor."

"Thank you, thank you so much for rescuing me; I was so sure that I was going to die," Alonso stared off in front of him for a brief moment before looking back at the Commodore, "were there any other survivors on the Sao Luis?"

"Sao Luis? That was the name of your ship?" asked Adam, Alonso nodded, Adam let out a sigh before answering. "Sadly there were no more survivors on the ship, how many people were on board?"

"About two hundred, maybe less."

"Then it would appear that most of the crew abandoned ship," said Adam "from what we could see there were about thirty sailors left on the Sao Luis." Alonso scratched his cheek and looked at all three men.

"You found them?" Amir took a step forward between the Commodore and Major.

"Alonso, perhaps now is not a good time to discuss this," said Amir, "you have already been through a lot, this information may…"

"No," interrupted Alonso "after all those months of being locked away, not knowing what was happening to my family. I want to know now, please." Adam looked over at the Commodore who nodded for him to answer.

"Once the Sao Luis was secured I and a few others searched the entire ship, we found many remains in the cargo hold. Based on their conditions we assumed that the lion had devoured them. From the bones we were able to identify at least thirty men."

"Ricardo," said Alonso, all three men looked at each other in confusion.

"I'm sorry, did you say 'Ricardo'?" asked the Commodore, Alonso nodded.

"Who is Ricardo?" asked Adam.

"Ricardo is the name of the lion."

"He had a name, you mean he belonged to you?" asked Amir, in a very perplexed manner.

"Not me, the Captain, Fernando de Mendoza, he acquired the lion when it was only a cub." The three men were left speechless; it had never occurred to them that the lion was actually a pet.

"But why…why did the captain have a lion, where did he get it from?" asked the Commodore in complete shock, Alonso smiled and almost appeared to laugh to himself.

"It must appear so strange hearing this; to be honest we became so use to it that it almost became normal to us. You see Captain Mendoza was a successful sea merchant and would trade a lot between Western Africa and the rest of Europe. About seven or eight years ago, while in Africa, he came across several lion cubs in the market place, he agreed to trade some goods for one cub. As the years went by the crew just became use to having the lion on board, you don't realise the absurdity when you see it growing from a cub. I know that sounds crazy but Ricardo became one of the crew members." Adam looked over at the Commodore who seemed baffled at the words he was hearing.

"One of the crew?!" said the Commodore angrily, "This was a wild animal, an animal that has no place being on a ship or around people for that matter!" the doctor placed his hand on

the Commodore's shoulder to remind him to calm down as
Alonso was still sick and suffering from trauma. The
Commodore stopped speaking and lent back on his stool, he
let out a long breath to calm himself down.

"I know…I know," replied Alonso, "but it was the Captain's
choice, and we trusted our Captain."

"So what happened?" asked Adam.

Alonso remained quiet and then looked up at the overhead.
He took deep breaths before giving his account.

"It happened one night; many of us were a sleep below when
we heard screaming, when we got up to the main deck we
saw that the Captain was dead, Ricardo had killed him and
brought his body outside. He then started attacking anyone
near him, due to the darkness, unsteady waters and…and the
death of our Captain everyone just panicked and ran."

"Nobody tried to stop him?" asked the Commodore.

"We could barely see, there were people running and bodies
on the floor. I just ran and locked myself away in the great
cabin, I remember," Alonso began to cry, "I remember the
screams and the sound of people running I…I can't," Alonso
began to tremble and his voice started to break. Amir stepped
between the two men and placed his hand on Alonso's
forehead.

"Sir I think that's enough," said Amir, the Commodore
agreed and got up, as did Adam.

They both walked out and headed for the poop deck
above. Once there they both looked out at the sea and clear
skies during the beautiful afternoon breeze.

"Because of one man's stupidity and arrogance two hundred
men have probably perished and an innocent creature has
been slain," said the Commodore, Adam nodded in
agreement but couldn't find any words to add to the
Commodore's.

8.
Benghazi

The Damascus finally arrived at the port of Benghazi. The ship anchored about one hundred meters from the peer. A long boat was being loaded with the belongings of all the three travellers, as both Ali and Umar descended down to the long boat Adam spoke with the Commodore on the main deck.

"I hope these events have not affected your mind-set for the mission you are about to embark on Adam?" said the Commodore, Adam shook his head and smiled.

"No Commodore, this is all part of my mission," Adam scanned the upper decks and saw sailors preparing to unload cargo and other goods to the peers. They would need at least another hour to prepare everything before setting forward. He noticed Alonso coming out the door from the passageway and setting foot onto the quarter deck. He had progressed well over these past few days, the colour in his face was less pale and his eyes seemed more alert and energised. He had been given new clothes to wear, the Commodore had ordered for a navy uniform to be given to him. Adam was surprised to see Alonso in the uniform.

"He is wearing a navy uniform?" Adam pointed out; the Commodore looked over to Alonso and smiled.

"Yes, after speaking with him I found out that he had nowhere else to go, no family or home to return to. He asked if he could remain with us and hopefully build new ties here, how could I refuse the request of someone that has been through what he has." Adam smiled and nodded, they both stared at Alonso who was enjoying the fresh air and the feel of the breeze rolling over him. Adam shook the Commodore's hand.

"May Allah protect you on your journey and make you successful in completing the request of the Sultan."

"Ameen," Adam responded "hopefully our pasts will cross again Commodore; it has been a pleasure serving you on this vessel." The Commodore patted the Major on the back as he turned to board the long boat.

Ibrahim rowed them to the peer, Umar looked back at the Damascus as they approached the coast of Benghazi he wondered if he would make it back to the capital and see the Sultan again. He looked over to Ali who was staring ahead at the peer; he seemed clear headed and focused preparing for the next stage of their journey.

Adam looked ahead and saw the two stone peers coming forth from the great city. The city was protected by a large stone fortress that surrounded it by going across the beach and up and along both sides. On each side of the city the fortress travelled up the high hills, the back was protected by a large mountain covered in greenery. Adam could make out several large buildings behind the fortress; first he saw two large towers which turned out to be churches. The city had previously been under the rule of Christians and many of the churches built still stood today. There was a large three storey building at the centre of the city, the flags of the empire were on top of each tower point, all six of them. The various sea merchants and trades people were gathered on the beach, selling all kinds of items, the scene reminded Adam of what he had witnessed when he left the capital. On the left peer Ali pointed to the large gathering of people that seemed to be waiting.

"I can see the Governor and his soldiers waiting to meet us." Adam and Umar both squinted hard in an attempt to see what Ali saw.

"How you are able to see them from that distance I will never know," said Umar, Adam laughed.

"Well thank Allah he can, otherwise I would be in the belly of a lion right now." All three men laughed, including Ibrahim, the long boat eventually made it to the peer and several soldiers dressed in uniform helped the three men up onto the peer.

As the group of soldiers parted in the middle an old man walked between them towards Adam. He was dressed in a red and white robe with a small black turban. He used a long walking stick that would often be used by animal herders. His skin appeared golden and his eyes light grey, almost his entire beard was white with the exception of a few black hairs on his moustache. Adam lowered his gaze to the floor as a sign of respect when the Governor stood in front of him; Adam kissed his hand, as did the other two.

"Praise be to Allah, Most High, that you made it to us safe and sound, I trust your journey was a good one?"

"Yes it was Governor," replied Adam immediately. Both Umar and Ali traded brief looks to one another.

"Governor please let me introduce you to my men," the Governor walked a few steps to the pair of them, "please meet Captain Ali Ibn Osman and Lieutenant Umar Ibn…"

"Idris," finished off the Governor, "how are you old friend?" Umar smiled and walked up to the Governor and hugged him. "When my men described you as you were arriving I knew immediately it was you, well enough talking we have more pressing matters to deal with. Major, I will escort you to your lodgings where you can rest, after the Isha prayer my men will take you to the Bani Khalid where you can speak with them." The realisation that he will finally be speaking with his kin had a sudden impact on Umar, long had he wanted to meet members of his tribe but now he was feeling conflicted because of the nature of the meeting.

They all walked up the peer, led by the Governor with a soldier at each side; they made their way across the stony beach. Adam, Umar and Ali walked in a straight row behind the Governor followed by seven armed soldiers behind. They walked to the centre of the fortress towards the small arched entrance; as they walked through the sound of street life immediately fell upon them. The fortress walls worked well at containing energy levels within themselves.

The buildings were all closely compacted to each other, ranging from small one storey huts to large three storey buildings. There was a stone cobble pathway that lead from the entrance and travelled gradually uphill to the large building that Adam had first seen from the long boat. The pathway was one kilometre in length with additional pathways trailing off to the right and left that went round the outskirts of the city.

Children could both be seen and heard running around and playing along the streets and on top of the small huts. Residents in the city were out selling, cleaning, working, conversing and eating all along the streets, but they would all pause and acknowledge the Governor when he walked past.

All three men were shown to three small houses, well within the town centre that were reserved for ambassadors and other dignitary figures. The Governor encouraged them to rest well and prepare their approach carefully in gaining the information required.

Adam had advised Umar and Ali to change out of their uniforms in order to portray a more welcoming appearance for the Bedouins, which was different to their previous experiences in Benghazi. Adam was dressed in a simple long white shirt and black trousers, Umar wore a traditional green, red and white robe with a dark red turban and black coat, he hoped that this would have a positive effect on the Bedouins. Ali was dressed in a long grey suit with a white turban and a thin black robe on top. All three men met together in one of the small houses, they sat on a large white and golden rug, surrounded by small red cushions and the smell of musk incense. On the walls were various coloured rugs to keep the rooms warm during the winter periods, which was bitterly cold due to being by the coast.

"Do you have some idea how you are going to engage with them Umar?" Adam asked, hoping that Umar had everything planned out.

"I have been trying to think of various angles to approach but every time I imagine the conversation in my head I see problems arising."

"What kind of problems?" questioned Ali.

"Problems of how to keep the conversation flowing. Figuring out how to direct the conversation to the attack and how long to wait before approaching that topic?" Ali nodded appreciating the complexity of the situation, after all he realised that Umar only had one shot at this, if he didn't win both the hearts and trust of his kin it would prove impossible obtaining the information at all.

The adhan for the Isha prayer echoed across the streets of Benghazi, the three men made their way to the large building in the heart of the city. As they walked through the red open doors of the grey structure, Adam noticed on the walls and the ceiling was Christian iconography. Previously this had been the main church of the city but had since been converted to a mosque once the empire took control.

The Governor slowly walked to the front of the large prayer hall and began to lead the many people in prayer. Umar noticed at the end of the prayer hall three black men dressed in long red and black robes, with a black head scarfs. He knew immediately from their attire as well as their mannerisms that they were the Bani Khalid. Once the prayer had finished the Governor approached Adam, who was sitting next to his two colleagues on the side of the prayer hall.

"Those are the Bani Khalid," said the Governor pointing to three men that Umar had already noticed.

"Shall I introduce you to them? You can then return to your houses and speak with them." Both Adam and Ali looked towards Umar, the Governor then realised that Umar would be taking charge at this point. He looked over at Umar.

"Well, what is your wish ibn Idris?" Umar thought quietly for a few seconds before answering.

"Governor Abdul Muiz, would it be ok to speak with them in the mosque alone?" The Governor looked confused at the request.

"You mean you wish me to evacuate everyone from the mosque Umar?" Umar nodded, the Governor turned round and looked at the many worshippers still remaining in the mosque and then at the three Bedouins congregating further down.

"It is a bit irregular but very well Umar, please give me some time to clear the mosque."

"Thank you Governor, may Allah reward your efforts," said Umar, the Governor smiled and nodded appreciatively at the comments. As the Governor walked away Umar lent in closer to Adam and Ali

"I think it would be best if you both left as well", Adam nodded and gestured to Ali for them to leave. Both men got up and wished Umar well in succeeding.

Both Adam and Ali were sitting on the roof of where they were staying; the night sky was covered in stars and a thin crescent moon. Ali turned round and looked at the mosque behind him; he saw the glowing light of the candles coming through the ground floor windows.

"Staring at the mosque is not going to make it finish quicker Ali," said Adam, Ali smiled and turned his head back.

"Neither is us sitting on this roof staring at the stars Sir," Adam laughed quietly and then let out a sigh.

"Unfortunately this is all we can do Ali, I'm guessing patience is not one of your strong holds as oppose to firing an arrow?" Ali shook his head and stared back at the stars.

"No it isn't, that is part of the reason why I try to stay silent most of the time, it's easier not to lose your patience when you speak less Major," Adam nodded in agreement. Ali looked back at the mosque; Adam laughed again and gently smacked Ali on the back of his head.

"Quit looking they'll let us know when they're done," Ali let out a small grunt of frustration before standing up and pacing up and down on the roof.

"What if he doesn't get the information we need Sir?" Adam looked back at the mosque and then towards Ali.

"All of this is out of our hands Captain, Allah is the Provider. All we need to do is focus on conducting ourselves in the best way possible." Ali stood at the edge of the roof top and looked over at the coast; he could see the ripples of the sea under the dim light of the moon.

"Do you know what the main reason for failure is Ali?"

"You mean when you're on a mission Sir?" Adam shook his head.

"No Captain, in every situation for everyone," Ali thought about the question for a moment.

"Is it impatience Sir?" Adam shook his head at Ali's answer.

"Arrogance?" again Adam shook his head; Ali thought longer this time but was unable to think of anything else.

"Sorry Sir I don't know," Adam smiled at Ali.

"Good that is the first step to success," Ali was puzzled at Adam's words, "the main reason for failure is manners, to be specific lack of manners; Ali sat back down next to him.

"I don't understand Major."

"Manners is the key to everything Ali, it is through manners that we know our place in this world. Accepting what we know and what we do not. Many people get involved in situations that do not concern them or fail to acknowledge that they do not know and therefore refuse to go to someone that does." Ali was beginning to understand the lesson that Adam was teaching him, many years ago Adam was being taught this same lesson by his father and Sheikh Abdullah when he was a young lad.

"If you can both accept and understand your place in this world, the place that Allah, Most High, has chosen for you then you will be successful. Our place now is to obey the words of our Sultan, to have belief that Allah will guide us. We do not have the knowledge or ability to get the information we need from the Bani Khalid, but Inshallah Umar does, so take yourself out of the equation and be patient."

Adam stood and stretched his legs, as he was bending forward to relieve the tension in his lower back he noticed movement from the corner of his eye, he looked fully and saw that Umar was standing outside the mosque alone. Both of them quickly made their way down to the mosque, when they got there they could clearly see that Umar's expression was not a positive one.

"Did it not go well?" asked Ali, the suspense clearly showing the effect on his face and tone of voice, Umar shook his head and remained silent. All three men had no words to speak; they simply stared at the ground, up at the stars or at the entrance of the mosque.

"What are they doing now Umar?" questioned Adam, in the back of his mind he was thinking what else needed to be done, he knew that they were on a mission from the Sultan, the representative of the Creator of the Heavens and the earth, what had they missed he thought.

"Praying and doing zikr. I'm sorry; I have failed you and the Sultan." Umar stared at the ground looking dejected and broken; Ali placed his hand on Umar's shoulder in an attempt to lift his spirits.

"Go through the discussion from start to finish, maybe there is something that was overlooked," said Adam.

Umar explained how he discussed their connection through his mother's side; he then went on to describe the character of the Sultan and his mission to help them. He could not tell them about the dream as the Sultan had forbidden the three men from divulging it to anyone that was not part of the mission. The Bedouins still refused to share the information or show them where the attack took place. Even after all this time, Umar explained, the fear was still in their voices when the attack was mentioned by him. Adam shook his head and began pacing up and down slowly by the mosque; he kept going over the words that Umar spoke as well as the words in the Governor's letter. All of a sudden he stopped in mid-step.

"Everything ok Sir?" asked Ali, Adam quickly walked up to Umar.

"We have been going about this the wrong way, it's fear." Umar and Ali stared at Adam and then each other.

"Sir, we know that they are afraid," mentioned Ali, before Adam interrupted him.

"No you don't understand, our entire line of questioning should be centred around fear, Umar?" Adam placed his hand on Umar's shoulder, "You have been trying to win their trust but that isn't what's stopping them, clearly whatever they're afraid of is not just from that night this is something deeper. You need to make them believe that we can stop whatever it is they are afraid of, Inshallah." Umar looked around; his face in deep thought when all of a sudden he smiled.

"What it is?" asked Ali, Umar raised hand indicating for them to wait a bit before rushing back into the mosque. Both Adam and Ali looked at each other confused.

"Do we stay here or go back to the roof again?" asked Ali, before Adam could respond Umar came rushing back out smiling even greater than before.

"They will show us where they were attacked providing the three of us will escort them back to their tribe in the White Mountains soon after." Adam and Ali were in utter shock, both at the result and the short amount of time it took.

"Ho..How did you do that? I mean you were in there for hardly a minute," asked Ali who still could not believe it, Umar looked at Adam.

"It was his idea," said Umar, pointing at Adam.

"All I said was 'fear' Umar, I didn't tell you what to say. What exactly did you say?"

"I told them if you take us there tomorrow you will have with you a man who fought off a bear with nothing more than sticks and stones, as well as a man who killed a lion with one arrow thirty meters away."

"That's it?" both Adam and Ali said simultaneously, Umar nodded and smiled.

All three men stayed silent looking at each other and then back at the mosque doors.

"Ok then," said Adam still in a confused and shocked manner, "I guess, that means we leave tomorrow." Ali nodded, still trying to fathom what just happened.

"I will just let them know that everything is confirmed for tomorrow Sir, I will see you in the morning at Fajr time," said Umar, Adam nodded as Umar went in. He looked back at Ali who was staring blankly at the red doors of the mosque; Adam smiled and smacked his back. Ali awoke from his daze and looked at Adam, who motioned back to their houses with his head.

"Let's get some rest Ali, we have a long day ahead of us tomorrow," Ali agreed and walked back with the Major to their rooms.

9.
The White Mountains

Six horses lined up outside the main mosque of the city. Each horse was geared with all the necessary equipment and items for the long trip. The Governor, Abdul Muiz, stood in front of the red closed doors of the mosque; he had led the Fajr prayer and was now preparing to see off both the three travellers that had arrived from the Sultan, as well as his three long staying guests, the Bani Khalid.

To his right stood the three Bedouins, dressed all in black, with medium length robes and black head scarfs held in place by golden colour agal-ropes. The Governor had offered each of them the gifts of swords, bows and arrows to aid them on their journey back to the White Mountains. To his left stood Adam, Umar and Ali, they had chosen not to wear their uniforms again, preferring to remain discreet when out in the open on the mountain lands and the desert. Instead they wore civilian clothes that were given to them by the Governor. All three wore plain long white shirts with black trousers and long camel skin boots. On top they wore waistcoats, which were leather on the outside and lamb wool in the inside. Adam's waistcoat was dark maroon, and both Ali's and Umar's waistcoats were black in colour.

Before the prayer was lead Adam and Ali were introduced to the three members of the Bani Khalid. The names of the three men were Sayed Ibn Musa, Idris Ibn Musa and Hamad Ibn Saif. Sayed was the oldest of all three, he was also the one that led the group in terms of authority. Within the tribe he was both a shepherd and a teacher, he was responsible for teaching his tribe reading and grammar.

The communication level of the Bani Khalid was very advanced. It was a skill that was preserved and passed down all the way from the time their founding fathers emigrated from the Kingdom of Macuria, many centuries ago. With each generation only a few people were chosen to continue the tradition of preserving and teaching to others within the tribe, it was deemed an honour to be anointed to this position by the tribes' chief. It was Sayed that was in charge of the group as well as their herd when they were attacked that night.

Syed was a very tall man, thin in stature and almost statuesque in appearance, his head was shaved and his eyes dark. Idris was the younger brother of Syed and although he was similar in height and appearance as his older brother, his physique was much broader and stronger. Adam was impressed by his appearance and was somewhat surprised that a man of his size and strength would be afraid to speak. Lastly there was Hamad, who was a distant relative of Syed and Idris. Hamad was much younger than the other two; in fact he was not even really considered a man but was on the verge of becoming one. He was much shorter and chubbier; his physique had not fully developed yet and was still growing into himself. His hair was longer than his relatives; his eyes were much softer and face rounder also. Despite his youth he seemed more engaging and positive than Syed and Idris, maybe lack of years had prevented pessimism and mistrust from engulfing him yet, Adam thought.

Just before the prayer Adam had spoken with Syed alone in one of their houses. Despite the difference in dialect Syed had been able to pick up the differences quite quickly, in the past five weeks he had stayed in Benghazi.

"Syed I have many unanswered questions on my mind regarding the attack…"

"Sir before you continue…"

"Please don't call me Sir, Syed," interrupted Adam, "we are both in charge of our men and therefore equals." Syed nodded in acceptance and continued.

"Adam, although we have agreed to take you to the scene of the attack it does not mean that caution has been forgotten. I will gladly answer your questions once we have crossed the mountain and are in the desert."

"Why then Syed?" asked Adam.

"Because at that time I will be sure that we are alone and safe to speak," Adam was taken aback at Syed's words.

"But Syed you are safer here than you are out there."

"Are you sure about that?" responded Syed in a deep tone; Adam was becoming increasingly confused the more that Syed spoke.

"We are in the heart of one of the biggest military cities in the empire; you have absolutely nothing to fear about being attacked…"

"Not attacked Adam, but heard," Syed could see that none of his words were satisfying Adam.

"Adam I will gladly speak when we are in the desert, agreed?" Adam looked at Syed for a moment before holding out his hand, Syed shook it and they both nodded in agreement.

The six men slowly made their way to the mountain that stood behind the city, which seemed to watch over the people in Benghazi. There were several routes that they could take but the Bani Khalid advised using the longer route as the gradient was not too high. The other advantage was that the riders could remain on their horses for most of the journey through the mountain.

Adam and Syed rode in front, with Syed taking the lead. Umar, Idris and Hamad rode in the middle followed behind by Ali who was able to monitor the situation with his strong sight. The riders slowly began ascending the mountain; they travelled along the right side slope, which thankfully was very shallow. Syed would occasionally keep looking around both in front and behind, Adam noticed the concern on his face the further they ascended along the side of the slope.

"There is no need to worry Syed," said Adam, in an attempt to relieve his concerns. Syed continued to scan the mountain before looking at Adam.

"You cannot be sure of that Adam; you are not familiar with these lands and those that wonder through them." Adam responded with an agreeable nod.

"True, but I can be sure of my soldier's strong sight," Syed look behind at Ali, who was also scanning the area regularly, "with these low slopes as well as being on horseback, it will be almost impossible for anyone or anything to sneak up on us without Ali seeing it first."

"Very well Major, I'll trust your words, for now." Adam smiled at his cynicism, but knew he couldn't respond until he had all the information. Maybe Syed was right to behave as he did or maybe his whole demeanour was unwarranted, either way Adam could only respond accordingly when they reached the desert.

The sun began to set behind them as they reached the half way point on the mountain.

"Syed!" Idris shouted from behind, Syed turned to his brother but kept trotting ahead while doing so, "If we do not stop at the Cave of Light we will not find any other shelter before nightfall." Syed looked up at the sun and realised his brother was right.

"We have taken longer than expected," Syed said to Adam, "we need to take shelter at the cave further up." Adam agreed and informed the riders that they would be stopping soon.

"Why is it called the Cave of Light?" asked Umar to Idris and Hamad.

"If we get their before nightfall you will see why," replied Hamad with a cheeky expression. The riders saw the mouth of the cave appearing, it was almost oval in shape and nearly three meters high.

"Will the horses fit in there?" Adam asked Syed.

"Yes, there are several large chambers inside; we should have plenty of room. But do not venture too far as there is a deep shaft at the back of the cave." The riders dismounted and began entering the cave with their horses, led by Syed.

Inside the cave was a passage, it lead to a large chamber. The chamber was lit up from a hole in the ceiling that allowed a beam of sunlight to pass through and reflect off the moist walls.

"I see," said Umar turning to Hamad.

"The Cave of Light," responded Hamad with a giant smile and his arms spread out wide as if he was performing for an audience. On the right-side of the chamber was a long column, Syed pointed towards the beam of light.

"About ten meters pass that beam is the shaft, so everyone stay in front of the beam." Towards the left wall were two separate openings that led to small rooms within the cave.

Using some wood and dry weeds they found outside the cave, Ali and Idris built a small fire as the temperature would drop rapidly in the mountain after sunset. Five of them sat round the fire eating bread and dried meat, Adam stood by the passage looking out through the mouth of the cave. Umar walked up to Adam with some food, he sat by the Major. "You haven't eaten anything since we left this morning," said Umar as he placed the bread in Adam's hand. Adam thanked him and began to eat.

"What do you make of our travelling comrades Umar?" Umar looked over at the three of them as they were chatting amongst themselves, Ali seemed content on being silent and watching the fire glow.

"They are hiding something Sir," Adam nodded in agreement, "there is something more to this attack."

"Why do you say that?"

"Call it a hunch Sir," at that moment Syed appeared.

"Go and get some sleep Umar, I will take the first watch," said Adam.

"Yes Sir," replied Umar, "wake me up when you wish me to take the next watch Sir."

"No need Umar, I will take the next watch, if that is ok with you Adam?" asked Syed, Adam nodded and Umar left the two of them. Syed sat on the other side of passage entrance facing Adam, who was still staring to the outside of the cave.

"I can see there is something on your mind Adam, it has been with you ever since we left the city. Adam looked over at Syed with a cautious expression.

"Yes, but you have made it clear that we cannot speak until we have entered the desert, so there is no point discussing what is on my mind." Syed looked over at his kin chatting round the fire and then up at the opening at the top of the cave.

"You may ask your question Major, if I am able to answer them now I will, otherwise you will have to wait."

"Fair enough," said Adam as he adjusted his seating position, "no doubt you have family left at the White Mountain I assume?" Syed nodded, "Then how can a man, from such a strong and noble tribe fall into fear rather than going back to protect his kin, that he has abandoned?" Syed stared at Adam with a blank expression; he remained silent, wiping his mouth with his hand.

"You think I submitted to fear at the expense of the wellbeing of my family?"

"How else am I supposed to see it?" replied Adam, Syed stood up and stared down at Adam, he looked over and saw the others were still socialising round the fire, except for Ali who was watching Syed. Syed walked over slowly and sat by Adam, he lent over so his words could not be made out by anyone else.

"I do not fear death, and neither do those who I travel with."

"Then tell me why you..."

"Will you be silent for one moment and let me finish?" sharply replied Syed in a low tone, Adam backed off and allowed Syed to continue.

"The fear that we have is not for us but rather our tribe, we long to go back but we couldn't risk being spotted and then followed. Our tribe has survived by being hidden, but that would all change if the enemy found out where we were based." The frustration was beginning to grow in Syed, Ali had been watching and stood up. Adam signalled for him to remain seated and not to come over.

"Who is this enemy Syed?" Syed laughed at the question and got up.

"Wake me up when you are ready to swap shifts," said Syed before he walked back to one of the rooms. Ali got up and walked over to Adam.

"What was all that about?" he asked Adam, the Major looked over at the room where Syed entered.

"I have no idea, you better get some rest Ali, I'll take the first watch. Tell the others to retire too."

"Yes Sir," Ali walked off and informed the others.

Adam was trying to make sense of what Syed had spoken. He got up slowly and made his way down the passage to the entrance of the cave, the wind was blasting through the passage which acted like a giant funnel. Adam made his way through and stood at the entrance of the cave, he turned round and with the dim moonlight he was able see further up the slope for at least two hundred meters. Aside from the trees and the curves of the naturally made footpath there was nothing else to see, he turned round and looked down, again nothing except what they had passed previously.

In the morning all six riders began making their way down the slope of the mountain, as they got closer to the bottom the greenery began to disappear. The trees grew fewer and the heat more intense, Adam looked over his shoulder and saw the rest of the group were no longer conversing as they had been the previous night. This was largely due to the change in demeanour of the three Bedouins. Zuhr had now come in and Adam thought it best that they pray while riding on their horses as the Bani Khalid were growing more anxious with every yard they covered.

Several hours later the riders reached the base of the mountain, the group was standing by the edge of a dried up lake bed, the ground was hard and cracked. Umar looked down at the dried up clay.
"How long has this lake been dry?" he asked.
"About four months," replied Idris, "the rain should come in about a month's time and fill the lake once more," all this talk of rain made Ali look up at the burning sun.
"How, long till we get to our destination?" Ali asked.
"About two days travel, and from there another day till we get to the White Mountains," replied Syed.
"How long till you are ready to tell us?" asked Adam, Syed looked behind him at the mountain and then ahead of him

towards the open desert. The desert was completely barren and apart from the giant sand dunes in the distant and the dried up lake, there appeared to be nothing else to see. "There are some boulders about half of day's journey due north, once there we can make camp and I will tell you everything". Everyone looked at Adam to see his response. "Very well Syed, but if you do not tell us everything then we will abandon you there and head back to Benghazi immediately, is that understood?" Syed nodded respectfully, Ali and Umar both knew that the threat was a complete bluff but Syed and the rest of the Bani Khalid seemed to have bought it.

After a couple of hours the sand beneath them began to appear much lighter and softer, the horses which had been conditioned to travel on loose deep sand began to increase their speed the more loose the sand became. The sand began flying up under the riders and so they all manoeuvred themselves in a single row, with Syed slightly ahead.

Eventually they reached the large black boulders, which were seven in total. The giant boulders appeared to have a desert varnish to them, due to the many years of being exposed to the natural elements. All the boulders were spaced out in an almost triangular shape. Apart from two small boulders, the rest were of similar size, around two meters high and six meters in circumference. They were all round in shape, hardly perfect spheres but still impressively curved for natural erosion.

All the riders dismounted and began to set up camp, both Umar and Ali checked the supplies of all the riders and rationed out the food and water for that night. Adam walked up to Syed who was resting his back against one of the boulders.

"Would you prefer to tell me alone or in front of my colleagues?" Syed smiled and stood up from the boulder.

"I will speak in front of everyone; you have been patient and stuck to your word." Adam appreciated this and walked to the rest of the riders, followed by Syed.

"Can I have everyone's attention please?" asked Adam, the rest of the group stopped what they were doing. Adam walked up to the middle of the group and sat down, facing Syed, who remained standing. The rest followed Adam's lead and seated themselves also. Syed took a few steps forward before looking up at the sky; the sun was beginning to set.

"The Bani Khalid has lived around the White Mountains for many generations," said Syed, "we have always travelled the land freely, utilising the blessings that Allah, Most High, has surrounded us with, until one year ago." Both Hamad and Idris seemed to become more dejected as the words came from Syed's mouth. Ali would occasionally look over to the two men; he could see that the situation they were in was having a great impact on their spirits.

"Initially we were getting reports that strange people were being sighted, roaming on and around the mountains. Nobody had seen them clearly; they would stay hidden in the shadows, keeping their distance. Eventually the Chief ordered a large army to go and find out what was going on."

"Which was a mistake," added Idris, Syed nodded in agreement.

"Yes it was Idris, it was. You see the enemy had been watching us the whole time and anticipated we would despatch a large army. As soon as the army had left they came and stole many cattle and other items we hold dear."

"Was anyone hurt?" Umar enquired.

"Alhamdullilah no, they were very organised and we didn't even know they had been there until after they left," replied Syed, "once that happened the Chief ordered that we relocate deep within the mountains, which we did. Up until now our location has remained hidden, the only time we venture out is to trade or source out better pasture for our cattle."

"Were there any other incidents when people left the village?" asked Ali, Syed remained quiet; Ali looked over to Hamad and Idris.

"A few times those that ventured out never returned," said Syed with a sad tone.

"And you still have no idea who these people are?" asked Adam, Syed shook his head.

"We are the first people that have seen them up close…"

"But you haven't returned Syed; right now your people will have assumed that you have disappeared too," said Adam.

"Which is why we are desperate to get back, we need to tell them what we saw," replied Syed quickly.

"What exactly did you see; can you describe your attackers?" asked Ali.

"It was one attacker," replied Idris. Adam, Umar and Ali were shocked at the response.

"One man over powered all three of you?" asked Adam, Syed nodded.

"I have never seen a man like I did that night, his strength and ferociousness was like that of a wild beast, he even looked like a beast," said Syed.

"How so?" enquired Umar.

"His body was covered completely in animal skin and bones, even his face," Adam tried to picture this person in his head; he had seen similar attire worn by fighters from mountain tribes in Eastern Europe, but never here in the desert.

"Did he say anything?" Adam further asked.

"Yes, he spoke some words but it was a language that I had never heard before."

"This is very odd," added Umar, "for someone to speak a language that is completely different in this area is strange indeed. You would need to travel a great distance to find a language that was completely detached from what is spoken in these lands."

"Unless," spoke Ali, "they are people that have remained hidden for a very long time."

"Never engaging with the societies around them," added Adam, Ali and Umar both nodded in agreement."

"Unless they were attacking them," Idris concluded. The group remained silent digesting everything that had been discussed. Adam got up and started walking towards Syed.

"You thought they had followed you back to Benghazi, which was why you were afraid to speak," said Adam to Syed.

"Yes, for one year they had watched us and waited patiently to strike. It would not have been difficult for one or two of them to follow us from a distance. Hiding in a large city like that would've been very easy."

"But you said that they spoke a different language, how would they understand your words if you had spoken to the Governor?" asked Ali, Adam answered before Syed was able to.

"Ali don't assume what they know and don't know, we have no idea how many languages they speak. Just because we don't know their language doesn't mean they don't know ours." Adam put his hand against the bolder beside Syed who was now resting his back against it.

"There is one thing that I am having trouble understanding Syed," said Adam.

"What is that?"

"The precision and planning that is needed to observe an entire tribe without detection is immense. Not to mention staging certain manoeuvres in order to coax them out, which they succeeded in doing." Adam walked away from the boulder and started walking amongst the others that were seated. They all listened to Adam's words as well as followed him with their eyes.

"They were also able to infiltrate the village, as an army, and not be detected by anyone, and yet when you encountered this 'soldier' shall we call him, he was a wild beast. I ask everyone here, how does an army of wild men carry out such organised tactics against an already strong foe?" nobody could answer this question, for the rest of the day and night few words were spoken until they retired for the night. Adam ordered that two people should remain on watch and alternate amongst the remaining four throughout the rest of the night.

Syed led Idris and Umar in the Fajr prayer, while Adam, Hamad and Ali kept guard on the outskirts of the boulders. Once Syed completed the prayer Adam then led the remaining men while Syed and the others stood guard.

After the prayer Adam approached Ali and Umar while they were preparing their horses to set off.
"Listen, I don't think it would be wise to search the area where they were attacked," both Umar and Ali stopped what they were doing and faced Adam fully.
"But the mission Sir?" enquired Umar.
"The mission still goes ahead, whatever evidence was there is long gone, it's been over a month since the attack. I believe our path lies with this hidden army and I don't think we are going to find them if go back to the point of attack."
"You want to go straight to the White Mountains," said Ali, Adam nodded.
"Yes, we know they are still there, somewhere, attacking the Bani Khalid. Maybe this strange city is connected to them; maybe they are the threat to its destruction." Ali signalled to Adam that Syed was making his way to them.
"Quickly give me your response before he is in earshot," both men agreed with the Major.
"Are you ready to set off Adam?" asked Syed, Adam signalled for Ali and Umar to leave them, which they did.
"Syed we have decided not to visit the scene of attack but rather go straight to the White Mountains," Syed was taken aback with Adam's statement.
"Why the change to the plan Adam?"

"You said yourself this hidden enemy is still attacking you around the mountain, it would be foolish wasting our time when we know they are based around the mountain area. If we can try and locate them and then arrange for the Sultan to send an army to wipe them out, your tribe will be able to live in peace again." Syed was relieved to hear these words, he held out his hand which Adam shook.

"May Allah bless you and your Sultan, from now on you are the sole leader of this camp, I will obey your orders completely Major."

"Good, first order is simple, have you told me everything Syed, is there anything else connected to this enemy or your tribe?"

"No Sir, I have told you everything, I promise," Adam nodded to show he believed his words.

"Ok, get your men ready, we set out as soon as possible.

For the next three days the six rode in the direction of the White Mountains. The mountain range in that area were Fold Mountains by design. They had been named by an ancient civilisation that no longer existed on paper, but their traditions and signs lived through folk tales and language. From generation to generation their stories and names had been passed down; one of those signs was the name of the White Mountains. The type of granite on the faces of these mountains would reflect the sunlight greatly, from a distant the mountains appeared to be made entirely from light rather than stone. This was the reason the ancients named them the White Mountains.

Adam dismounted his horse and walked up close to the base of the mountains. He looked up and scanned the faces of this stone beast; he was able to make out the peak of one of smaller mountains towards the east side. The rest were covered by the clouds that moved quite quickly over the area.

Syed walked up beside Adam and placed his hand on his shoulder.

"Would you prefer to rest Sir before heading to our village?" Adam looked over at his men, as they were eating their last remaining rations. He could tell from the mannerisms and expressions of the Bani Khalid that they were holding back their excitement.

"No Syed, we will march on once they have finished eating."

"Are you sure Major?" Adam smiled at Syed.

"Brother Syed, I have no doubt you and the rest of your tribe are desperate to see your family, let's not make them wait a moment longer than necessary." Syed smiled and showed his appreciation by getting his companions to kiss Adam's hand, which he did also.

All six men walked while holding the reigns of their horses through an almost passage-like path towards the east-side of the mountains. Idris had warned the group that the mountains would prove difficult even on foot and so to pace themselves, for the journey would take at least half a day.

As the hours passed by all six men walked in a single file through the narrow walkway of the mountains, Syed walked ahead with Adam behind. Throughout most of the time the party remained in silence with the occasional exchange of words between Adam and Syed. The high rocky walls meant both sight and sound was very restricted which made Ali unsettled. The gift of strong sight was something that he had become accustomed to and now to be without it was like walking into open battle with no armour. Adam also felt they were very vulnerable and so instructed everyone to put on their chain-mail armour and to keep their swords unsheathed. Hamad was kept in the middle of the group as it was the safest position; Ali took the rear as he was the most experienced in combat, after Adam.

The walls in the side began to lower and the path widened until eventually it was completely open. The temperature suddenly dropped and the view became foggy. Syed stopped walking and signalled with his hand for everyone to remain still and silent. Everyone remained in their positions for two minutes before Adam slowly made his way to Syed's side.

"Is there a problem Syed?" he whispered, Syed did not respond for another minute before turning to Adam.

"No, everything is fine," Syed tried to continue ahead before Adam took hold of him by the arm.

"Why did you stop Syed?" Syed gestured with his hand for him to lower his voice.

"Some of our tribe have gone missing from this spot; I just wanted to be sure that there was nothing else. Until we get to the village we need to keep our noise to a minimum," Umar made his way up to the front.

"How are we able to make it back to the tribe without being sure that we are followed?" he asked Syed.

"We have two checkpoints, each checkpoint is guarded by at least four men," Syed pointed towards the fog ahead, "the first checkpoint is further up that mountain."

"Ok, from here on no one speaks, if you see something, quickly come to me or Syed and let us know in a low voice, only raise your voice if absolutely necessary," said Adam. The group continued walking into the mist; their speed was slow and their attitude more cautious.

As they started to ascend further up Ali quickly rushed ahead and grabbed Adam's arm.

"There is something ahead," he whispered. Adam looked ahead and saw nothing, he turned to Syed.

"Are we close to the checkpoint?" Syed shook his head.

"There it is again," said Ali. Idris, Ali and Hamad armed their bows; Adam knelt down and continued to focus in front him. He heard a sound, like a something tapping on the ground. The sound repeated continuously. Syed immediately recognised the sound and smiled, he told everyone to lower their weapons. At that moment a black mountain goat leaped out of the mist towards them.

"No exactly a hidden enemy," remarked Umar, the group smiled and started to make their way up the mountain when all of a sudden a huge rumbling sound came ahead. The ground began to shake and the mist started to become denser. Hamad and Idris ran towards Syed, all of the horses ran back towards the passageway.

"The horses!" shouted Umar, both Ali and Umar tried to retrieve them; suddenly many huge boulders began falling down towards them. Adam tried to grab the Bani Khalid to run down but several large boulders fell between them, Adam could no longer see them and was just about avoiding the falling giants. He knew that he would be crushed if he stayed there so he started to run back the way they came. He saw the passage ahead; both Umar and Ali were standing by the entrance, shouting for Adam to hurry.

"Move right!" shouted Ali, Adam quickly side stepped and narrowly missed a boulder from crushing him. He leaped into the passage and was caught by both men; several boulders smashed into the entrance and sealed the walkway. All three remained on floor taking deep breaths.

"The Bani Khalid?" asked Umar, Adam slowly got up and dusted himself off; he looked at the boulders blocking the path.

"I couldn't get to them."

"Were they killed?" continued to ask Umar, Adam shook his head.

"They were alive before we were separated, Inshallah they managed to find a safe place." All three men stood there looking at the boulders and occasionally each other.

"What do we do now Major?" asked Ali.

10.
Through the darkness

Umar reached up to the ledge like formation on the large boulder that blocked the path. He was supported below on the shoulders of Adam, which he stood on; gradually he pulled himself up and stood on the narrow ledge.

"Can you reach the top?" asked Ali, who was standing by Adam. Umar reached up but was about fifteen inches shy.

"No I can't."

"Is there room for one us on the ledge with you?" asked Adam, Umar looked below at the ledge; it would be a tight fit he thought.

"Maybe Ali could, Inshallah," Adam ordered Ali to climb on his shoulders and then support Umar to the top from the ledge. Eventually Ali was able to help Umar up, then, while Umar held onto Ali's right hand with both of his, Ali was able to grab hold of Adam's hands below. Slowly Umar walked back pulling them both up, Adam helped by using his legs to partially walk up the boulder.

All three stood on top of the boulder, the dust in the air brought by the landslide, as well as the mist, made it impossible to see beyond ten feet in front of them.

"It's impossible to find the path that we were on before," said Ali.

"We'll have to wait for the dust to settle," replied Umar, Adam shook his head.

"No we can't, it will take a long time before it does, by then it will be nightfall. We have no food or water plus the temperature will be freezing." said Adam.

"Not to mention we have no weapons in case we're attacked," added Ali.

"Exactly, we need to press forward, Inshallah we will hopefully find the path again and more importantly Syed and the rest of the group," said Adam. All three men slowly climbed and slid down the large boulder.

The many boulders that had fallen from above had created an almost labyrinth style maze. Slowly they began making their way through the newly created passages formed by the boulders, as the pathway had no clear structure it was impossible to tell what direction they were heading in.

"We can't continue like this, unless we have a reference point there is no way to tell where we are going," said Umar. Ali looked above at the size of the boulders.

"Maybe we could find a smaller boulder to climb on to, hopefully we will find a reference point from there," he said.

"In this fog?" questioned Adam; Ali looked at the boulders again.

"How about we try and leap our way through, from boulder to boulder?", said Ali, both Umar and Adam thought it was worth a shot and started scanning for a boulder small enough to climb.

As they searched they were able to come a across a few weapons that had been dropped during the landslide. One sword as well as a bow with a few arrows, Ali took the bow and Umar the sword. Eventually they found a boulder that they could scale. Umar gave Ali a boost up and was about to climb up the boulder when they heard a shuffling sound not too far away. Adam signalled for Umar to lower him back down, Adam took the sword from Umar and slowly made his way towards the noise, followed by Ali who had armed his bow.

Adam slowly made his way round a right-hand bend, the fog was quite thick and the strange sound had stopped. Adam paused and waited to hear it again, a huge roar came from above; they all looked up to see two figures falling on top of them. Adam was able to dodge the first figure, the second landed on both Umar and Ali. Adam was only able to make out horns and a black furry hand. Adam swung his sword but it was blocked by a large axe. Umar tried to grab the second figure but he got struck by their fore-arm, the force of the blow forced Umar to fly back and crash into a boulder. Ali saw the face of the figure; it was a skull, with brown animal fur covering the top and sides. He quickly launched his arrow which struck the attacker somewhere on the upper body, but Ali could not see where due to the fog. The attacker let out a huge roar, the first attacker quickly turned to his partner. They both ran back in the direction that Adam and his party had come from; Adam quickly ran to check on Umar, who was already trying to make it to his feet, both Adam and Ali supported Umar up.

"Shall we go after them?" asked Ali, Adam looked at Umar who still seemed slightly off balance.

"It's too risky chasing them in this fog while Umar is still dazed, give him a bit more time to recover, after we'll try and follow them," replied Adam, "did you hit any of them?"

"I'm pretty sure I did, possibly in the stomach or the side." Umar started to look stronger on his feet and signalled that he was ok to continue.

"If you hit him then that means we should have a blood trail, hopefully these things will know a way out through this mess," said Adam.

Slowly they were able to locate the blood trail on the floor; there was quite a large pool at first which then became a thin line.

"You got him good Ali, hopefully he won't die before reaching their destination otherwise we're lost again," said Adam. They continued to follow the trail through the maze of boulders, Ali, who was at the rear armed with his blow, was keeping a look out up top in case they launched another attack.

Eventually they made it through the boulders and were welcomed by some dark pine trees; the area was open and covered in the white fog. After a while the ground started to go down-hill, quite sharply, they all slid down for about twenty feet. At that point the fog seemed to mostly disappear and they saw an almost small valley type lay out in front of them. The walls on either side seemed to create a V shape design with some partial greenery running through them.

As they continued forward the blood trail then took a sharp left almost into the wall, Adam crouched down to get a better look.

"There's a small hole here," he said. Ali and Umar came over and saw the hole which was around three feet in diameter. "This attacker has a lot of will and strength to continue all this way with a wound like that," said Umar. All of them crawled through the space, led by Adam. It lead to a plateau that seemed to connect to another mountain about two hundred meters away. The temperature was now falling rapidly and the light was starting to go also.

"Shall we continue Sir or find some shelter?" asked Ali, Adam knew that they risked possibly freezing to death but he also knew that these attackers could potentially regroup and attack them in large numbers in the middle of the night. He decided to continue ahead and placed his trust in Allah, Most High, that he and his team would be kept safe.

As they reached the other mountain Ali noticed that the trail seemed to stop about three meters ahead. Adam checked to see if there was some kind of trap set up for them, in anticipation that their mystery attackers knew they were going to follow the trail. He told the others to stay put while he went ahead to investigate. As he approached the end of the trail he saw a small shaft, he waved the others over. All three peered down the hole, unable to see the bottom.

"It looks like they escaped through here," said Adam, Umar leaned over and peered deep within the shaft.

"There is no way of knowing how deep it is," he said.

"Well it can't be that deep if they were able to use it," responded Ali.

"But it's hard to prepare for a drop when you don't know where the ground is. You could easily break something in that situation," said Adam, he looked around and saw a large stone which he brought over and dropped down the shaft. They heard several thumps before the noise trailed off.

"That's not a vertical drop," said Ali, "they slid down a steep path from the sound of it, Adam and Umar agreed. Adam decided to go down first at the behest of his soldiers. Adam sat on the edge of the shaft with his feet dangling inside, he said a prayer before dropping in, he immediately hit the ground and started to slide down, the steepness was so vast that he had to lean back to ensure he didn't fall forward and break his neck. Once he landed at the bottom he shouted at the rest to come down, when all three were down they saw a small arch that was four feet from the ground. It was almost pitch black in there but they were able to see a large stack of broken twigs, beside that was a load of quartz stones.

"I guess this is how they got through here, in the darkness," said Umar, he looked around and saw two unlit torches on the ground behind the stack of quartz. Umar bent down and started using the quartz to light up some of the kindle, once he did Ali lit both of the torches and handed one to Adam.

All three men crawled through the arch led by Adam, then Umar and finally Ali. As they came through they entered a narrow yet tall passage, Adam looked ahead to see any sign of light from the attacker's torches ahead, which he didn't. They began walking through; Adam was keen not to be detected so he instructed everyone to whisper if they needed to communicate. After a while the passage began to open until it was almost treble in size, the walls seemed to glisten against the light of the fire, Ali rubbed his hand against the wall and saw that it was the same quartz that they had used to light the torches.

"This is a quartz mine," he whispered, Umar and Adam also examined the wall upon hearing his words.

They were surprised how long they had kept walking without changing direction, always in straight line. After three hours Adam decided to stop and rest for a while.

"I wonder if this path goes straight through the mountain range?" he questioned.

"If it does then we could be here for days," replied Ali.

"At least it is warm, up there we wouldn't last the night", said Umar, Ali nodded in agreement.

"Umar, do you know of any other villages around the White Mountains?" Adam asked.

"No Sir, there is only desert around here."

"There is no way any enemy or mystery city could survive in the middle of the desert, this is how they survived, through this tunnel," said Adam.

"You mean they use it to travel though the desert?" asked Ali, Adam nodded, "that means we will be here for weeks?" Adam nodded again.

"But we have no water Sir," said Umar.

"I know," replied Adam, "Inshallah something will turn up, we just have to keep moving forward."

They walked for hours, having to roughly guess the prayers as they couldn't see the sky. Eventually they decided to stop and rest for the night. Adam took first watch while the others slept; the temperature never changed and always remained warm and slightly humid. Adam then just realised the air, it was humid. He felt the walls and sure enough they were moist which meant there was water nearby. After he woke up Umar to change shifts, he told him about the humidity and moist walls. Umar's spirits seem to lift as there seemed a chance to escape this tunnel.

Umar sat cross legged on the floor with his back against the tunnel wall. He also rested the lit torch against the wall beside him while listening carefully for any sounds within the tunnel, from both directions. His mind began to wonder and he started thinking about the Bani Khalid and the landslide. He was so engrossed in his thoughts that he didn't notice Ali getting up until he sat beside him.

"Can't you sleep?" asked Umar, Ali shook his head and took a few deep breaths.

"How can anyone sleep down here?" responded Ali, Umar smiled and pointed towards Adam who was in a deep sleep. Ali smiled and shook his head.

"Did he fall asleep straight away?" asked Ali, Umar nodded, they both laughed softly. They sat in silence for a brief period, constantly checking the tunnel.

"Umar, we never actually spoke about what happened up on the mountain," Umar looked to the ground.

"I know," Umar responded, "actually I have been trying to keep the images out of my head but with not much success."

"Yes so have I, Inshallah they made it safely back to their village." Umar looked over Ali.

"Do you really think they did Captain?" Umar asked sincerely, Ali knew deep down that the chances of them making it through that carnage were slim at best. "We have to have hope Umar, Allah, Most High, can do anything, so we must always have hope, always." Umar nodded in appreciation of Ali's lifting words.

Ali was getting up when Adam sat up in mid sleep with a shocked expression on his face, which made both Umar and Ali jump.

"Are you ok Sir?" asked Ali worryingly, Adam immediately got up and started looking both ahead and behind, pacing between two spots over and over again.

"Sir is everything ok?" asked Umar, Adam continued to pace and then stopped. He pointed in the direction they had come from before.

"We need to go back that way," both Ali and Umar stared in the direction that they had just come from.

"But Sir," replied Umar "we have just spent hours travelling in this direction, how can you be so sure that we are on the wrong path?"

"I'll explain later just trust me," both men stared at Adam in silence; they shared brief glances to one another before Ali spoke.

"Can you share with us a little Major?" asked Ali.

"Yes, but we need to walk while talking," Adam started walking quickly while the others quickly got to their feet and tried to catch up with him, "there was something bothering me the whole time we were walking through the tunnel but I couldn't figure out what, then it dawned on me."

"What was it" asked Ali, Adam stopped walking and placed his torch to the ground, both men looked at the ground by Adam's feet.

"In all this time walking through this tunnel we haven't seen one drop of blood or a body," said Adam. It had now just dawned on Umar and Ali also that they had not bothered checking the ground for any of these signs.

"So what is it we are looking for Sir?" asked Ali, "A small hole or a hidden door?" Adam started walking again.

"I don't know Ali," Adam handed the torch to Ali and gestured for him to go ahead of him, "but I'm hoping you will see it when we get there." Ali took the lead, while Adam and Umar walked side by side behind him, with Umar holding the second torch.

They had walked for several hours, mostly in silence when Ali stopped suddenly, Adam bumped into his back because he was scanning the ground at the time.

"There!" shouted Ali, who pointed to the wall on the right. Adam walked up to the wall but couldn't see anything out of the ordinary. He looked over to Ali and showed his confusion. Ali smiled and held the torch closer to the wall; he then saw what Ali did. The wall shined as the flames flickered close to the quartz, except for the spot that Ali pointed to, it was a different material. Adam placed his hand on the wall and felt that it was a different kind of stone; it was rough and uneven, compared to the silky smooth feel of the quartz next to it. He gestured for both Ali and Umar to lower their torches to the floor, when they did they saw both a trail and large pool of blood on the floor.

"Good work Ali," praised Adam, he turned to the wall and placed his hands on it. He tried to push it but the wall didn't budge. All three men tried pushing together, the wall started to give and they felt it moving slowly forward. After pushing it five feet they cleared the walls beside the stone door, a cool humid breeze engulfed them from the right. They entered the hidden path to the right, towards the breeze. After walking about ten feet the ground began to go downhill steeply.

Carefully they walked down the dark passage until they heard the gushing of water. As the passage opened up they were greeted by a narrow river that flowed left, they walked up to the bank of the river. Umar noticed three boats stacked on top of each other against the wall.

"They must have used those," pointed out Umar, Ali walked up and investigated the boats. It was a similar size to the long boats on the Damascus, but they were slightly narrower with a much more pointed tip. Both Umar and Ali lifted one of the boats and placed it on the side of the river. Umar held it in place while Ali and Adam jumped in.

"I can't see any ores," said Umar, "do you think they took them?" Adam examined the flow of the river.

"I don't think we need them," he said, "I think we just let go and let the river take us there."

"But how do we change direction or get off without them," asked Umar. Adam shrugged his shoulders.

"Guess we'll find out when we get there," he said, "c'mon Umar jump in and let's see where it takes us." Umar obeyed and jumped in, Adam and Ali sat in the back with Umar up front. They were surprised at the speed of the current once Umar let go of the bank. The river was mainly straight with a slight curve to the right. The boat travelled at a steady speed, all three men stayed alert until the bank disappeared; at that point Ali suggested that both Adam and Umar get some sleep while he sat watch.

The journey through the river would prove to be very long indeed, hours turned to days. For four days they travelled deep within the mountain in pitch black, as the torches died within the first day on the boat. With just five dates to sustain them for the journey as well as the freshwater from the river they were able to keep themselves going.

The darkness started to effect the minds of the three men, they began to feel unbalanced and paranoid due to the lack of vision and the constant sound of the river flowing. Adam asked Ali to recite the Quran to help them on their journey. For most of the three days in darkness they would recite the Quran in turns to help their minds stay focused and not be deterred by the constant darkness.

On the fourth day Umar woke up both Ali and Adam from their sleep, to both their surprises they were able to see Umar's face when they opened their eyes, they quickly sat up and looked ahead. In front they saw an opening further down the river; the bank had now appeared on their left. The opening was allowing streams of sunlight to pierce through and gently light up the tunnel. The current was very mild and slowly the boat headed towards the opening, all three men used their hands to paddle to the edge of the bank. They all climbed out of the boat, Adam and Ali picked up the boat and placed it by another boat which was against the wall by the opening. No doubt this was the boat used by their would-be attackers, they all thought. Adam looked back at the river and saw that it continued round, past the opening and started to go back in the opposite direction through another tunnel. There seemed to be a small drop further ahead where the current sped up.

"I think this river goes round in a circle, it probably heads back to where we came from," said Adam.

"So where is the source coming from?" asked Ali.

"Probably somewhere higher up the mountain, deep inside," replied Umar. Adam walked up to the opening, his legs felt weak and his head dizzy from the lack of food and the constant motion of the river, for the past four days.

The opening was a large arch two meters wide and five meters high. It was covered by thick weeds. Adam slowly walked through the weeds and entered an open plain. He saw a large green field with a huge forest behind it. To his right he saw the White Mountains far in the distance and to his left was nothing except the field that continued into the open space. He turned round and saw the mouth of a cave that was engulfed in weeds, grass and moss. The three men stepped out into the field and into the bright sunlight, which burned their eyes.

"I can't believe this hidden cave travels all the way through the mountains," said Ali, the rest wanted to comment but were too exhausted and hungry. They all started walking towards the forest in the hope that they would find something to eat, or at least find some signs of life.

The ground felt soft beneath their feet as they approached the forest; to their surprise they found several apple trees on the edge of the forest. They began reaching up to pick some, for the next hour they sat on the ground enjoying the sweet crisp flavours of the fruit. The heat grew intense so they took off their waistcoats and chain mail.

Adam noticed some strange markings on the trees that were on the outside of the forest, he got closer to the tree to examine them. On each trunk he noticed three carved diagonal lines which stretched all the way along the trees of the forest.

"What do you think that means?" asked Umar, Adam touched the markings with his fingers.

"I think it is some kind of warning," said Adam, "no one goes to this much trouble unless they have major reasons to do so." They all stood looking at the markings.

"Shall we go in or walk around?" asked Ali.

"We'll walk around for now," replied Adam.

They began walking along the forest admiring the scenery, after a few minutes they heard the sound of movement ahead of them, the forest curved round to the right creating a blind spot. Adam wasn't sure to wait and see who it was or hide in the forest, as the sound grew louder Adam quickly dived in the forest and hid behind a small boulder, followed by his colleagues. As they waited they saw at least thirty figures walking along the outside of the forest. They couldn't make them out completely due to the trees blocking their vision. All of them appeared to be dressed in black;

from their posture and mannerism they all seemed to be men. Some were carrying large sticks and others nothing at all, there were no signs of weaponry. As the last one past, Adam told his colleagues to leave their weapons and follow him. Adam slowly walked out of the forest and looked at the travelling party who now had their backs to him. One of the men at the end felt someone was watching him; he turned round and saw the three strange men looking at his group. "Chief Akbar!" he shouted, the rest of the group stopped and quickly turned round. They were shocked to see the three strangers; a large man began making his way through the group. They were all dark skinned but varied in size, some were broad and others slender. They were all dressed in long black robes with small black turbans or caps on their heads. He didn't walk towards them but instead stayed staring at Adam and his soldiers.

"Follow my lead," whispered Adam, who began walking slowly towards the group. His arms were open outwards and his hands open, palm side up, to show that they were unarmed and not a threat. When they were within three meters the large man held out his hand.

"Halt!" he bellowed in a deep voice, he was broad like an ox and had a thick short beard. His appearance was quite like Hasan, both Adam and Ali thought at the time.

"State your name and business strangers," said the large man, Adam thought for a moment.

"Apologies, I and my colleagues were travelling through the mountains and got lost after a landslide, we barely made it through with our lives. We are lost and not sure where we are, could you please offer us some help?" The man looked at them for a moment and then to rest of his group.

"My name is Akbar and I am Chief of my people, we are happy to aid you but we need to know more about you before we do so."

"Of course Chief Akbar, we have nothing to hide," replied Adam.

"Your names and where you come from?"

"My name is Adam and these are my friends Umar and Ali. We are tradesman from the city of Benghazi, we came to the mountains to do business with some of the tribes in the area," the Chief appeared confused at Adam's words, "we got caught in a landslide on the mountains and ended up here."

"I have never heard of this city," said the Chief, "consider yourself fortunate that you encountered us as oppose to others, there welcome would have been much different to say the least." The Chief took a few steps closer; he studied the appearances of the three tradesmen in more detail.

"We will allow you entry to our city, but remember you are guests so therefore you must respect the customs and laws of our people, is that clear?"

"Of course, thank you Sir," replied Adam; the three men followed their new acquaintances along the outskirts of the forest.

11.
Chief Akbar

The three soldiers of the Sultan walked in the front row of their new acquaintances, only Chief Akbar walked ahead of them. As they walked in silence beside the forest, Adam could not help examining the markings on the trees that he analysed previously.

"Chief Akbar?" he asked, the Chief continued walking but let out an acknowledging grunt, "what is the name of this land?" the Chief didn't respond at first, he rubbed the bottom of his chin and muttered something to himself.

"Our lands have no name," the Chief responded.

"No name?" questioned Adam in a confused tone.

"That's correct," the Chief remained silent and just continued walking. Adam briefly looked at his colleagues and then towards the back, at the rest of the party. The majority seemed to look towards the ground or off to the far distance. Adam thought best not to press any further.

"Sorry to ask Chief Akbar," asked Umar, "but you all seem to be wearing the same type of clothes is there a special occasion amongst your people or is it simply part of your custom?"

"We have just returned from a funeral, we buried some of our fallen."

"I am sorry to hear that Sir," said Adam, "to Allah we belong and to Him we shall return." The Chief stopped suddenly and turned to face Adam, his face became even harsher than before; he pointed his finger towards Adam's chest and poked firmly.

"As you are guests I will allow that comment, just this once, but know we are people who trust in ourselves we do not need support from anyone else, especially false gods that do nothing!" The Chief turned round and carried on walking; Adam exchanged brief looks to his comrades who looked relieved that the incident did not escalate further.

They walked for just under two kilometres, during that time Adam studied the mannerisms of the Chief and the rest of the group, whenever he got the opportunity to look back. What stood out immediately was how disengaged they appeared to one another; nobody exchanged any words or even looked at each other. For the most part they simply walked in a rather zoned out state, not seeming fully awake.

Adam and his comrades were rather shocked when they saw the city appearing ahead of them; based on the actions and behaviour of their hosts they assumed their homes to be rather modest and simple. The four meter high fortress started to appear in the distance, as they got closer the intrinsic detailed carvings of various geometric shapes and circular patterns became apparent. The fortress stretched along the front of the city for three hundred meters and then continued round the sides.

Behind the city was a single dark brown mountain that covered the entire width of the city, the layout reminded Adam of when they first arrived at the docks of Benghazi. The mountain was considerably smaller than the mountain in

Benghazi or the White Mountains but was still fairly big in comparison to the city. Right in the centre of the fortress stood a huge double wooden door, with an arch top.

"Your fortress is incredible Chief Akbar," commented Ali, "the stonemasonry work is very highly skilled." The Chief smiled slightly.

"Our elders were gifted in the use of stone, we owe them everything," responded the Chief. As the group got closer to the city they heard someone shouting within the fortress walls, immediately the doors began to open slowly. Adam looked around the area and saw nothing else apart from the huge forest in the distance, which they had just passed.

As the doors opened they were greeted by two large figures dressed in long robes of brown and cream, their complexion was slightly darker than the Chief's but there facial structure was very similar.

"This is Orhan and Kamal, they will show you to the guest quarters," said the Chief, "we need to finish off the funeral procedures so please excuse us." They thanked the Chief and their group as they walked off around the fortress to the far right-hand side. Orhan was the taller of the two, his head was shaved and he had a long goatee beard, Kamal had curly long hair that went just below his ears, he face was clean shaven and both men had strong dark blue eyes.

"Please follow us," said Orhan. As they walked in they were equally surprised by what they saw within the fortress walls. The buildings and workmanships were similar to those in the capital and Benghazi. From the tall three storey structures to the small simple huts, as well as the many stone pebble pathways that outlined the various streets and sections of the towns.

As the three visitors studied the buildings they were taken aback at how decrypted and worn down the entire area was. Not a single building was void of some kind of damage or severe erosion, parts of roofs and walls were either missing or majorly damaged. There were mediocre attempts at fixing these problems with poor materials such as thin pieces of wood or poorly mixed mud cement, which had not been applied properly. The pathways had also not managed to avoid the spreading damage and the simple minded attempts to fix them. The roads had become uneven due to missing or cracked stones; the town's people had simply left the damage or covered it up with poorly mixed cement. The three men found themselves being cautious as to where to place their feet for fear of falling over or injuring themselves on the dangerous pathway.

The people within the city seemed to reflect what they had already experienced from their initial meeting with the towns people.

The streets were predominantly quiet, the children, if there were any, were not to be seen. The few that were on the streets were men and woman that wore similar colour course garments, which were worn and dusty. Most of the women either wore loose scarves or not at all. Their garments were all brown and cream in colour, as was the colour of all the men's clothes; they were either wearing long robes or long shirts and trousers. None of the people engaged with each other or their new visitors, they simply hurried along and kept their focus elsewhere.

"Is there a reason the streets are so quiet?" asked Ali, the two large men at the front looked at each other for a moment.

"We tend to keep to ourselves here, most of the time we remain indoors," replied Orhan.

"Why is that?" further asked Adam.

"It is just our way," replied Kamal in a more forceful tone, clearly not happy with the questions being asked.

Eventually they reached a small hut that had major cracks travelling all the way across the front of the building and along the right hand wall.

"These are your quarters," said Kamal, pushing the door open, "make yourselves comfortable, we will bring you some water and food a bit later." The three soldiers thanked them for their hospitality before they left. They entered the room and found three straw beds on the floor, along with an old chair and a small table. The flooring was comprised of partially rotten floor boards with large stones placed in the damaged holes. The three men stared at the room in silence, Adam noticed something on the wall, it was a marble tile and in the middle was a carving of the sun with a hole in the centre. The hole was blocked by a small cylinder shaped piece of wood, Adam pulled firmly to release the wood. Nothing came out except for a few grains of sand and wet mud.

"That is incredible," said Adam. Ali and Umar walked up to the tile.

"This is hundreds of years old," further said Adam, "you can tell by the colour of the marble. They had running water back then?" Ali rubbed his finger by the rim of the hole and felt the grains between his finger and thumb.

"There hasn't been water through there for many years, I wonder what ceased the water," said Ali. Adam looked through the front window at the street and the few people walking through.

"Is this the city Sir?" asked Umar.

"Definitely Umar, the way the Sultan described it in his dream is almost identical to what I'm seeing here."

"So what exactly is the danger we are trying to save them from Major?" asked Ali, Adam walked away from the window and looked at the damaged flooring.

"Take a look around Ali; many years ago this area was more advanced than almost any other city in the world, but something has changed the path of these people and this city."

Adam walked over to a straw bed and sat down; he took off his boots and laid down, letting out a pleasurable groan as he did so.

"Let's use this time and rest, we haven't had a proper sleep since we left the Damascus, hopefully tomorrow we can start to search for clues," said Adam, both Ali and Umar also got into their beds.

"The Chief is not going to be happy about us snooping around," added Umar, Adam closed his eyes and smiled.

"Well I guess we'll have to be subtle, keep our conversations and questions to a minimum and only call each other by our names, not rank and also…," Umar and Ali waited for Adam to complete his sentence, until they heard him snoring a few moments after. Ali shook his head with a smile at Umar before both men also fell asleep.

After several hours Umar woke up to find two large wooden buckets in the centre of the room, he slowly sat up to look over at his two colleagues that were still snoring away in their beds. Umar investigated the buckets and found they were filled with light brownish water, he then noticed a wooden plate behind the buckets that had several pieces of very stale and very hard brown bread. Adam also got up and looked at what was brought by their hosts.

"There seems to be some kind of problem with their water supply," said Adam, he placed his right hand in the bucket and took a sip from his cupped hand, Adam winced slightly; "yes the water tastes and feels very grainy and bitter." Umar picked up a piece of the bread and took a hard bite in order to break a piece of the bread away.

"I don't know if it's the water that has affected the bread or maybe they have some kind of problem with their crops, but this bread is close to being inedible." They knew they had to eat something so they took a few bites and some sips of water to keep them going. Ali eventually woke and had some food before they decided to venture out and explore the city.

As they stepped out of their door they noticed the silence in the streets, there was not a soul about, not even any animals. They walked down the street in the direction of the main entrance of the city. All the buildings were locked up and seemed deserted; occasionally they saw some movement through the dark dusty windows.

"Are they hiding from us or is this how they live here?" asked Ali, they continued walking in the warm air. The clouds had gathered above them and the sunlight was blocked out completely.

As they got to the main entrance, which was locked from the inside, they heard the sounds of footsteps behind them. They turned round and saw a young man walking towards them with speed, what surprised all three of them about the stranger was his demeanour; he was actually smiling and seemed happy to see them. He was a young man, maybe late teens or early twenties, Adam thought. He was dressed the same as everyone else in the city with his brown and cream shirt and trousers, with a thick brown cloak on top. He had the hood on top of his head but they could see the long curly brown hair that seemed to go down to the middle of his ears. His face was covered by a thin patchy beard and his skin was a golden olive colour, his frame was of medium build and was slightly short in height.

"Greetings visitors, welcome to our city, I hope you rested well?"

Adam needed a few moments before replying because he wasn't expecting that kind of welcome, based on their treatment thus far.

"Yes we did, thank you Sir," replied Adam.

"Oh sorry, where are my manners, my name is Najib." He shook the hands of all three men, who also introduced themselves.

"I am the Chief's son."

"You seem very different from your father," said Umar, Najib smiled.

"Yes, I hear that a lot. I take after my maternal uncles mainly. Were you heading out of the city?"

"Yes," said Adam, "we were hoping to search the surrounding areas, get a feel of the land. We are kind of in the dark here as we haven't spoken to anyone, nor do we know the names of the city or the land." Najib smiled politely at Adam's words but they could see that he appeared slightly awkward, as if he was not sure how to respond.

"I am guessing that you've been told that these areas are nameless?" The three men nodded at the question, Najib looked around to see if anyone was in close proximity.

"This was not always the case, there use to be names for these lands and our once beautiful city, but alas those times are far from here."

"May I ask what the name of this land use to be called?" asked Adam; again Najib looked around before speaking.

"We are forbidden from talking of such things, please let me show you around these lands," Najib began to unbolt the doors and was about to open the front gates.

"Najib!" came a voice from the right; all four men knew who the voice belonged to. They turned to face the Chief, who was marching with thunderous strides and a look that showed the aggression one would see on the battlefield. Najib quickly locked the gate and took a step to the side; he placed his hands to his side and lowered his head. The three visitors took a few steps back away from Najib, not wanting to get involved in this family dispute. The Chief grabbed Najib by the arm and dragged him several meters away from the rest of the group. He was speaking quietly into his son ears and although his words were quiet his eyes showed utter malice. He would occasionally strike Najib on the shoulder or back while pointing to the three men and the front gate. After several minutes of berating his son the Chief stepped back and took a few deep breaths. He walked over to the group and stared strongly at Adam.

"I'm afraid that my son didn't realise the time, it is forbidden for people to leave the city so close to sunset, he will be happy to show you round first thing in the morning," the Chief paused and passed his glare at everyone in the group and then back to his son, "I trust you are ok with that?" asked the Chief menacingly.

"Of course Chief Akbar," replied Adam, "would it be ok for Najib to walk us back to our quarters so we can thank him properly for his hospitality." The Chief looked back at Najib who had remained still and silent the whole time, not even looking back at his father or the visitors while they were talking.

"Najib," called the Chief in a less angered tone, "show them back to their rooms." The Chief then walked off back down the pathway he had appeared from. Najib remained silent for a few moments before turning to face the rest. They were surprised that he didn't appear upset or saddened but instead frustrated.

"Please follow me," said Najib. As they approached the doors of their quarters both Ali and Umar walked ahead and opened the door, they turned and saw Adam speaking with Najib a few meters away. He signalled for them to go in and leave him with Najib, which they did.

"Najib, I can see that something has plagued this city from its glory days and still continues to do so," Najib was reluctant to speak.

"It would be best not to speak about such things Adam; you've already seen the attitude of this city, I will see you in the morning." As Najib turned round to walk away Adam stopped him by placing his hand on his shoulder.

"I understand you're sceptical about this but just hear my words before you go, you don't have to reply to anything I say, only listen." Najib thought for a moment and then turned to face Adam with his whole body, he signalled for him to speak.

"I can see that the city has gone through massive changes, none of it for the better," Najib concurred on his findings by nodding, "myself and my friends have travelled to many different lands and fought in many battles. Your people have took us in and offered us safety, let us return the favour by aiding them."

"I wish it were that simple Adam, but, I'm afraid that this city and its people are beyond saving, right now all we can do is survive."

"Are you giving up Najib?"

"Yes...yes I am, we have tried many times to rescue ourselves but each time will fall further and further into darkness..."

"Darkness?" interrupted Adam with a curious tone, "What exactly has happened here Najib, we can help you." Najib smiled and placed his hand on Adam's shoulder.

"Hopefully my friend you will not be here long enough to find out, now please go back to your quarters and I will meet with you after sunrise. Najib walked off leaving Adam more bewildered than when he first arrived.

Umar and Ali were attempting to eat more of the bread when Adam walked in.

"Did you manage to get anything from him?" asked Umar, Adam shook his head and stared out of the window. He then walked over to the sun tile and stared at the hole in the centre. "What happened here?" Adam said quietly to himself. Ali got up and handed Adam some bread, Adam grimaced as he looked at it.

"We have to eat Sir, otherwise we'll struggle tomorrow. Adam nodded and began taking small bites from it.

The three men performed wudu and prayed, led by Adam. They had agreed not to pray out in public nor talk about their faith in the company of others, for the moment. The hostile reaction that they had received from the Chief when Allah's name was mentioned was the only clue they had, as to why this city was decaying away.

In the morning Najib knocked on the door of his three guests, Ali opened the door and invited him in. Both Umar and Adam were putting on their boots; they greeted Najib warmly as he sat on the chair.

"Was there anywhere in particular that you wanted to visit?" asked Najib.

"Well we only saw the forest when travelling to the city, maybe that could be our first place of call?" said Adam, Najib stood up.

"I'm afraid that won't be possible, we are forbidden to enter the forest," Adam exchanged glances at his friends and then walked up to Najib.

"It seems there are many prohibitions in this city Najib."

"I know, but in the case of the forest the prohibition is warranted."

"Can I at least ask why?" asked Adam, Najib looked at him in silence, "Let me guess, you are forbidden to tell me?"

Najib nodded and looked to the ground.

"Are we allowed to go to the outskirts of the forest? That is where we met your father," said Umar.

"Yes that will be fine," replied Najib.

The four men left the city and made their way south to the forest, Najib remained silent for the whole journey often walking five strides ahead of everyone else.

When they made it to the forest Najib seemed to peer through the trees into the darkness further in. His shoulders and back seemed rigid and stern. The hot sun was bearing down on their heads and back, Adam took a few steps closer to the forest and saw the markings again on the trees. He reached forward and touched the markings with his hand.

"Your people made these markings didn't they?" Adam asked, Najib walked up and looked over Adam's shoulder. "Yes, we are sent here every year to check the markings are still visible and to make new ones where needed."
"What do these markings mean, are they a warning?" asked Umar, Najib remained silent, still looking at the markings on the tree.
"Is it because of this darkness that you mentioned yesterday?" asked Adam, Najib snapped out of his trance upon hear that word and stared at Adam.
"Yes," he replied, he took a few steps back and looked at the many markings spread across the trees, "I know it seems strange that an entire city is scared of venturing into the woods but we have lost many men that have gone into this evil forest."
Adam looked over at Umar and Ali who both seemed stumped as to what to say next. Adam walked to Najib and looked him square in the eyes.
"What is in their Najib?" Najib remained silent, the fear starting to engulf him; he turned round, back towards the city.
"I think it best that we make our way back to the city," said Najib, Adam quickly ran up to Najib and grabbed his arm. He spun him back round towards him.
"Enough of this foolishness, what is in this forest Najib!" demanded Adam, Najib became frozen, unable to speak. He tried to get away from Adam but he threw him to the ground and pinned him to the floor with his knees on his chest.
"Major!" shouted Ali, afraid that the anger Adam was showing was real, Najib immediately looked over to Ali in a perplexed manner.
"Major?" said Najib, the words seemed to make the fear evaporate from him. Adam stood up and then helped Najib to his feet, he patted away the grass and moss that were on Najib's back.

"I'm sorry for my outburst Najib," he held out his hand, Najib looked at him for a moment before shaking it.

"He said 'Major', who are you people?" asked Najib, still holding on to Adam's hand.

"My name is Adam ibn Mustafa; I am the Major of the Sultan, the Caliph and Leader of the Believers. The representative of Allah Law's, has sent me to your people." Najib was shocked and confused.

"Sent? I don't understand what is going on…"

"We are soldiers," interrupted Umar, walking up to Najib, "the Sultan, leader of the Islamic Empire, the largest and most powerful empire on this planet has assigned us the task of rescuing your people and your city from this darkness that you speak of."

"But how does he know…"

"He was sent a vision, a dream," interrupted Ali, who also walked up to Najib, "by Allah, your Lord and ours. Because of this dream we have been sent thousands of miles, through many obstacles to get here."

"You are all soldiers?"

"Yes," replied Adam, "this is Captain Ali ibn Osman and Lieutenant Umar ibn Idris." Najib smiled, he went over to Adam and hugged him.

"This is not a dream? Tell me this is real," pleaded Najib, Adam gently moved back away from Najib's grasps and placed his hands on Najib's shoulders.

"No brother Najib this is not a dream, we are here to help. But we need two things from you."

"Anything!" replied Najib eagerly.

"Good, firstly you must keep our true identities a secret, especially from you father," Najib nodded in agreement, "secondly, you must tell us everything that has happened so far, everything."

"Ok," said Najib in a gentle tone, "but not here, let's go to the city and I will tell you everything in your quarters, in case my

139

father or his men appear." Adam agreed and they all set off back to the city.

Back at their quarters Najib sat on the chair, while the others sat on one bed together side-by-side.
"Ever since I was born, I and the rest of the younger generation have been told that a curse has been upon our city."
"A curse?" let out Ali instinctively; Adam quickly gave Ali a look to keep silent. Ali silently apologised to Najib and signalled for him to continue. Najib smiled briefly before taking a deep quiet breath.
"For years we have been told never to discuss such matters, even amongst ourselves. But although belief in a Creator is deeply frowned upon in our city, my heart, for some reason, finds comfort in you being here. Whether it is because of our desperate situation or perhaps something deeper, I feel compelled to tell you all that I know." Najib sat in silence trying to structure what he was going to say, the three other men sat silently. All three of their hearts were beating heavily for all their travelling and hardship had led to this point, this moment.
"We were told that a curse was upon our people, before we were strong and very prosperous. As you can see from our buildings we were once powerful and advanced in many areas. Our homes were solid, our crops vibrant and our people strong. Any tribe or army that tried to attack us regretted it instantly; our skills in battle along with our weaponry were second to none." Najib stood up and began pacing slowly up and down the room.
"How do you know all this Najib?" asked Adam.
"My grandfather, our Chief, told me once when we were alone. He told me not to say anything to anyone as the hearts of most people in our city were too fragile to carry this,

especially my father." He stopped and looked out of the window before sitting back on the chair.

"My father believes that hiding is the only way to survive, but I know that we cannot continue like this anymore, this curse that appeared many years ago almost destroyed the whole city. Our food, our homes and everything else within the city just started to decay and then the will of the people also started to crumble. In the short time that I have been alive I have seen the characters of people become weaker and weaker, I wish that I could say that this curse is a myth but look around!" Najib started to cry and quickly got up and turned away from the others, not wanting them to see him in that state. Adam looked over at Umar and Ali once more before getting up and walking over to Najib. He patted Najib on the back.

"Najib, we can help, Inshallah, have hope…hope in your Lord that sent us here." said Adam. Najib wiped the remaining tears away before turning round to face Adam.

"Now Najib, tell us about this thing that lurks in the forest."

"The curse?" asked Najib.

"I don't believe this thing is a curse, but I do believe that something is in there, so what do you know about it."

"Hardly anything, nobody has seen it."

"Then how do you know it exists?" asked Umar.

"Because of the many men that it is killed, my father told me that you met them during the funeral yesterday."

"That's right," confirmed Adam, "he said they had fallen, I assumed there had been some kind of battle," Najib shook his head.

"No, they had tried to kill the curse that was in the forest; they left a few months ago but never returned."

"How many men?" asked Ali.

"Thirty," replied Najib.

"Thirty?" said Adam in shock, "this thing killed thirty men, were they armed?"

"Yes, they were the best soldiers that we had left, over the years different groups have marched to the forest, hoping they will save the city, but they never return."

"Do you find their bodies?" asked Umar.

"No, we can't go in the forest; if we do then we will also perish."

"So what do they bury at their funerals?" further asked Adam.

"Some of their clothes, it's all we ever have left." Adam and the rest remained in silence; Najib looked out of the window, "I must go back, my father will be wondering where I am, I will meet with you later this evening and tell you the rest, I promise." Najib quickly ran out before any of them could protest. Adam walked to the chair and sat down.

"What next Sir?" asked Ali.

"Good question Ali," replied Adam, he smiled for a moment before standing, "I'm going back to the forest to find out what this thing is."

"But Sir it's already killed many people, you can't go alone," said Umar.

"His right," confirmed Ali, "we've spent all this time travelling here; it would be foolish to take a risk like that."

"So what do you both suggest instead?" asked Adam.

"Let's wait to hear what else Najib has to say; maybe he'll shed some more light on the situation. Until then why don't we just explore the land around the forest and see what we can find."

"Do you agree with that plan Umar?" asked Adam.

"Yes Sir I do," replied Umar.

"Very well then, I will go out and explore the area, you two stay here in case anyone comes asking for us."

"And if they ask where you are?" replied Umar.

"Tell them I went site seeing," said Adam, smiling before walking out. Ali rolled his eyes and looked back at Umar.

"Site seeing? I can really see the Chief being happy with that."

12.
A friend in the woods

Adam walked along the outskirts of the forest, running his hand against the markings on every tree that his passed. It was almost impossible to see beyond ten meters within the forest, as the trees were many and the shadows inside were so dense. After walking along for several minutes Adam stopped and faced the forest, he closed his eyes and tried to listen carefully. He hoped that something would make itself known; he didn't believe that a curse lurked within the forest but he knew something did.

A sound started to come through, he could barely hear the almost humming sound slowing coming from within the forest. Adam focused harder but something else broke his concentration, a young child's laughter.

He turned round to see two children, a boy and girl running about in the field chasing one another. They must have been around four or five years old, thought Adam. They were both dressed in cream colour clothing; the boy had a long robe and the girl a dress. Her hair was dark and long, tied in a big ponytail in the back with white flowers placed in her hair. The boy's hair seemed to match the girl's in colour and thickness, but not length, his hair stopped just above his ears. Adam noticed another figure walking slowly behind the children, a woman; she was dressed similarly to all the other women that he had seen in the city, except her hair was fashioned the same way as the little girls, but with more flowers in her hair. The woman knelt down as the children ran up to her; she embraced them warmly in her arms and playfully pushed them to the ground and started tickling them. From the distance Adam could see her features and skin tone was similar to the children's. They were all light brown in colour with round faces and prominent cheeks.

Adam didn't want to scare them, so he turned back round to the forest and tried to listen again. After several moments he felt a tugging on his shirt from behind, he turned round to see the little girl smiling at him from below.
"What are you doing?" she asked, showing her bright white teeth with her large smile. Adam smiled back and knelt down so he was eye-to-eye with the little girl.
"I thought I heard something in the forest," he replied. At that moment Adam noticed the woman running towards them with the little boy in her arms, she stopped several meters away and held out her hand.
"C'mon Sarah let's go back," said the woman in a slightly shaken tone, it was apparent she was trying not to scare the children by not appearing scared herself, even though she clearly was. The young girl reached out and grabbed Adam's hand.
"No I want to stay with the man," she said, the woman's face started to become more worried and seemed close to panicking. Adam realised that there would be an incident if he didn't do something.
"Sarah is it?" he asked, the girl looked at him and nodded, still with a large smile. "I think you should listen, the forest is not a safe place for children to be running around and I'm

sure Chief Akbar would not be happy if he knew you were here. Once Adam mentioned the Chief's name the woman appeared to relax slightly, but now her fear had become curiosity. Adam walked Sarah towards the woman, after a few meters he let go of the girl's hand and she walked over to the woman. She never stopped staring at Adam while she reached out and grabbed Sarah's hand tightly.

"You're with the visitors that came from the mountains yesterday?" she asked, Adam nodded silently.

"My name is Adam, what is yours?"

"Amina," she replied, "I am the Chief's daughter."

"Would your father be ok with you out here by yourself?" Amina didn't answer and looked back at the children.

"We need to be heading back now," Amina said in a gentle tone, both of the children waved at Adam, who waved back with a smile. As the children started walking back Amina looked over at Adam.

"My father would also be unhappy if he knew strange visitors were lurking round here alone too." Adam nodded that he understood the agreement.

The humming sound started coming from the forest again, but much louder than before. Amina and the children froze and looked back in the forest with absolute fear.

"Adam!" yelled Amina, "quickly, come with us back to the city, it's not safe here." Adam looked back at the forest, trying to pinpoint where the sound was coming from.

"What is that sound?" asked Adam.

"There is no time to explain, quickly come with us!" she shouted while running back. The children began screaming and crying as they ran, Adam began to run too when the humming became even louder. Adam froze, he turned round and faced the forest once more, the sound was familiar. It didn't cause fear in his heart but rather solace, he looked over and saw Amina and the children still running in the distance.

As Adam made his way slowly to the edge of the forest the sound kept becoming louder and louder. He still could not make out what the sound was, Adam just stood there listening to the humming. It seemed to be only a few meters ahead of him but he couldn't see anything beyond the dark shadows in the forest. Without even realising it Adam had walked ten meters into the forest. He looked back and could just about make out the sunlight from outside the forest, he looked up and saw the thin sunlight beams that pierced through the tree branches from above. The ground appeared solid and level, he kept walking slowly towards the sound.

Adam had expected to see or at the very least, come across some abnormalities within the forest; however that was not the case. The forest appeared the same as all previous forests that he had ventured in before. He smelt the aroma of earth and wood; he felt the twigs and stones beneath his feet as he walked forward as well as the sounds of creatures inhabiting the forest both above and below. The trees became less and the spacing between them larger the deeper he travelled within the forest. Strangely the humming sound did not increase but stayed constant, Adam kept scanning the area of the forest; the trees appeared to be Lalob trees. He had seen them before when travelling through Egypt, during a major drought his army had survived the harsh deserts by eating the bitter yellow fruit and the fresh shoots. The trees were around ten to twelve meters high; he rested against one and ate several of the brownish yellow fruit that hanged from its thorny branches. At first appearance you would not have been blamed for mistaken them as dates but upon further inspection, as well as taste, you would quickly realise that they weren't.

As Adam removed the seed from his fifth piece of fruit the humming began to sound even louder. It was only then that Adam was able to make out the words that were being spoken. In an almost instinctive manner he quickly popped the deseeded fruit into his mouth and ran forward between the trees. After running about one hundred meters, almost tripping several times, he saw the source of the noise.

The man was sitting on a large fallen tree trunk, the tree that it once belonged to was clearly not a Lalob tree but a different species all together. The man was dressed in a long dark green robe, with a white turban on his head. The whiteness of his turban matched the colour of his long beard. His skin was very dark and his physique slender, Adam thought he had similar resemblances to the Bani Khalid, in particular Syed. He held on to a long stick, the base of it was almost rooted into the earth below, along with a wooden bucket that was on the other side of the man. The elderly man had his eyes closed and was softly speaking words that had appeared as a rhythmic hum from the distance. Adam was surprised that he had heard the man from such a far distance. On the left side of the man was a stone well, the circular wall was just over one meter in height, there were some wet puddles around the wall on the earth as well as wet patches on the man's clothes.

The nature of the words was the reason that Adam had ran to the man, the words coming from his lips were the words of the Quran, more specific it was Surah Ikhlas. The man was reciting the Surah repeatedly, each time he completed the Surah he would say 'Allahu Akbar' and then start the Surah again. It was something that Adam had seen various prominent Sheikhs and Scholars do back home. Adam didn't want to disturb the man but at the same time he felt he was being disrespectful standing above him so he sat down on the spot he was standing on and waited for the man to finish.

After an hour the man stopped reciting and remained silent, Adam kept his eyes on him the whole time, observing his movements and mannerisms which were very minimal.

Eventually the man opened his eyes, which were light hazel brown. He smiled at Adam, but not enough to show his teeth. "Salam Alaikum, I was wondering if you would ever show up soldier," the elderly man said. He grabbed hold of his beard and ran it down to the tip. Adam returned the greeting and then remained silent; he had spent enough time around learned and righteous elders to be able to spot them. He knew after several minutes of being in the man's presence that he belonged to this category and so adhered to the required manners necessary when in their presence.

"I pray that the Caliph is in good health and representing Allah, Most High, as He should be represented, please speak soldier."

"Yes he is in good health since I last saw him my Sheikh, he has held the title of Leader of Believers the same way as his fathers before him."

The Sheikh smiled and nodded.

"Alhamdullilah, we must be thankful to our Lord for blessing us with leaders that look out for the welfare of their people, we never know when this blessing can be taken away from us as it was taken away from previous nations before us." The man reached down and scooped out a handful of water from the wooden bucket and drank, he gestured for Adam to come forward and have some of the water. As Adam took some water from the bucket the elderly man inspected his attire, he grabbed hold of the corner of Adams white shirt and felt the material with his thumb and index finger.

"Do you like the shirt my Sheikh? Please take it, if it is to your liking?" Adam started to unbutton the shirt but the man stopped him by putting his hand on Adam's chest.

"No my son, I was just seeing if you had adopted the uniform of my friends, on the other side of the forest."

"You mean those that live in the city?" asked Adam, the man nodded gently while holding his stick with both his hands.

"It is a uniform?" further enquired Adam.

"More or less," responded the man, he used the stick to try and pull himself up. Adam immediately helped by placing the man's hand on his shoulders, "now then soldier let's officially introduce ourselves, my name is Yusuf ibn Muhammed," Sheikh Yusuf held out his hand which Adam immediately held and kissed.

"It is pleasure to meet you Sheikh Yusuf, my name is Adam ibn Mustafa."

"Well then Adam, could you help an old man by carrying his water back to his home?"

"Of course my Sheikh!" replied Adam enthusiastically. Slowly he walked behind the Sheikh. as he made his way further into the forest.

After walking for about ten minutes there appeared an open clearing, Adam saw a small wooden cabin with a large wooden tree stump by the side of it. The trees seemed to encircle the area like a fortress, the open clearing allowed sunlight to pour in. Adam then noticed some crops growing on the other side of the cabin. As Sheikh Yusuf walked past the tree stump he tapped it with his stick.

"Place the water there and take a seat, I will be back in a moment." As the Sheikh entered his cabin Adam sat on the floor by the stump, after placing the bucket on it. He noticed a large piece of rock by the stump, the Sheikh came up to him holding a small piece of bread. He handed it to Adam and then sat down on the large rock, he gestured for Adam to eat. As Adam ate he noticed that the bread, as well as the water, was far better then what he had received from Chief Akbar's people.

"Sheikh Yusuf, how long have you lived in this forest?" The Sheikh looked up to the sky and closed his eyes; he appeared to be counting the years by tapping his finger on the stick.

"At least twenty years, maybe more."

"Twenty years? And you have been safe this entire time?"
Sheikh Yusuf chuckled a little and then rested his stick
against the stump.
"You mean why has the curse not killed me by now?" the
Sheikh said pointing at Adam with a glint in his eye. Adam
was surprised at the Sheikh's choice of words.
"So you're saying there is no curse, which is what I first
assumed."
"Oh no," said the Sheikh immediately, "there is a curse
Adam."
"There is?" replied Adam in complete shock, "You mean
what Chief's Akbar's people told me in the city is true?"
"Almost," said Sheikh Yusuf, Adam appeared confused at his
words, "the situation is more complex then you realise, then
they realise also." The Sheikh looked over to his cabin.
"It is because of this confusion that I have been in this forest
for so long."
"Why do you not go back to the city, the people are lost.
They need someone like you there."
"No," responded the Sheikh firmly, "if I went there I would
make things worse…"
"I can't believe that Sheikh Yusuf, you are…"
"It doesn't matter what you think Adam," interrupted Sheikh
Yusuf, "you know nothing of what's happened and what is
continuing to happen. If you want to save these people you
need to keep your eyes open, for many years I tried to help
them but things got worse." Sheikh Yusuf reached over and
grabbed his stick.
"It was then that I realised my role was not to help these
people, but it was to guide the one who could."
Sheikh Yusuf got up and started making his way to the cabin.
"I suggest you make wudu and pray Zuhr, I'm going to take a
nap. Use this time to search the forest but don't take anything
with you, go empty handed. Hopefully you will learn
something…hopefully, Inshallah.

"Earlier you said that you were 'expecting me', how did you know I was coming and how did you know I was a solider of the Sultan?" Sheikh Yusuf gave Adam a smile and a nod before entering his cabin. Adam knew that he wouldn't be getting the answers to his questions anytime soon, so he focused at the task at hand.

Adam made his way through the forest, he kept thinking about this suppose 'curse' that was in the forest. Now that the Sheikh had confirmed, albeit not entirely, he knew there was at least some merit to what Najib and his people had been saying. The trees were now more in number and the space much more restricted. The clouds above began blocking some of the light that was seeping through. Adam kept walking forward, sometimes squeezing past the gaps between the trees, then he saw some light ahead. He could make out another clearing in front of him. As he made his way through the last row of trees he was welcomed by a large opening that must have been half the size of a small city. He guessed it would take him at least an hour to just walk the perimeter; the ground was made up of long grass that was just above the knee in height. The welcome of sunlight and space was short lived; as he took a few steps forward he encountered another large piece of this mysterious jigsaw. He saw row upon row of graves, because of the long grass Adam couldn't quite tell how many graves were buried there so he climbed up a tree to gain a better view. When he reached up the top of the ten meter tree he looked ahead, to his horror he saw hundreds of graves stretched out as far as he could see. As he scanned the site he realised that almost all the clearing was made up of graves.
"To Allah we belong and to Him we shall return," he said to himself quietly. Adam climbed down and walked up to several of the graves. They were all unmarked, for each grave there was a small mound of earth with a large stone at the top

end. Adam stared at the graves and tried to imagine the names and faces of the people buried here. Were the thirty men, who died recently, buried here? Did the people of the city know about this place and who was burying them? So many questions running in succession, Adam closed his eyes and took a deep breath. It was clear that something was killing the people.

He knew he had to find this creature and kill it before it wiped out the city; he started walking across the cemetery, making his way to other side of the opening. As Adam made it to other-side rain started to come down, the dark grey clouds blocked the sun out completely and Adam's vision was poor at best. Adam walked slowly through the forest to try and see or hear something, thankfully the trees were able to block out most of the rain from coming through. Adam noticed several large craters in the ground, upon closer inspection it seemed like something large and heavy had hit the ground with great speed. Almost like a large cannonball, he then noticed several trees had been knocked down, and others appeared to have been pulled out of the ground along with the roots.

Adam saw something strange on the ground, it was a circular shield made of metal. It was dark grey in colour with thin circular lines going around the edge. There was another circle made up with a lighter metal in the middle, Adam picked up the shield. As he walked further he saw pieces of red clothing and armour scattered around the floor. "This is where they were killed," he said to himself quietly. He quickly started looking around, trying to see if their attacker was still close by. He tried to trust the words of Sheikh Yusuf, but how could he feel safe with what he was seeing. The clouds started to open up and the sunlight began to make its way down to the forest, as the sunbeams cut through Adam noticed something small and bright on the ground. As he walked up to it more shiny spots started to appear on the ground, Adam bent down to examine one, it was gold, a golden nugget the size of a small stone. There was gold all over the surface, he placed the gold in his pocket and walked further ahead. He hit something with his foot, it was a sword, the tip was broken and the handle was wide and made of metal. He picked up the weapon, he felt safer armed, along with the shield.

As Adam walked even further into the woods the ground began to tremble slightly, was it an earthquake he thought? The tremors grew stronger and the trees began to shake wildly. Adam tried to steady himself by holding onto the trunks of one the trees. As he grasped on to the tree Adam heard the sound of something ripping or breaking ahead of him. The sound was so loud that it almost sounded like a roar; all of a sudden Adam saw something in the sky flying. As it got closer he saw it was a large tree flying towards him, the tree must have been at least fifteen meters tall. Adam quickly dived to the ground and the tree just flew over him and crashed some ten feet behind him. Before he could get up another tree came flying towards him again. He quickly turned and started running; in his panic he dropped his weapons. He ran back towards the cemetery, he could hear something running behind him. The sounds of its feet hitting the ground sounded like cannons being fired in the distance. Adam knew he wouldn't make it to the opening at his current speed, he saw a hollow tree trunk on the floor. He quickly climbed inside and prayed that whatever was following him didn't see him climb inside. The footsteps got closer and the ground felt like it was going to spilt open, but then they stopped.

Adam could hear something large breathing deeply; there was a small hole in the trunk above him. He tried to look through it but couldn't see anything. Adam knew it was close, he thought about wriggling up slowly to the other end of the trunk to get a better view, but before he started to move the trunk was lifted from the ground. Adam held on to the sides of trunk, he then felt the trunk being launched high into the sky, the floating feeling was interrupted by a large crash as the trunk hit a large tree. He fell to the ground still hidden inside the trunk. He could hear the sounds of footsteps coming closer, he was partially dazed. He felt himself being lifted again and throw even harder. The trunk smashed against another tree and broke into several pieces; Adam fell to the ground with large pieces of the trunk falling down on top of him.

Adam found himself standing on a mountain top staring up into the sky. He saw the top of the forest that stretched out for miles and miles. He then saw the Sultan, dressed in a pure while suit and turban that almost seemed to shine like the moon. He was standing on top of a mountain on the other side of the forest; he looked over at Adam and smiled. The sky was blue and the sun shone down, the Sultan pointed down to the forest, Adam looked down and saw a ball of light emanating from within the forest. The ball of light then transformed into a ball of fire and started to consume the entire forest. The forest then changed to the unnamed city of Chief Akbar and the fire destroyed everything within the city. Adam could hear the sounds of the fire roaring through buildings and the screams of the people in them.

13.
A hidden treasure

Adam woke up to find himself laying on a low straw bed, he didn't recognise the small room which had one black leather cushion and a prayer mat in the corner. Apart from the bed there was nothing else in the room. Adam sat up and felt a sharp pain travel up along his spine, along with soreness on his upper right thigh. He slowly made his way to the door and hobbled his way through.

As he breathed in the fresh air he immediately recognised the large tree stump that he had sat by previously with Sheikh Yusuf. He walked closer to the stump and saw some food on a small wooden plate. He sat down, trying to ignore the excruciating pain in his body and ate some dates and drank several handfuls of water from the wooden bucket. Moments later Sheikh Yusuf emerged from the forest holding a small black bag in his right hand. He sat himself down next to Adam on the large rock.

"How are you feeling?" asked the Sheikh, Adam rubbed his back with his hand and felt the sharp pain intensify.

"Sore, but at least nothing appears broken, Alhamdullilah."
The Sheikh started to recite some Quran quietly and then
asked Adam to stand, which he did. The Sheikh then rubbed
his hands on the injured section, still reciting as he was doing
so.

"I was attacked by something in the forest; its strength was
unlike anything I had ever encountered before. How did I end
up in your cabin?"

"After you didn't return I went out looking for you. I found
you under a pile of broken wood, unconscious. Did you see
what attacked you?"

"No."

The Sheikh removed his hands and sat back down; Adam also
sat down and noticed that the pain was far less than before.
Sheikh Yusuf reached and grabbed his stick that was resting
against the stump.

"I need to find a way to stop this beast from killing anymore
of the people, but I don't know how to do it with the
resources I have plus the resistance of the Chief.

"Some things cannot be rushed Adam, there are many
problems that must be tackled, you are trying to take a short
cut and get to the end, but it won't work." Adam had no idea
what the Sheikh meant, he felt the frustration building inside
him, thinking about all the problems and deaths that he had
encountered so far. He didn't want to go through these riddles
and games; he just wanted to save the city and its people.
Adam took a few deep breaths and looked around at the trees
that surrounded them.

"Sheikh Yusuf, please help me to save the people. I can't do
this myself. Just tell what I have to do." The Sheikh tapped
Adam firmly on the top of the head with the tip of his stick.

"That frustration you just felt earlier before speaking, that is
the problem we need to tackle. If you have that in your heart
then you cannot help the people."

"I'm just getting tired of these secrets and mysteries; there is something in these woods that has been killing the people for many years. If I stop this thing then the city will be saved."

"Will it?" asked the Sheikh, he smiled and then stood up. "How do you expect to save someone when you don't even know what they need saving from?" The Sheikh walked over to the trees on the west side of the cabin. Adam got up and made his way to his side.

"What do I do Sheikh Yusuf?" The Sheikh smiled and looked at the trees.

"When you have a bad infection you must clean out the wound before wrapping it up. It hurts and is very unpleasant, but it is necessary," the Sheikh ran his fingers through his beard and looked up at the sky. Several light brown desert sparrows flew over them while singing.

"The people have simply been covering their infections for generations, and right now this infection is beyond cleaning. They need to amputate in order to save themselves, do you understand what I am saying Adam?"

"I think so Sheikh, I need to find out everything before responding, otherwise I'm just reacting, which means things will get worse." The Sheikh nodded.

Adam made his way to the city, as he approached the fortress he was greeted by Umar and Ali who were relieved at his arrival.

"We thought something happened when you didn't return yesterday," said Umar.

"Yesterday?" said Adam, "how long have I been away?"

"Since yesterday morning," replied Ali, "Chief Akbar has asked to see you several times."

"I'm guessing he is not too happy about that?" said Adam.

"That would be a yes Sir; he is waiting for you in the city centre. Are you able to see him now?" asked Ali, Adam nodded.

Umar and Ali led Adam down the damaged stone path, pass their quarters. As they walked through the narrow streets they entered an open square which had various markets open. The market stalls were very basic, selling grains, clothing and small furniture mostly. The people selling and buying in the markets seemed closed off to everything around them; there was no chatter or shouting that you would expect from a market place. Behind the stalls was a large table covered by a partial grey tent that blocked out the sun.

At the table sat the Chief, with his children, Najib and Amina sitting to his left. Behind him stood Orhan and Kamal, they appeared to be standing guard, monitoring the market place and everything else around them. Najib signalled to his father that the three men were approaching, the Chief ordered Orhan to fetch some food for his guests. As Adam walked up to the table the Chief signalled for him to sit down in front of him, along with his friends.

"Thank you Chief Akbar," said Adam as they sat down.

The Chief remained silent, staring at the three men intensely, Najib and Amina stared at the table not making eye contact with anyone. Orhan also stared at the three, not masking his contempt with his facial expressions. Kamal arrived with two plates, one with bread and the other with dried meat.

"Oh," said Adam, "I didn't realise that you had livestock, I hadn't seen any since we arrived." The Chief took some food and handed it to his children, he then started eating himself.

"Yes, we keep our animals towards the back of the city, near the mountain. We only bring them out for grazing in the open fields just outside the fortress."

"Are you fearful of bandits or poachers?" asked Ali, the Chief looked at Ali for a moment before taking another bite of meat.

"No, we are simply cautious people that prefer to be vigilant." Everyone remained silent for the next minute, the two guards behind the Chief continued to stare at the three visitors, but deep down they saw them as intruders. The Chief ate one more piece of meat before wiping his mouth with the back of his hand. He looked over at Najib and signalled for him to speak.

"Where did you go to yesterday Adam? Myself and my father were hoping to meet with you yesterday evening but your colleagues said you were not available." Adam looked over to the Chief who avoided eye contact by staring into space to his right, the guards however were all too happy to keep their gazes fixed.

"I was wondering around the open fields as well as the outskirts of the forest. I guess I lost track of time."

"The whole night?" asked the Chief, whose stare was now fixed on Adam and nothing else.

"Yes Sir," replied Adam "by the time I realised it was late it was too dark to work out my route back so I decided to sleep out under the stars." The Chief continued staring at Adam in silence, as if deciding whether to accept his words as truth.

"Did you happen to meet anyone while you were out there?" asked the Chief. Adam paused for a moment; Amina looked up briefly to Adam before looking back at the ground.

"Yes Sir I did," Amina's eyes widened and her heart pounded.

"Who did you meet?" further asked the Chief.

"An old man who came from the forest," the sense of relief poured over Amina like a cool breeze, she knew first-hand the repercussions of disobeying her father. Everyone stared at Adam with stunned expressions; the guards looked at each other and back at the Chief.

"I see," replied the Chief in a low tone, clearly trying to keep his anger at bay, "and who might this man be that you met Adam?" Adam realised that the Chief was setting him up for another barrage of angry outbursts directed towards him. He could see that the Chief used bullying tactics to assert his authority over others, much like other leaders that he had encountered while travelling the world. He knew that being passive would not progress his chances of finding out the problems that this city was under.

"I think you know who this person was Chief Akbar," said Adam, whose tone and posture seemed to transform before everyone's eyes. Ali and Umar could see the Major materialising in front of them and so they anticipated some form of resistance from the guards and got ready to launch a defensive if need be. The Chief was taken aback at the sudden change of character from his guest. He quickly signalled for his guards and daughter to leave their presence, Amina seemed reluctant to leave but her father gave her a stern glare and she left soon after.

"What did Yusuf say?" the Chief asked in a deep tone.

"He said that the people of this city were in trouble, he also mentioned some kind of curse within the forest that has plagued your people for many generations." The Chief slammed his fist on the table and yelled several obscene words.

"Of course this snake knows of our troubles, he is in league with this evil that torments us!" yelled the Chief, Najib placed his hand on his father's shoulder.

"Please father don't get too excited, it's not good for your health."

"I'm fine," replied the Chief sharply, while pushing his son's hand away.

"For years Yusuf has helped this curse grow and fester within our lands, nobody has remained untouched by this evil, nobody I tell you," said the Chief. Adam looked over to Najib for reasoning to this madness.

"I'm afraid he is right Adam," added Najib, "for years everything and everyone has been infected with this evil, except Yusuf.

"That doesn't mean he is the cause of this…"

"Yes it does!" interrupted the Chief, "He would tell us not to focus on the evil but rather look to the skies for help. We needed to look within ourselves and root out the evil there, complete rubbish!" the Chief started to wheeze a little and placed his hand on his chest, Najib quickly brought his father some water. After a long sip the Chief was able to compose himself again. He looked back at Adam with tiredness rather than rage.

"Yusuf's misdirection meant that the evil grew too much for us to defeat it and now he stands on the verge of claiming what he has always wanted."

"Which is what?" asked Umar, unable to remain silent.

"Everything," replied the Chief in a low tone, "to be the ruler of everything." The Chief leaned back in his chair and closed his eyes, the strain clearly draining him of his energy. He signalled for Najib to come closer to him, he whispered something in his son's ear before getting up and leaving without saying goodbye. Once he had left the square Najib got up and sat closer Adam.

"My father's words may seem hard to accept but he is not lying." Adam looked back at his colleagues who seemed bewildered by this whole conversation.

"Who was this man that you met Major, could he really be the reason for all this?" asked Umar.

"No he's not," replied Adam firmly.

"My father is not lying!" yelled Najib, Adam grabbed Najib's wrist tightly.

"Lower your voice, if you draw attention to our actions then all hope for your people is gone, understand?" Najib nodded apologetically.

"I know your father is not lying Najib" said Adam in an empathetic tone. Ali leaned with a confused expression.

"But Sir, you just said that his father was wrong about Yusuf…"

"He is wrong," interrupted Adam, "but he believes his words to be truthful. What makes this situation so difficult is for years these people have been told a lie believing it to be true, and they hold on to it without any doubt. But now we have to open their eyes to the truth in order to help them."

"So hold do we do that Major?" asked Umar.

"Well, first thing we have to do is find out what the truth is ourselves, at the moment I only have a few parts to this puzzle. We need more information before we can decide our next course of action."

"You are asking me to go against the orders and beliefs of my people," said Najib in a concerned tone.

"No Najib," replied Adam, "I asking you to help us find out what is plaguing your city."

"And how do I do that?"

"By helping us to sneak back to the forest, I have no doubt that your father will be watching over us from now on," Najib remained silent and then stood up.

"Very well, I will help you to sneak out tomorrow before sunrise, but on the condition that you take me with you."

"I can't do that Najib," replied Adam immediately, Najib was angered by his response.

"It is my people Adam; I have every right to be there…"

Adam reached over and grabbed his arm. He pulled him back down to his seat.

"Will you refrain from your emotional outbursts; if you want me to trust you then you must show me that you can handle your actions and emotions, understood?" Najib realised that he was copying the actions of his father, he raised his hand apologetically and asked for Adam to continue.

"I was attacked yesterday by something in the forest."

"Attacked?" asked Ali, "Attacked by what?"

"I don't know what it was, but it was powerful and big…"

"It's the curse!" said Najib loudly.

"We don't know what it was Najib, but that's what we need to find out."

"We?" asked Umar.

"Yes, we need to go back into that forest and find out what this creature is and where it is based."

"Do we go armed?" asked Ali.

"No," replied Adam, "based on its strength even if we went armed from head to toe we still wouldn't be able to kill it. Which is why I can't bring you with me Najib, you are not a soldier and I can't risk your life, understand?" Najib nodded acceptingly.

"So we search the forest, unarmed, to find a powerful creature that has already killed many people?" asked Umar.

"Basically yes," said Adam.

After the Fajr prayer the three men were escorted to a small hut close to the fortress front wall. At the main gate stood four men, all of which were tall and broad, Adam looked at the four men through the front window.

"Are there normally guards at the front or is this simply a welcoming for us?" asked Adam. Najib walked up beside Adam and looked through the window.

"Ever since you told my father about Yusuf he has been worried. It's been many years since he's heard his name, now he is convinced that he will come and take the city." Adam walked away from the window and sat on a short stool next to the table. Ali was sitting on the other side, staring at the wall in front while Umar was praying in the corner, Najib watched Umar as he prostrated to the floor.

"You follow the same religion as Yusuf, don't you?" asked Najib to Ali and Adam.

"Yes we do, we follow the religion of Islam," replied Adam, "do you know of the religion?" Najib nodded while watching Umar rise up from prostration to start his second rakaat.

"Yusuf would speak of the religion a lot, at least that's what I was told by my elders. My father hated the idea of looking up to the heavens for help when the problem was occurring on the land in front of him. That is why he banned all religions once Yusuf was banished from the city." Adam leaned forward and looked over at Najib.

"He banished him?" said Adam in a baffled tone, "How can you banish a man of his character and faith?" Umar had finished praying and sat on the floor cross-legged.

"Your father thought that he was using the religion to gain power and trick the people, didn't he?" asked Umar. Najib went back to the window and looked at the guards again.

"They will be doing a search of the fortress wall soon, once they do there will only be two on guard. I can distract them for a moment while you sneak out." Adam got up and walked over to Najib, who was still looking out of the window.

"Is that true, did he think that Yusuf was using religion to take over the city?" asked Adam, Najib turned round and look at Adam.

"Yes he did and he also warned everyone that if they followed his ways then they will be banished too." Adam went back to his seat and sat down.

"Sheikh Yusuf is a true servant of Allah, Most High. He is the last person in this city that would be interested in gaining power. It's because of him that I was able to find out what I know so far, we cannot save the city without his help." Najib looked at Adam and the rest of the men.

"Very well Adam, as difficult as it is I will trust your words."

"Thank you Najib, I know going against tradition and previous teachings can be hard but we must follow truth when it becomes clear from falsehood." Najib walked over to the table and sat beside Adam.

"I hope that you are able to rid us of these difficult times," said Najib. "I don't believe that the city will survive much longer."

"You mentioned earlier that the people had been suffering, when we first met. Apart from the deaths in the forest what else has been happening?" asked Adam, Umar got up and also sat by the table to hear Najib's response.

"The people's characters have changed, along with their health. They have become weaker and more distant. Our food and water has also become infected, I'm sure you noticed that when you first ate," the three kept silent, not wanting to appear rude by commenting on his remark.

"It is hard to sum up exactly what the problem is, but overall this place and its people have become shells of what they use to be."

"I think that description sums it up perfectly Najib," said Adam.

"The men are leaving," said Ali.

Najib quickly looked through the window.

"How did you see from over there?" he asked.

"He heard them," said Umar, while getting up off the floor.

"Incredible," said Najib.

Najib ordered the two remaining guards to check the market as he thought he saw some of the livestock running around. As soon as they left the three men quickly went through the front gate, Najib agreed to meet them on the outskirts of the forest just before the sun started to set.

They marched through the cool air, over the bright green fields. Occasionally they would look back to the city to check if they were being followed. Adam led them through the same route that he took to Sheikh Yusuf's cabin, when they arrived they saw a small fire burning away by the tree stump. As they walked up to the fire Sheikh Yusuf came out from his cabin holding his familiar stick.

"Ah Salam Alaikum brothers," said the Sheikh warmly as he made his way to the stump. The three men returned his greeting and kissed his hand after he sat down.

"Sheikh Yusuf, these are my companions, Ali ibn Osman and Umar ibn Idris." The Sheikh smiled at each one of them as their names were introduced.

"What brings you three men here?" asked the Sheikh kindly, Adam sat by the stump, followed by the others.

"After what happened to me yesterday and also hearing your advice, I thought best that we come and search the forest for more clues. Inshallah we will find out more about the situation and how to help the people of the city." The Sheikh sat silently for a moment before looking in the direction that Adam took yesterday when he encountered his attacker.

"And what do you plan to do in the forest while you search?"

"Nothing, we just want to gather information, nothing more Sheikh Yusuf."

"Good," replied the Sheikh, "remember keep your eyes open and do not..."

"Bring anything with us," said Adam, completing the Sheikh's sentence." The Sheikh smiled and pointed to Adam. "Hopefully you will follow my words this time and not just remember them."

"But Sheikh Yusuf I did..." the Sheikh held out his hand to stop him.

"No more talking Adam, you three needs to get going." Adam stood up and looked at the direction they needed to go in.

"I had a few questions that I wanted to ask before we left," said Adam.

"When you return Inshallah, you can ask me as many questions as you want." Adam nodded and kissed his hand before marching off.

As they approached the clearing of the cemetery they felt a slight tremor, Adam quickly froze and fell to the floor, the others followed and quietly crawled up beside Adam.

167

"Is that what attacked you yesterday?" whispered Ali, Adam nodded. After several minutes they got up and made their way into the opening.

"There must be nearly a thousand graves here," said Ali, as he walked between the rows.

"I know," added Adam, "because they are unmarked it is hard to work out the time span. Are they all recent or have they been burying people here for generations."

"By 'they' I assume you mean Chief Akbar's people?" asked Umar.

"Yes, because I wasn't sure I didn't want to bring it up in front of the Chief or his son." After scanning the area they carried on marching forward. As they walked through the narrow gaps between the trees Umar noticed something on the floor.

"Is that a sword?" he asked, as he bent down to pick it up a huge tremor came from the ground. All three men dropped to the ground and tried to find some bushes or trees to hide behind. They managed to find a large green and brown bush close to a fallen tree.

"Nobody pick up anything," whispered Adam, "that was the mistake I made yesterday. I was too busy focusing on stuff around me that I didn't have the chance to see what attacked me. Remember keep your eyes open." Adam looked ahead, as his eyes focused he realised that there was something far ahead behind the trees.

"What is that dark mist ahead?" whispered Umar.

"I don't know," replied Adam. Adam started to crawl forward when Ali reached out and grabbed his ankle.

"Don't move," he said. Ali remained staring at the darkness in front, "it's a shadow of something, it's looking towards us or maybe watching us."

"It's huge," said Umar, "that can't be a shadow it's probably a large hill behind the trees.

"No it's not," said Ali, "I can see it moving slightly." All three men remained still and stared at the darkness in front. After what seemed like hours, the dark shape began to slowly fade away, the ground shook slightly as it did. Adam got up onto his knees and turned to Ali.

"Can you still see it?"

"No," replied Ali, Adam stood up and dusted himself.

"Let's see what this thing is." said Adam.

The three men continued to go forward with a lot more caution. They came across many craters and fallen trees on the way, until eventually they came to an open clearing. They saw a small stream running past a large cave mouth that must have been five meters in height and four meters wide. Behind the cave stood a large white mountain that was similar to the mountain in Benghazi.

"Do you think it went in their?" asked Ali, Adam looked into the dark mouth.

"It must of," Adam replied, "I can't see any light in there." As Umar stepped forward he noticed something on the ground in the mouth of the cave. He reached down and picked it up; it was a handful of gold dust.

"I think this is a gold mine," Umar said, Adam reached into his pocket and pulled out the gold nugget he picked up yesterday.

"I found this in the forest before I was attacked; the ground was covered in them."

"Do you think Chief Akbar and his people know of this place," asked Ali. Adam placed the gold back in his pocket.

"I don't think so," said Adam, he took a few steps into the mouth when he noticed an unlit torch resting by the cave wall, "well someone has been here," Adam picked up the torch and handed it to Umar. He used several stones to light the old rag wrapped around the tip of the torch, once lit he handed the torch to Adam.

"You know whatever is in there will see you a mile away with that torch in the darkness," said Ali.

"I know, but we don't have any other choice. We have to know what this thing is." Adam slowly walked into the cave with the others following on either side. After only walking a few meters the walls lit up with the gold reflecting the light of the torch.

"Subhan Allah," said Umar, "I have never seen so much gold before." He reached over and rubbed his hand against a large piece of gold submerged in the rock. All three men gazed at the bright gold all around them, astounded by its beauty. As the light reflected off the gold Adam remembered the dream he had, the ball of light that he saw emanating from the forest was the same as the light reflecting off the gold.

"This cave has something to do with what's happening to the city," said Adam.

"But you said it's unlikely that they know about this place," whispered Ali. At that moment the ground began to shake and chunks of rock began falling from the ceiling, they quickly ran from the cave and back outside. The tremors began to increase and so they hurried back towards the forest and kept running until the tremors stopped.

Slightly shaken the three men walked back to the cabin of the Sheikh, who was still seated by the stump doing zikr with some prayer beads. They sat by the stump in silence, waiting for Sheikh Yusuf to finish. Once he finished he looked at the three men.

"Did you find what you needed?" he asked, Adam looked over to his colleagues.

"We think we did Sheikh Yusuf," said Adam.

"Then speak," ordered the Sheikh.

"It's the cave," said Umar.

"Or more specifically the gold," said Ali. The Sheikh tapped his stick on the heads of each them lightly.

"Good, you are starting to make progress, now then, ask me your questions Adam."

"The first time we met you called me soldier and mentioned that 'you had been waiting for me', how did you know I was a soldier and that I was coming?" The Sheikh rested his stick against the stump and placed his hands on his knees.

"I was the one that asked Allah, Most High, for help. When Chief Akbar banished me I knew that I didn't have the power or the ability to change their hearts, that power belongs to Allah only. So when I first arrived I begged Allah, that night and every other night from then on."

"You begged Allah for twenty years, even after they banished you?" asked Adam.

"Of course, I failed them and my Lord; I couldn't get them to see what they were doing and to guide them back to Allah. That's when I realised that the task of helping them was not mine, so I asked Allah to send someone that could help them."

"So you've been waiting for us to come for twenty years?" asked Umar, the Sheikh nodded and smiled.

"About one week before you arrived I had a dream that the Leader of the Believers had sent three orbs of light to the Bani Hakeem."

"Hakeem? That's the name of the people in the city?" asked Adam excitedly, the Sheikh nodded slowly.

"Sheikh Akbar thought that by forgetting history and breaking away from their past they could escape the fate that they had created for themselves." Sheikh Yusuf reached over to his stick and used it to stand up; he walked over to his cabin and went inside. The rest of the men waited by the stump, thinking about what they had just heard. Sheikh Yusuf emerged from the cabin with a small black bag with him; he placed it on the stump and sat back down.

"This was the only thing I took with me when I left the city, he slid the bag over to Adam, "it is yours Adam," Adam opened the bag and emptied its content onto the stump, it was an old key.

"What is this key for Sheikh Yusuf?" asked Adam, the Sheikh placed his hand over the key and slid it to Adam's hand."

"This will help you with your journey, Inshallah. I have been holding on to it, waiting for the one that will complete the task that I couldn't do. Adam took the key and showed it to his colleagues.

"What does it open Sheikh Yusuf?" asked Ali, Sheikh Yusuf didn't respond, he remained silent with his eyes closed.

"Sheikh Yusuf?" called Adam who reached forward and touched his knee. The Sheikh still didn't respond, Umar got up and placed his hand close to the mouth of the Sheikh.

"He's not breathing Sir," they stared in shock at the body of the Sheikh. It took several minutes before they were able to speak.

"Allah, Most High, allowed him to finish off of his mission," said Umar. Adam cried a few silent tears before reaching over and kissing the forehead of Sheikh Yusuf. They quickly washed the body and buried him by the stump using their hands and pieces of large wood to dig the ground. Adam performed the funeral prayer and then raised his hands to the sky.

"Oh Allah, Most High, please send Your Blessings and Mercy to Your servant that has passed. He died serving You, please raise his station in this grave and in the Hereafter, Ameen," a few tears trickled down Adam's cheek as he finished off the prayer.

14.
Invasion

The dejected three men walked out of the forest after burying their guide and teacher, Sheikh Yusuf. None of them had spoken a word to one another since the funeral, they didn't feel it was appropriate to engage in conversation so soon after.

As they emerged from the trees they heard a voice calling them from their far left, it was Najib. The passing of Sheikh Yusuf had caused them to forget about the agreed time to meet with him; Adam looked up and saw that the sun had already started to set.

"Where have you been, I thought you had perished in the forest!" yelled Najib, as he came running up to them.

"Apologies Najib, we were held up and couldn't leave," said Adam.

"Is everything ok, what did you find out?" Adam looked back up at the sun, which was slowly coming down.

"We need to pray Asr Najib, after the prayers we will make our way back and tell you what happened on the way."

As the three men prayed together Najib stared into the forest, imagining the evil that lurked within the shadows. At that moment a group of ten men came running towards them, Najib recognised them straight away as he saw Orhan and Kamal leading the group. All the men were armed with swords, they charged with anger in their eyes and voice. Najib quickly turned to his three colleagues, expecting them to be fleeing from the attack, but they remained in their positions continuing to pray. Orhan grabbed Najib by the arm.

"You support these men, you are a traitor Najib!" yelled Orhan, the rest of the group, led by Kamal, surrounded the three men as they prayed.

"Look!" shouted Kamal, "they pray like the old man they are in league with him; he probably sent them to spy on us and help them invade the city.

"Let's kill them now, it will be easy!" yelled one of the men from the group. Najib broke away from Orhan and stood in front of Adam, who was on his knees finishing off his last rakaat.

"No!" yelled Najib, "you must let them meet with my father; they are trying to help us." The men began to get angrier, Orhan started to approach Najib, while pointing his sword at him.

"Lies Najib, you have been tricked. Step away and let us finish these servants of evil, if you do not then we will consider you one of them and kill you."

"You will have to kill me," said Najib in a fearful tone.

"Very well then, by order of Chief Akbar we execute you, a traitor to the city and…"

"Enough!" shouted Adam as he stood up, Ali and Umar stood by his side, not showing any signs of fear or intimidation. The men were shocked at their bravery and strong zeal, as they stood unarmed in front of ten men with swords. Adam placed his hand on Najib's shoulder.

"May Allah bless you brother Najib, do not sacrifice your life, step away from us and let us deal with whatever Allah Decrees."

"I can't Adam; you three have opened my eyes and my heart. I would rather die alongside you then go back to the city without you." Adam smiled at his words as did the rest of his group. He gently positioned Najib behind them, as he walked a few steps towards Orhan and Kamal.

"Very well Najib, you can die with the rest of your new friends," said Orhan coldly," he quickly lunged forward and swung his sword at Adam's face, Adam quickly ducked under the sword. Before Orhan and the rest realised what was happening Adam threw two punches to Orhan's kidney, as he fell forward Adam elbowed him in the face and grabbed his sword. Orhan fell to the ground, his face bloodied. The rest of the men began to come forward, Adam put the blade close to Orhan's neck who was laying on his back, still dazed from the attack.

"One more step and I will cut his head off!" shouted Adam, the rest of the men stopped.

"Drop your swords!" yelled Adam, the men dropped their weapons and stepped back.

"All we ask for is a moment to speak with your Chief, if he wants to kill us after that then so be it, we will not resist." Najib came running out from behind and stood by Adam.

"Adam don't do this, my father will kill you no matter what you say." Adam looked back down to a bloodied Orhan, whose pride was more damaged than his body.

"Do I have your word that you will allow us to speak with the Chief?" asked Adam, Orhan sat up slowly and spat a mouthful of blood on the grass.

"You ask like we have a choice," said Orhan coldly, Adam immediately flipped the sword round and placed the handle in front of Orhan's hand.

"Take the sword and tell your men to pick up theirs too," Orhan was shocked at his gesture. He took the sword and signalled for his men to do the same, he stood up and faced Adam.

"Why would you give up your weapon?" Orhan asked in a bewildered tone. Adam looked back at his friends and then to Najib who now look scared, Adam patted him hard on the shoulder.

"Because we are here to help your people Orhan, you can't help someone with a knife to their throat." Orhan stared at the four men for a moment.

"Very well, we will escort you back and allow Chief Akbar to decide your fate." Adam thanked him; they marched back to the city, with the four prisoners being positioned in the middle of the large group.

Once they arrived in the city they were escorted back to their quarters, where they were imprisoned until Chief Akbar met with them and decided their fate. Adam sat on his straw bed, with Najib sitting beside him. Ali stood by the window, watching the guards that stood by the door and Umar was sitting on his straw bed performing silent zikr.

"Did you find out what was lurking in the forest?" asked Najib.

"No, but we have uncovered more information. Hopefully your father will allow us to…" the door burst open and in walked Chief Akbar, with Kamal standing behind him, sword in hand. The four seated men quickly got to their feet not wanting to increase the Chief's anger further. Chief Akbar immediately rushed over to Adam and punched him full force in the stomach, Adam fell to his knees. Both Ali and Umar rushed towards the Chief and Kamal, in an effort to stop Adam being hurt anymore. Adam immediately signalled for his men to stop, coughing heavily, he was unable to voice his instructions. Najib grabbed his father's arm.

"Father please don't hurt them!" the Chief struck his son across the face; he then tossed him towards Kamal who restrained him.

"I suggest you stop worrying about them and be more worried about yourself." He walked up close to his son's face.

"You are no longer my son and your punishment will be severe!" Adam slowly stood himself up, resting his back against the wall; the Chief grabbed Adam by his collar with both hands and slammed him against the wall, causing him to hit the back of his head against it. Again Umar and Ali came forward to help.

"No!" shouted Adam to his two companions, "Stand down now!"

"But Adam," objected Umar.

"I said stand down Lieutenant, you as well Captain."

"Yes Major!" replied both men loudly, they immediately went back to the corner and stood firm. The Chief loosened his grip on the collar but still kept Adam against the wall.

"Major?" questioned the Chief in a confused tone, "You are soldiers of Yusuf, he has assigned you to infiltrate this city, so he can take over. Admit it, admit it now!" shouted the Chief as he slammed Adam against the wall a second time. Adam pushed his head forward to avoid hitting it again against the wall. He grabbed the forearms of the Chief firmly and looked deep into his eyes.

"Sheikh Yusuf passed away; we buried him with our own hands this afternoon." The words hit the Chief like a boulder; he slowly released his hands, as did Adam.

"His gone?" said the Chief, in a whispered tone. The Chief took a few steps back. He looked over at his son, who was still in the clutches of Kamal.

"Release my son Kamal." Najib quickly ran over to Adam and placed his hands on his shoulders.

"It can't be Adam, what are we to do? How can we stop this without him?" asked a distraught Najib.

"What are you whimpering about you child?" asked Chief Akbar in a firm tone, "The city is now free, we can live in peace knowing that he can't harm us anymore." The Chief laughed out loud, along with Kamal.

"You know that's not true," said Adam, focusing his eyes on the Chief, "you know that Sheikh Yusuf wasn't a threat to your safety, he was a threat to you and your lies!" The Chief immediately lunged forward to grab Adam a second time, but Adam blocked his attack and threw him to the ground. Kamal stepped forward with his sword but was blocked by Umar and Ali who overpowered and disarmed him.

"You see Najib!" yelled the Chief from the floor, "they are enemies…"

"You are the enemy Chief Akbar," interrupted Adam. He kneeled down and pointed his finger to the Chief's face.

"You have lied to everyone within the Bani Hakeem." The Chief tried to hide the fear in his face upon hearing the name of his people.

"That…that name is forbidden to be spoken," said the Chief struggling to control his tone due to the fear "we are not…"

"Enough!" shouted Najib, who kneeled down beside his father with tears in his eyes.

"Why must we forget our history and name, you keep us locked away in this dungeon…you won't even say the name of our city! The name our father's used!" Najib grabbed his father's arm and shook it violently.

"You have destroyed us!" Adam pulled him away and tried to calm him down; the Chief got up looking clearly shaken by the turn of events.

"You don't understand," said the Chief, his voice almost like that of a scared child, not the fearful tyrant that he depended on for keeping his people inline.

"I had no other choice; it was the only way to ensure the survival of the people."

"The Bani Hakeem, say it father, say the name that we have gone by for generations, say it!" The fear was no longer present in Najib's voice or body, the anger fuelled him completely. It was a frustration and negativity that he had bottled up and repressed for many years and now, without control, it was spewing out of him like lava from a volcano. Adam continued to hold him back, the Chief was shocked at what his timid son was now manifesting into, a manifestation; he knew was mostly his to blame.

"Najib! We can't allow the anger to take over; this situation is bigger than you and everyone else. Stay focused, please!" pleaded Adam, eventually the anger began to subside and the tiredness set in, Najib slumped to the floor on his knees.

"None of this matters anymore, without Sheikh Yusuf we can't survive," said Najib, as he dropped his head into hands. By now Kamal had stopped resisting and was no longer restrained by Ali and Umar, instead he joined them in witnessing the unfolding of events in front of his eyes. Adam walked over to Chief Akbar, who was still supporting himself against the wall.

"You know what things lay in that forest don't you?" asked Adam, the Chief refused to make eye contact with him and instead looked upon his son, who was a crumpled mess on the floor.

"It's all over now, that forest and everything in it no longer matters to my people," said the Chief in low a voice.

"You have constantly spoken about Sheikh Yusuf, but not what else lurks in those woods, why? Why have you hidden this from your people? The Chief refused to speak; he slid down to the floor and stared up at the ceiling. Najib also

looked up and slowly crawled over to his father. He sat
beside him and placed his hand on his father's knee.
"We can't continue like this anymore, the secrets have to stop
father. It's the only way." Adam walked over to Ali and
Umar, to allow them to speak privately as father and son.
Kamal sat down on one of the straw beds, with the others
standing by the closed door.
"He knows more than we realise," whispered Adam to his
two colleagues.
"About the gold?" asked Ali.
"Perhaps, there is a link to everything but I can't think of
what it is." They looked over at Najib and his father, the
Chief appeared to be silent while his son seemed to be
pleading to him. Adam walked over to Kamal, who was still
sitting on the bed. As Adam approached Kamal he stood up.
"How is Orhan?" asked Adam.
"He'll live." Adam nodded and smiled, hoping that would be
the end of any future hostilities between the two of them.
Najib approached Adam and pulled him towards his
colleagues.
"My father is not saying anything; he keeps repeating the
same words over and over again."
"What words are they?" asked Umar.
"He keeps saying 'To stop the deaths, to stop the deaths,' do
you know what he is going on about?" Adam looked over at
Ali and Umar.
"The cemetery?" asked Adam.
"It has to be," confirmed Ali, the door burst open, which hit
Umar and Ali hard on their backs. One of the men, from the
group that attacked them earlier, rushed in.
"What is it?" asked Kamal, rushing towards him.
"Sir! They are coming; they have been spotted on the fields
close to the forest." Kamal immediately rushed to the Chief
and told him the same information. The words woke him

from his partial slumber, his posture and aura seemed to return to him at that moment.

"Najib!" shouted the Chief, "quickly go to your sister, make sure she gets there safely as well as the rest of them!" Najib obeyed without question and rushed out of the house.

"Kamal go to others and make sure that everybody has been evacuated, quickly move!" Kamal also ran out in the same desperate manner. Adam and the rest looked on with utter confusion.

"What is going on?" asked Adam as the Chief walked up to them.

"I know your anger and mistrust towards me is high," said the Chief, "but right now the people of the city have only a few moments to escape…"

"Escape wh…" Adam was interrupted by the hands of the Chief over his mouth.

"Please Adam! We don't have the time; you must trust me, please!" Adam could see the fear and desperation in the Chiefs eyes and voice. He could feel the sweat on his palms on his face, as the Chief removed his hand Adam nodded obediently.

"Very well Chief Akbar, what do you need from us?"

Adam and the rest ran out of the house and headed down the pathway towards the city square. For the first time, since they came to the city, they saw masses of people out in the open. Men, women and children were all gathered on the streets, walking in the same direction. As the men passed the square they soon saw the lone brown mountain towards the back of the city, just behind a row of buildings that marked the end of the square and the city itself. In between the houses was a large wooden arch with no doors underneath it. As they approached the arch they saw two lines of men, each by one end of the arch, they supported others going through and uphill on the stone path. Adam looked though the arch and saw a man made path that had been carved along the front face of the mountain. The path seemed to go up about half way through the mountain.

The men from the village ordered everyone to go up the path carefully and not cause a stampede. The orders were also issued to Adam and his men, who obeyed without question. As they walked up the path they saw elderly people and small children, who were being helped by others in the city. What surprised Adam most was seeing the unity and solidarity amongst the people, something which seemed lost up until now.

As the people made their way up they were met by another group of men that were directing the people around a sharp right-hand bend. The path led to a big open space that looked out upon the city. As Adam walked into the space he saw children immediately being led to the back towards the mountain face. Adults were giving the children toys and playing with them, Umar could see they were distracting them from whatever was coming to the city.

Ali walked to the edge of the ledge and looked down at the city; he could see the final numbers of people walking up the path with the group of men making the final row of people. He saw livestock running around the square along with large sacks and barrels that seemed to have been brought out, just after they started ascending the mountain path. Soon after the Chief, along with his son, Kamal and Orhan joined them on the ledge. The Chief stared anxiously to the city before looking back at the children.

"Najib, make sure the children are distracted the whole time," ordered the Chief. Adam walked up to the Chief's side.

"Sir, what is going on?" the Chief looked back at the city.

"You will see soon enough Adam," replied the Chief as he pointed down to the open square.

The sun began to set behind the mountain and the darkness of the shadow began to slowly engulf the city. As the shadow appeared from the northern part of the city Adam saw something coming from the south. Hundreds of people appeared to be coming through the front gate of the fortress. They appeared to flow through city pathways like water spreading through cracks on the floor. As they walked through some would go into buildings, people's homes, and take things from them. A large number from this strange invading army appeared to head straight to the open square and take the livestock, barrels and sacks. Adam realised that these were left out on purpose for the invaders. Ali turned round and saw that personal items and food had also been brought up the mountain and were placed by the children, almost acting as a wall to block then from seeing what was happening to their homes. There were sacks of grains and flour as well as barrels of dried fruit and livestock sitting by the people on the mountain.

"Who are these people?" asked Adam to the Chief. The Chief remained silent, constantly watching the developments down below.

"They come from the south," Adam turned round to see Amina standing behind him, "they come every two months and take what they want." Adam could see the pain in her face, how could anyone witness this personal invasion on a frequent basis thought Adam.

"Can you make them out Ali?" asked Umar, Ali stared down, focusing hard.

"Just about, the shadow from the mountain is making it difficult. I can't tell what they are wearing but they don't seem armed. Adam walked up close to the edge.

"Let's go down and take a closer look," whispered Adam to Ali, he nodded in agreement. They walked back to the pathway, followed by Umar, at the entrance of the pathway stood Orhan and some of his men.

"Where do you think you're going?" Orhan asked suspiciously, his voice muffled due to his nose being very swollen.

"We want to get a closer look at these strangers to see who they are?"

"Why?"

"We were attacked by some strange figures just before we arrived here; we wanted to see if they were the same attackers." Kamal squared up close to Adam.

"You can't go down, if you do you will be captured and they will come up after us."

"No they won't," said Najib appearing from behind, "you know very well they'll just kill them on the spot and leave, as long as there's enough food for them they don't care about us."

"They still can't go down unless your father gives them permission." Adam smiled at Orhan and patted him on the shoulder, the anger still burned inside of him because of the beating he received from Adam earlier.

"Come now Orhan, I know you still hate me. This is your chance to finally get rid of us, let us go down and sees what's going on." Kamal looked over at the Chief who was still watching the city. Kamal stepped aside and Adam and his men rushed past, Amina quickly ran to the path but was stopped by Najib.

"What are you doing Najib, they'll be killed!" said a frantic Amina, Najib tried to calm her down by holding her.

"Don't worry Amina; you don't know these men like I do," whispered Najib to his sister's ear. Amina took a step back and looked upon her brother with confusion.

"What do you mean?" she asked.

When the three men made it to the bottom of the path, they saw the square filled with these strange figures. They quickly ran through under the arch and climbed up a small single storey hut that's was close beside it. They laid on their stomachs looking ahead, immediately they recognised the men that were dragging the sacks from the square. They were covered in different types of animal fur with bones and horns also adorned on them.

"It's them," whispered Ali, "they are the ones that attacked us on the mountains."

"They are the ones that have also been attacking the Bani Khalid, I'm sure of it," said Umar. The three men stayed there watching the lives of these people being chipped away slowly by these mysterious figures.

"They don't seem like wild men, they are coordinated and efficient," said Adam.

"Yes, I noticed that as soon as they arrived. Everyone knew what to do and where to go immediately," added Ali.

"So are they organised or have they just been doing this long enough to remember everything?" asked Umar. Adam cautiously raised his upper body up in order to get a better look at the invaders. It was impossible to see any of their natural features as they were all covered from head to toe in fur and bones; there movements seemed heavy and forceful. Although they were working as a team it didn't hide the fact that they all seemed to lack any kind of grace or stealth-like abilities.

"These people walk like the animals they cover themselves in, maybe even worse," said Adam, "Syed was right, they are like wild beasts." The fur covered strangers were growing increasingly excited or angry, they couldn't tell as their faces were covered and they couldn't understand the language they were speaking. Their speed seemed to increase as they started throwing the barrels and sacks down the pathways towards the group by the fortress entrance.

"I've never heard speech like it," said Umar.

"I know, their language is unlike anything that I have encountered before," said Adam, "and I have travelled across every continent on this planet."

A tall, broad and fierce figure appeared at the city square entrance. His wore a long black fur robe, which seemed to be made from bear skin. The robe covered him completely, overlapping at his front so his arms were also blocked from sight. On his shoulders were two metal shoulder plates with small animal horns, on his head he wore a large animal skull and attached horns from a bull on top.

"Is that the leader?" asked Ali.

"It could be," replied Adam.

The dark figure opened his arms slightly and a large silver axe came from within his robe, he looked around the square before slowly turning round and walking back to the fortress entrance.

"He was checking that everything had been collected," said Umar.

"Yes," replied Adam, "he may be the leader or perhaps a senior officer." As the army left the city, Adam and the rest climbed down and made their way to the centre of the square. They looked upon the bare surface and the damage they had incurred on the city, the three men realised why the city had deteriorated so much, it was because of these pillages. Adam looked up at the mountain towards the large ledge where the people gathered, he could not see them but he knew they saw them.

"What should we do now Major?" asked Ali, Adam looked ahead down the pathway.

"Let's follow them, see where they go."

The three began to run down the pathway, led by Adam. As they approached the entrance of the fortress they saw the army in the distance, their lit torches appeared like beautiful stars in the night sky. The army were unable to travel fast due to the heavy items they were carrying;

eventually they made it to the forest. Adam and his men remained at a distance, lying on the floor in the middle of the field. The large figure they saw in the city square seemed to be speaking with the others as they circled round him.

"Can you make out anything Ali?" asked Adam, Ali focused hard but shook his head.

"No Sir, it's too dark." After a while the army began walking again, to their surprise the army went into the forest.

"They are going into the forest! Amina told me they came from the south," said Adam. Once the last row of men entered the forest the three soldiers quickly got up and began making their way over, as they approached the trees they noticed that the army had extinguished their torches. They could still make out some movement as well as the noises of them stumping through woods, dragging their stolen cargo behind them. In a single file, led by Adam, they began to walk through the woods; Adam knew he had to be cautious as he would not be able to see if they had a look out until he was face to face with him.

The army walked in a controlled manner, there was no talking or shouting just the sounds of their feet on the earth below. Adam was able to work out that they were heading away from Sheikh Yusuf's cabin which was west; the army was heading south-west.

The trees were a lot more spaced out and the ground mostly downhill, albeit mildly. There were also few boulders and craters compared to the ground north-west of the forest, where they encountered the mystery beast and the gold mine. As Adam strolled through he was both relieved and annoyed that the invaders were heading away from the beast's stomping ground. On the one hand he was glad that he didn't have to worry about encountering the mystery beast but on the other hand it would have been a good opportunity to see what the beast was with a large army standing between them.

Due to Adam's mind wondering he did not notice that the mystery figures in front had slowed down considerably. It was only when Umar grabbed him from behind and pulled him to the ground did he notice that they were only six meters away from them. The sudden drop to the ground made a sound loud enough for a few of the invaders in the back row to hear. Two of the men dropped what they were carrying and stood there, looking back towards the three soldiers. By now the sunlight had gone completely and the night sky with a half-moon shone down on the forest. Adam could make out the horns on one of the invader's helmet as the moon light reflected off the ivory. The two invaders slowly started walked back towards them.

"They're coming, don't move a muscle," whispered Ali. Adam and Umar subconsciously held their breaths. All three put their faces down so they were in the earth, in case the moonlight revealed their faces. With their faces down they had to rely on their hearing instead, they heard the two men coming closer, when they were about two meters away they stopped. Adam could hear their breathing, they were not breathing heavily or in a panicked pace but rather they seemed relaxed. The two strange figures waited a few more moments before turning back.

"We should wait a while before going ahead," whispered Umar, the rest agreed.

Eventually all three got back up and started following them once more, they could hear some commotion ahead as they started to approach the end of the forest. Adam had to restrain himself from not running ahead as he was nearly caught out before. When they were only a few meters from edge they saw intense moonlight coming through between the trees. They heard the sound of gushing water as they walked through the final row of trees, the beautiful dark lake that appeared like a mirror under the bright moonlight almost masked the tension that the three men were feeling. To their left they saw a tall waterfall that spewed out of a small dark mountain that sat in the middle of the lake like a stone island. Normally they would admire the beauty of the sight and sound of their environment but they were too puzzled to do so. The entire army had disappeared; they saw the footprints of the men on the muddy ground by the bank of the lake. "They entered the lake," said Adam, "so where are they?" All three men continued to look up and down on the bank, even retracing their last few steps in case they missed something. "Ali can you see anything," asked Umar, Ali looked for a few more moments out at the lake and towards the mountain. "They could not have crossed this lake and climbed completely over that mountain in such a short period of time," said Ali.

"Not a large army like that," added Adam.

"With their cargo," further added Umar.

"No," said Adam, he walked up to the lake with his feet submerged up to the ankles, he looked out at the lake and the moonlight reflecting over the ripples, "it's no good, we should head back. Maybe we will find something in the daylight to explain where they went.

15.
The fall

It was now the next morning, Adam sat in front of the Chief at his table in the city square. Just the two of them sat there, while the rest of the people worked together to clean up the city. The Chief watched on as his people worked through the city, trying to rebuild their lives after what had happened yesterday.

"It is easy to say we are weak," said the Chief, "that we are cowards but the fact is, these people are the strongest that I have ever known. Month after month, year after year they've endured this. Watching these animals go into their homes, steal their food, their children's food, and yet they still go on." The Chief tried to put on a smile but the reality of the situation made it too difficult. Adam knew that the Chief was lying with his words, either to him or to himself. Both men remained silent, the sound of the people cleaning and repairing behind them helped to alleviate any tension that would have been there.

"What is the name of this city Chief Akbar?" asked Adam bluntly.

"Abu Rashid," replied the Chief immediately, Adam was surprised at how quickly he responded. He was expecting resistance and having to drag the name out of him.

"Enough of this Major," said the Chief in a stern yet controlled tone, "you want answers from me, very well you can have them, on one condition."

"Which is?" asked Adam.

"That you tell me who you are and why you are here? If you do I will answer all your questions, agreed?" Adam nodded in agreement, the Chief gestured for Adam to start talking.

"My full name is Adam ibn Mustafa, I was sent by the Sultan, the Leader of the Believers to your people."

"Believers?" questioned the Chief, "Believers of what exactly?"

"Believers of the One true God, Allah, Most High. The One who sent His Beloved, the master of creation, the Prophet Muhammed, PBUH." Adam saw a strange look on the Chief's face, a combination of frustration and familiarity.

"You've heard these words before haven't you Chief Akbar?" The Chief smiled gently and nodded.

"It's like I have Sheikh Yusuf in front of me again, so you say that your Sultan follows the same religion as do those who serve and obey him?"

"Yes Chief Akbar, it is because of our religion that I am here now.

"But why? We do not even follow the religion or any religion for that matter."

"I don't know why, that knowledge has not been given to us." Adam went on to explain how they encountered the same enemy when journeying with the Bani Khalid.

"So these Bani Khalid, do they suffer the same plague as us?" asked Chief Akbar.

"I believe so, but only for the past year," the Chief listened to everything that Adam had to say about them, he then lent forward and poked his finger on the table.

"We have endured for many years in this city; we are not in need of your help or your leader's."

"Chief Akbar, these people have now started attacking other tribes because they are not getting enough from you. Eventually they will grow tired and angry with the Bani Hakeem and finish you off completely." The Chief laughed and waved his hand at his words.

"Why would they do that, without us they would have nothing?"

"They have already travelled through the mountains and discovered another tribe, once they expand further they will not need you anymore and so they will destroy you and take everything you have, everything." The Chief was no longer smiling; he looked back at his people.

"Our food has been growing less, we cannot feed ourselves and our young ones the same as we use to before, but I do not have the resources to flee nor to fight them."

"Have you tried?" asked Adam.

"Yes, many years ago, they massacred many of our people. I don't know why they allowed us to live?"

"Because they can live off your backs rather than work for themselves, I have seen this many times throughout my travels. Why work hard when you can live off the backs of slaves, a true tyrannical mind."

"Slaves?!" said the Chief in anger, "We are not slaves…"

"Oh come now Chief Akbar look around you!" The Chief sat back and looked to the table. He had nothing to reply with, he knew in his heart that Adam's words were true but he didn't have the strength or the will to fix it.

"Is there anything else that you need to tell me Adam?"

"No, that is everything from my side Sir."

"Very well, you may ask me your questions." Adam thought carefully about the order that he would ask them, he had discussed with his colleagues the previous night what they needed to find out.

"Do you know the Bani Khalid?"

"There name use to be mentioned many years ago by my elders, we use to trade with them before the curse came."

"What is this curse?" asked Adam carefully, the Chief clenched his hands tightly and released them while letting out a long breath.

"During my grandfather's reign our men started to die in large numbers in the forest, we couldn't understand what was killing them. After a while my father ordered that the forest was forbidden, which meant that our water supply for our crops and livestock had gone. Instead we had to use the old wells that no longer supplied the clean waters that they use to before."

"I saw the well when I first met Sheikh Yusuf, it is only a short journey into the forest, surely you could..."

"No Adam, that forest is a grave for hundreds of my people. How can we drink from that water when their killer still roams those woods?" Adam appreciated his words.

"So why did you blame Sheikh Yusuf and banish him?"

"Sheikh Yusuf caused us more harm than good; in the middle of this carnage while our sons and brothers were dying he was blaming us. That we had killed them and that we must turn to God, I ask you how can you blame the victims and then ask them to turn to the heavens for forgiveness?!" The Chief kicked the leg of the table in frustration.

"I knew he was not to blame but I also knew that he couldn't be in the city anymore so I banished him."

"And told others he was to blame in order to keep them away from him?" asked Adam

"Yes, once he went to live in the forest it became easy for them to believe."

"That is why you banished Islam or any other religion in the city?"

"I couldn't have any others following the same path as him, causing the same problems." Adam lent forward and looked at the Chief closely.

"Do you know what things lay in that forest, what killed your people?"

"No, which is the biggest pain of my life," Adam stood up and walked round the table, he sat next to the Chief.

"There is some kind of beast lurking in those woods Chief Akbar."

"You have seen it?" asked the Chief eagerly.

"No, but it did try to kill me, a few days later myself and my friends searched the forest and found a gold mine."

"Gold?!" shouted the Chief, "Where is it, does anyone else have claim to it?"

"I don't believe so, we weren't there for long."

The Chief got up from his chair; he started to walk round the table excitedly.

"With that gold we can rebuild our city be the Abu Rashid we once were and crush our enemies." Adam got up and restrained the Chief.

"Chief Akbar we can't do anything until we stop the invasions, no amount of gold will stop these invaders, we have to fight them. Also that beast seems to roam around the mine, attacking anything that comes near." The Chief's focus came back to reality and now appeared more dejected than before.

"We can't fight them Adam, they are too powerful. Why do you think I have kept my people hidden all these years? I'd hope that by getting rid of our names and history that the turmoil would pass over us, but it didn't."

"Exactly!" shouted Adam, "It hasn't, now listen to my words. I will help you to defeat these people but you have to follow my orders. Once we have defeated them I will then help you to destroy whatever is lurking in those woods, Inshallah, and then you can claim the gold and help rebuild your homes." The Chief began to have tears in his eyes; he felt a huge burden lifted from his shoulders that he had inherited from his father. Adam held out his hand to shake on the agreement but the Chief grabbed him and hugged him tightly.

"Thank you," whispered the Chief.

Adam, Umar and Ali began making their way through the forest again. All three men were armed with swords and daggers, Ali also carried a bow as he was the only one skilful enough to use it in the crowded wooded area.

"By their foot prints it seems they were walking in several single files," said Umar, who was examining the trail. Ali climbed up one of the Lalob trees and scanned the area, while Adam and Umar stood at the base of the tree.

"What are your plans Major, for the city and the invaders?" asked Umar.

"The only choice is to fight them Umar," replied Adam, "if we don't they will destroy them and then move on to the Bani Khalid."

"The Bani Hakeem are not warriors Major, how can we defeat an army like that Sir, with three soldiers and a bunch of civilians that spend most of their time in hiding?" Adam walked up to Umar and patted him on the chest.

"Come now Umar, have more faith than that, you clearly missed what I saw last night."

"What was that Sir," asked a confused Umar, at that moment Ali slid down the trunk of the tree and landed between the two men, as they parted just in time.

"What did you see?" asked Adam.

"There is nothing around us in terms of men, the lake and the bank also seems clear too." They continued to walk up to the edge of the forest but instead of going out onto the bank they remained hidden behind the bushes and the last row of trees. "What exactly are we waiting for Major?" asked Ali, Adam pointed to the waterfall that was pouring out of the mountain with great force.

"I don't understand," said Ali.

"Me neither," added Umar, Adam stood up but remained hidden behind the trunk.

"Last night we heard some commotion before we got to the bank, but we didn't hear the sound of splashing or people swimming," said Adam.

"They had boats," said Umar.

"Yes," replied Adam, "they loaded the boats and then set off."

"But where?" asked Umar, "There were no boats on the lake when we got to the bank and there wasn't enough time for them to cross the lake and disembark."

"Also they would need lots of boats Major to board all those men plus their cargo," added Ali, "surely we would've seen signs of all these boats on the bank."

"Unless it wasn't boats, but rather a large vessel," said Adam. Ali and Umar looked at each other not sure if Adam was being serious or not.

"A vessel?" questioned Ali, Adam nodded.

"Sir how could a vessel vanish so quickly?" further asked Umar.

"Through there," said Adam while pointing at the waterfall again, "do you see what I'm getting at now?"

"Through the waterfall!" said Ali excitedly, "There is a large opening behind it."

"Yes," replied Adam, "all we need to do is wait for one of them to come out to be sure, then we can report back to Chief Akbar and plan our next move.

The three of them remained there for a while in silence; they took it in turns to pray while the other two remained on look out.

"There," whispered Ali, while pointing towards the waterfall. A small black boat came through the waterfall, on the boat were two men covered in fur, using their shields as cover while they went through the waterfall.

"Why do they still cover their faces?" asked Umar. The two men on the boat used a paddle each side to move the boat forward, as they got closer Adam signalled for his men to get ready to attack them quickly and quietly. Adam was hoping to kidnap them back to the city for interrogation. So transfixed were they on the boat that they didn't hear the four other men coming from behind. One of the four men began shouting in his strange language to his comrades on the boat, no doubt warning them of their presence, thought Adam. Ali was able to arm his bow before turning fully around. The four men were ten meters away; Ali was able to put two of them down before they had to retreat. The three of them ran south along the outskirts of the forest, the two men on the boat had got to the bank and joined the other two in pursuit. Adam could hear the four of them getting closer; there breathing sounded more like growls.

"There gaining on us!" shouted Umar, Adam looked back while running and saw that they were only a few meters behind. He knew that they would have to stand and fight if they got any closer. He pulled his sword out while running and was about to order his men to do the same, he turned his head again to check how close they were but to his surprise they had stopped pursuing and were just standing there, looking on. Adam heard Ali screaming, followed soon after by Umar, before he could look back to his colleagues the ground suddenly went drastically downhill. The ground was so steep that it felt like they were falling off a cliff, all three men tumbled down the steep hill at high speed. They tried to avoid any trees or boulders in their path, which thankfully were few and far between. After what seemed liked ages all three men landed on the ground unconscious.

When Adam opened his eyes, he saw the clear blue sky, as he sat up he was surprised that he felt no pain. He looked down and saw no sign of injury, even his clothes seemed free from any damage.

"How can that be," he whispered to himself, he looked over to his right to examine the steep hill but it had vanished. Instead of a large hill there was nothing but endless open green fields all around him. Adam stood himself up and turned around several times examining his surroundings, he didn't recognise any of this. Just then he realised that Ali and Umar were missing too and his confusion changed to worry, for the wellbeing of his men. A soothing sound came from behind him, one that was very familiar. Adam turned round and saw Sheikh Yusuf sitting on his rock, by the tree stump. Adam was now by the Sheikh's cabin in the middle of the forest; Sheikh Yusuf was reciting surah Kahf in a low tone.

"I'm dreaming," whispered Adam to himself again, at that moment the Sheikh stopped reciting and stared at him with a small smile, he signalled for Adam to sit next to him. Adam walked over and sat in front of the Sheikh on the ground.

"What is happening Sheikh Yusuf?" Sheikh Yusuf still remained smiling and turned his head around towards his stick that was resting against the tree stump. He reached over and took it; he then tapped the top of Adam's head with the tip of it.

"What do you think is happening ibn Mustafa?" Adam thought for a moment.

"I'm dreaming?" asked Adam.

"Yes, but what else?" Adam didn't know what the answer was, he felt himself getting frustrated and angry again. He wanted to get back to his friends, to help the city get ready to defeat this army and then on to the beast. As all of this frustration and anger starting flowing through him he quickly took in a deep breath and held it. He then breathed slowly, emptying his mind of all the garbage that was flowing through it.

"There," said Adam, realising why the Sheikh was sent to him, "that is my enemy." Sheikh Yusuf smiled and nodded. "Yes my son, not just yours but many others, overthinking, panicking, impatience and reacting. That is what leads to the downfall of many, because while you're doing that what are you not able to do?"

"To see and hear," replied Adam, the Sheikh tapped him on the head again.

"You are beginning to understand, but to truly help these people you must not react. The answer is there but don't let yourself get in the way, understand."

"Yes my Sheikh."

Adam opened his eyes and saw Ali looking over him, the trees and the grey clouded sky also began to come into focus.

"Sir are you ok?" asked Ali, Adam sat up and immediately felt a sharp pain on his back and left shoulder, as well as the left side of his neck.

"Where's Umar?" he asked, Ali pointed to his right and there was Umar lying on his back with a bad head wound. Adam quickly got up and made his way over to him.

"Is he ok?"

"He was conscious when I awoke," said Ali, "but then fell unconscious soon after, he seems in bad shape Sir; we need to get back to the city as soon as possible." They both picked up Umar and placed him over the shoulder of Adam, they took it in turns to carry him as they travelled west through the wide open forest at the bottom of the large hill. For the most part the journey was quiet and uneventful until they heard some noises in the distance.

"Do you think that's them?" asked Ali

"Possibly," replied Adam, "I think they deliberately ran us off."

"Are you sure Major?"

"Yes Captain, they stopped chasing us just before we fell off, so they knew we were approaching the drop."

The ground began to go uphill, at some points quite drastically, which required both of them to carry Umar at the same time. When the ground began to level off they saw an object in the distance behind the trees, as they got closer Adam immediately recognised the cabin of the Sheikh. Once Umar was in the cabin resting in bed, Adam set off to the well to fetch some water. Nightfall had come and both Adam and Ali sat by the lit fire next to the tree stump.

They had found some food in the cabin and were able to feed some to Umar before having some themselves.

"Tomorrow morning we'll take Umar back to the city where they'll hopefully have someone that can take care of him. Then after we need to start preparing," said Adam while gazing at the fire.

"Preparing Major?"

"Yes, preparing for the next attack, Amina mentioned on the mountain that they attack every two months, so in the next two months we have to get the people and the city ready."

"Do you think two months is enough Major?"

"You don't think it is do you Captain?" Ali shook his head.

"These men are wild and strong, plus they are large in number. I can't see how we can prepare a city that has spent generations living in fear Sir." Adam appreciated the honest words he spoke but he knew that both Ali and Umar were not seeing the full picture.

"Battles are not only won by size or aggression Ali, it is the small details that win it," Adam grabbed a long branch from the ground and poked at the fire, "up until yesterday I would have thought the same thing but what I saw last night showed me we can defeat this army."

"What did you see Major?"

"I'll tell you tomorrow when we meet with Chief Akbar, there's a lot that needs doing Captain."

16.
We are Bani Hakeem

On the large ledge of the mountain, that covered the entire northern side of the city of Abu Rashid, gathered the people of the once great city. They were not strangers to gathering on this rocky beast as they had centred their life and safety on this very spot for the past four generations. The mountain itself, although had remained constant in its appearance, had gone through many changes in terms of titles and usages. The Bani Hakeem had referred to their northern guard as the 'Tower of Strength' in times gone by, for they would often use it as an aid when combating invading armies. Due to the awkwardness of the northern, eastern and western faces, it was not possible for anyone to climb the mountain from any side, except the southern face which was guarded by the city of Abu Rashid.

For many years, since locating to this area, the Bani Hakeem were able to strive and progress, not only developing the minds and hearts of their own people but those from neighbouring cities and tribes also. However as the sands of time fell so did the situation of the Bani Hakeem and although the mountain remained constant behind the people, the name and usage had changed. The new title was never spoken allowed, however in the hearts of the people they had come to know it as the 'Stone Prison', for that was how they felt whenever they gathered during the pillages, as prisoners.

As they gathered closely on the ledge, with the children and the elderly behind them, they were once again facing their once adorned city but the feelings and emotions that were circling in their minds and hearts were conflicted on this occasion. For although the past memories came flooding back, they were also curious too for there were no attack, no intruders bursting into their homes and taking what they had worked for. Instead they looked upon the face of a stranger and beside him stood their leader, Chief Akbar.

As Adam looked at the faces of the city dwellers he was reminded of the times he, with his army, had entered cities that were at the mercy of a tyrant. It was a look that unfortunately he had seen too often, the eyes always appeared the same. Even though the people may have been looking upon you, the hollowness and the spark in their eyes was gone or at the very list dimly lit. He knew that he had to reignite that spark within the people, it was the only way they would have a chance of defeating this external danger. "People of the city," bellowed Adam, his voice echoing off the face of the mountain, "I am a stranger here, amongst you. I have brought you here today to look upon your homes, your land," Adam turned sideways and gestured for them to look hard at the city below, "tell me what you see." the people were confused at the nature of the question, they looked at each other some whispering to one another, but nobody answered. Some of the people looked at Chief Akbar, hoping he would shed light as to what was happening.

"This is not a trick question!" shouted the Chief, "Tell him what you see."

"Our homes!" shouted a man at the front.

"No!" replied Adam sharply, "What do you see?"

"The city!" shouted a young woman on the edge of the group; again Adam shouted that they were wrong. The people began to get nervous at the line of questioning, which was beginning to appear more like an interrogation. As the people began to fall silent and unwilling to give anymore answers a small girl walked out in front, she was holding onto the hand of Amina, it was Sarah.

"What are you doing Amina?" asked the Chief.

"Sarah wanted to say something to our visitor," answered Amina, the Chief nodded acceptingly. He crouched down and looked upon the eyes of the little girl.

"What is it that you want to say Sarah?" asked the Chief in a gentle tone.

"I...I want to ask the man something," she replied, Adam walked over to Sarah and crouched down in front of her.

"What is your question Sarah?" asked Adam.

"What do you see?" she replied. Amina looked down at her and smiled, as did Adam. He patted her on the head gently and stood up.

"What a perfect question to ask," Adam responded, the girl began to blush and quickly turned and hugged Amina out of shyness. Adam walked back to his spot and looked at the city.

"What do I see Sarah?!" said Adam, "I see Abu Rashid!" the name bounced of the mountain wall like a hammer on an anvil; the people were stunned that the name was mentioned out loud, in front of the Chief. They all looked to the Chief and were surprised to see him smiling and nodding at the words of the stranger; Adam turned back around and faced the people.

"Behind me is Abu Rashid and in front of me I see the Bani Hakeem," the people began to get emotional, some cried at the mention of their names while others felt anger at the words being mentioned by an outsider, yet they were not allowed to speak it themselves. Chief Akbar walked up to Adam and stood by his side.

"My people for years I have tried to keep us safe, to stop us from being destroyed by outside forces in the best way that I could. But my actions were wrong," Amina was shocked to hear such words coming from her father's lips, she felt a hand on her shoulder, it was her brother, Najib. Both of them looked at their father as he took ownership of the setbacks of their people.

"I know that you are tired, that you angry and that you are afraid," said Adam, "but we can overcome this, we can stop them from coming into your homes…"

"We!" shouted a large man at the centre of the group, "Who is 'we', it's us that has suffered and it's us that has had to hide up in these mountains like scared children. Who are you to give false hope? We can never stop these animals they will kill us instantly and our families," tears began to come down the cheeks of the man. He quickly stepped back into the group and hid behind several rows of people to hide his emotional face.

"You're right," replied Adam, "I am not one of you. My name is Adam ibn Mustafa, Major to the army of the Sultan, ruler of the Islamic Caliphate and Leader of the Believers." The people were taken aback at the words coming out of Adam's mouth, although he was one man he appeared like an army coming towards them. He walked forward a few steps.

"The Sultan, your Sultan and mine, has commanded me to come with my brothers, Captain Ali ibn Osman and Lieutenant Umar ibn Idris," both men stepped out and stood behind Adam. Umar was still feeling weak from yesterday's fall but refused to stay in bed, he wanted to be with Adam as he spoke with the Bani Hakeem, for his Lord, His Prophet, PBUH, and his Sultan. He wore a wrap underneath his turban and was balancing himself by holding onto Ali's shoulder due to his weak legs.

"Why does he care what happens to us," asked Amina angrily, Najib tried to calm her down but she pushed him away, the Chief also stepped forward to calm her but Adam stopped him.

"It's ok Chief Akbar," said Adam, he looked on at Amina, whose eyes were like daggers, "please continue sister Amina." Amina walked forward and stood in front of him. "How do we know that your leader won't do the same as those invaders, once you defeat them you could take control and enslave us like they have, why should we trust you!" There were no tears, only anger, her fists were both clenched and her knuckles were red. The Chief looked at his beautiful daughter and was angered too, with himself; he knew he was to blame for the harm done to his children and his people. He walked over to his daughter and hugged her tightly, she was shocked at the support from her father, she had not felt his loving embrace since she was a small child. The anger left her like water turning into steam, she looked over at Adam. "I'm sorry…I shouldn't…I'm sorry," her voice seemed broken and strained.

"It's perfectly ok Amina, you are right to be suspicious after everything that has happened," said Adam gently. He walked closer to the group behind her and started walking up and down, along the front row while talking to them.

"You want to know why the Sultan sent me?" the people began to nod, some said 'Yes' in a low tone to avoid Adam focusing on them.

"Because Allah, Most High, your Lord, the Creator of everything in the Heavens and the earth has ordered his representative to come here and save you from this hardship. Yes you have forgotten Him, but He has not Forgotten you." Some of the people started to cry, for some of them it was out of happiness and joy for their Lord was still watching over them and for others the tears were out of shame for turning away from their Lord. Adam could see the frailty in some of the people and so he would place his hand on some of their shoulders and smile at them warmly.

"Do not grieve, rejoice and be thankful. In Islam we are all one, we are one unit, one body. If there is a problem in one area the rest of the nation feels it, right now the Sultan is hurting, because you are hurting. That is why we are here, to stop the pain so you can grow again. We will fight them together as one, knowing Allah, Most High, is with us. His Prophet, PBUH, taught us that a person who goes to bed with a full stomach while his neighbour is hungry is not a believer, well the Bani Hakeem are our neighbours and you have empty stomachs and broken hearts but know that your brothers and sisters in Islam are here to help you, every step of the way.

"Allahu Akbar!" shouted Umar.

"Allahu Akbar!" again he shouted, with Adam and Ali.

"Allahu Akbar!" shouted the Chief, the rest of the group were completely overcome with the words that Adam spoke, but hearing their Chief shout out the takbir broke down all the barriers of doubt in their heart.

"Allahu Akbar!" shouted everyone on that mountain; Allah's name echoed continuously across the face of the mountain, everyone kept chanting the takbir, again and again. Adam marched up and down along the front of the group shouting out with them. The Chief walked up to Adam and held his hand, everyone went silent to see what their leader was about to say.

"Oh Adam, please forgive me and my actions," Adam smiled and embraced him.

"There is no apology needed brother Akbar, we are family..."

"No," interrupted the Chief, "not yet, I need to embrace the religion of Islam so that we can be united." Adam nodded in appreciation of his words.

"Very well Chief Akbar, repeat after me, I bear witness that there is no God but Allah and Muhammed is His Messenger." The Chief repeated the words and the three soldiers said takbir, as they embraced him another person from the group stepped forward and asked to do the same, then another and another. Throughout the entire morning and most of the afternoon everyone in the group stepped forward and took Shahadah with Adam, once they had all accepted Islam Adam turned to the city and held out his hands to the sky.

"Oh Allah, the Most Merciful and the Most Compassionate, You are the only Lord that we worship please help us to overcome this enemy. We are weak and unable to do this alone but I am here under the orders of your representatives the Prophet, PBUH, and the Sultan. Please guide our hearts and our bodies in the right way so we can overcome this enemy, so we can raise our children to worship You and love You, the way You Should be worshiped and loved. You are the All Powerful and the All Knowing, please help us, Ameen."

"Ameen," said everyone behind him.

Kamal and Chief Akbar walked along the western wall of the fortress, followed closely by Adam and his party. Behind them walked Najib and Amina, side by side.

"What is it that you are looking for Adam?" asked Najib.

Adam ran his hand along the smooth dark wall of the fortress while looking up at the top.

"I need to see every angle of the city from the outside, are there any platforms inside that will enable us to see over the fortress walls?"

"The platforms have mostly all decayed," replied Kamal while pointing up at the fortress, "and we haven't been able to repair them due to lack of materials.

"There are trees further out past the mountain, but it would take at least one month to bring back enough wood to rebuild all the platforms," said Amina. Adam shook his head and looked back to the south.

"What about the forest in the south, we could retrieve all the wood we need in a matter of days," said Adam. Kamal, Amina and Najib all looked at the Chief. The cutting down of trees had also been forbidden since the reign of the Chief's father, by order of Chief Akbar himself.

"Kamal?" said the Chief, "Get your men and go to the forest, tell them to chop down enough wood to rebuild the platforms, but only from the eastern side of the forest, from the outer rows. They are not to enter the forest, understand?"

"Yes Sir, responded Kamal, who quickly left the group. The Chief continued to walk, now with Adam walking by his side.

"Do you know what numbers we are looking at if they fully invade?" asked Ali.

"At least three thousand but that was many years ago," said the Chief, "more than likely their numbers have increased. Ali looked back at the wall, scanning it all the way along.

"Well, that would mean we're looking at a thousand soldiers on each fortress wall, at least. It wouldn't be difficult for them to orchestrate an ascension over the walls from multiple points," said Ali.

"How many men do we have that can fight Chief Akbar?" asked Adam.

"No more than eight hundred," replied the Chief dejectedly, Adam looked at the Chief in silence and that back at the wall. He walked over to the greenery and sat down, still looking upon the tall fortress. He pictured the battle from start to finish, from every possible scenario. It was a tactic that he used every time when preparing for a battle. The rest of the group remained silent looking at Adam in deep thought, as the time passed Chief Akbar and his children started feeling the hope in their hearts melting away.

"It's not possible is it?" said Amina, her father placed his hand on her shoulder and smiled.

"We must never lose hope my daughter, while there is air in our lungs there is always a chance," Amina looked at her father's face.

"I can't believe these words are coming from you," said Amina with a stunned, yet joyous expression, "I never would've dreamed that you could be this way after everything we've been through."

"Especially now when we face an army of three thousand," said Najib with a smile on his face as he patted his father's back, "but at least we will face them together father."

"Right," replied his father holding both his children tightly, Umar and Ali looked on with warmth in their hearts as they watched a family united together.

"Ok I got it!" said Adam leaping from the ground, the Chief looked back at him with a confused expression.

"Got what Major?" asked the Chief, both Ali and Umar had smiles on their faces as they knew what the Major was going to say next.

"The plan," replied Adam, "the plan that we're going use to defeat them, Inshallah of course." The Chief and his children stared at Adam with blank expressions.

"You have a plan?" questioned Amina, still stunned as she spoke, "How is that even possible?"

"We are talking about three thousand warriors," said Najib, "strong and savage…"

"Against eight hundred," interrupted Amina, Adam walked over and stood between Najib and Amina.

"Numbers are not always the most important factor in a war," said Adam, he walked over to the ground close to the base of the fortress. He bent down and felt the earth with his finger.

"Chief Akbar I want you to round a large group of your people, men and women.

"Women?" questioned the Chief with a slightly annoyed tone.

"That's correct," replied Adam, "we have two months to get everything ready, so we have to utilise every pair of hands we can muster."

"To do what exactly?" asked the Chief, seemingly becoming more annoyed at the situation. Adam pointed to the ground and ran his finger along.

"We are going to dig a large trench all the way around the city, covering all three sides..."

"Like the Prophet, PBUH, did against the confederates?" asked Umar.

"Correct, exactly the same way," replied Adam, "the situation was almost identical." Adam walked out and then stopped; he turned round and faced the fortress walls.

"This is how far the trench must be..."

"But that's about four meters!" shouted the Chief.

"And I want the depth to be the same also," said Adam. The Chief's anger began to come through again, as he paced around the area. Amina quickly grabbed him by the shoulder.

"Father please, don't do this again," the Chief looked at his daughter's face and saw the same pain that he had witnessed on the mountain.

"I'm sorry Amina, you're right, that man is dead," the Chief looked over at Adam, "Major Adam, we'll obey your orders completely."

"I'm glad to hear that Chief Akbar," said Adam as he walked up to the Chief, "and while the trenches are being built we also need the platforms inside constructed too. Everything must be in place within a month,"

"Why a month, we have two months till they come again," said Najib.

"I know, but the trenches and the platforms are only the first half of the plan, next we have to develop your fighting skills as well as design and put into play the strategies we will be using when they come."

Throughout the first month the entire city worked together to complete the trenches and the platforms. Ali, Kamal and Najib monitored the work outside the fortress. The first week proved the hardest as the heat grew intense but as the days went by Ali saw the people develop into a rhythm as the soil was dug up. Adam had requested a portion of the earth to be brought into the city walls, whereby they were placed into medium size straw sacks along with stones and pieces of broken clay. The platforms proved slightly easier to complete than the trenches, Orhan and Adam lead the large group to retrieve the wood from the forest. The measurements by Orhan enabled the platforms to be built exactly to Adam's specifications and five days ahead of schedule. This meant more hands to help with the trenches.

As the sun came down behind the mountain Adam led the people in prayer in the city square, he knew that a mosque needed to be built, but it would need to wait until after the battle. After the prayer Adam met up with Chief Akbar, Ali and Kamal at the Chief's table by the city square.

"Have you completed your strategy for the battle Adam?" enquired Chief Akbar.

"Yes I have Chief Akbar," replied Adam who was seated in front of him, Ali and Kamal were seated to his left and right, "when they come we have to try and take out as many as possible before they even manage to reach the walls."

"That would mean archers," said Ali, Adam nodded; he used a piece of old coal to mark out the city on the table.

"We need to make sure that we are fully armed with archers on all three sides," said Adam, "eventually they will make it to the fortress wall…"

"How can you be so sure?" asked Kamal, "Maybe they will retreat after losing so many men."

"It's unlikely," said Ali, "with three thousand it would be near impossible to kill enough to hold them back completely." Chief Akbar studied the plan that was marked onto the table.

"But we don't have that many skilled archers," said the Chief."

"That's where Ali comes in," replied Adam, "he is the best archer I have ever seen, within a month your people will be able to make shots that you didn't think possible, Inshallah."

"What about once they enter the walls?" asked Kamal.

"Myself and Umar will be training the men on sword and hand-to-hand techniques; it will be tough and at times frightening but no more worse than what the people have be going through for all these years.

"Very well," said the Chief, "Kamal, instruct the blacksmiths to start repairing, as well as making new weapons as quickly as possible."

"Yes Sir!"

Twelve targets were set up outside the western wall of the fortress; Ali gazed upon the people, men and women lining up and shooting at the basic round targets. Over the past week a large number of them had improved greatly, this was due primarily to Ali's teaching techniques which had been handed to him by his father and uncles. Chief Akbar came to observe his people and saw Ali standing next to a group by the third target closest to him. The Chief was enraged to see that one of the people in the group was his own daughter Amina. As Chief Akbar stormed across to the group his eyes never moved away from them, particularly Ali and Amina.

"Oh no!" said Amina in a frightened panic, Ali turned round to see the Chief with several of his men behind him, closing in on him.

"Chief Akbar is everything…"

Before Ali could finish off his sentence Chief Akbar struck Ali hard on the chest causing him to fall to the ground. Once he landed on the floor Chief Akbar continued to strike him using the bow that he grabbed off his daughter.

"Father please stop!" screamed Amina, trying to pull her father away but was immediately pulled away by one of the Chief's men. Although the strikes were quite vicious and constant, Ali was able to deflect and avoid most of the shots. He knew that he could find room to leap back up and disarm the Chief but he decided against it, not wanting to escalate the situation further. Two arms wrapped around the Chief from behind and threw him to the ground. The four men that had escorted the Chief was stunned at the attack, the three that were not holding Amina charged at the attacker but each one was over powered and sent crashing to the ground with a variety of strikes and grappling techniques. The remaining guard of the Chief stood their frozen; still restraining Amina; at that point Amina stomped on the foot of the guard and pushed him away. The Chief looked up at Umar who was now giving Ali a helping hand to his feet.

"You dare lay your hands on me?!" screamed the Chief with venom, "Imprison these traitors now!" he ordered as he got up from the ground.

"No!" yelled a voice from the behind, everybody looked to see Adam marching forward with a large stick in his hand.

"You dare override my order!" screamed the Chief, as he reached over to grab Adam by the arm; he was hit by a hard strike to his side by Adam's stick. Adam then used the stick to lift the Chief of his legs by striking the back of his calves. The Chief laid on the ground holding his side.

"This is treason Major, I will..."

"Enough of this!" shouted Adam, he pointed the tip of the stick to the chest of the Chief, "As you are new to this faith I will let you off this one time, but if you ever lay your hands on my men or anyone else in this city for no justifiable reason I will punish you personally. Is that understood?!" The Chief was stunned at the warning, for generations his family had been the unchallenged voice of authority. He was helped up by his men that dusted his back and sides as he stood there in silence. He looked over to Ali and Umar, in his eyes the source of all this trouble.

"You had no right to involve my daughter in this Captain," said the Chief in a cold yet calmer tone." Adam looked on at Ali and Amina with a confused expression.

"Father we did nothing wrong…"

"I don't want to hear it; I told you already, you are not to fight." Adam began to understand what this was all about.

"Captain Ali?" called Adam.

"Yes Sir."

"Were you training Amina to be part of the battle?"

"Yes Sir I was, but I wasn't aware that she was forbidden to do so." Adam looked over at the Chief, trying to wipe away all signs of his annoyance to calm things down.

"You see Chief Akbar, Ali was not aware of your orders. I think an apology is definitely warranted." The Chief and the rest of his guards were shocked at the request.

"What? Is the Chief and his family above apologising when they make mistakes," said Adam.

"It is not common practise," said Amina.

"Well Islam does not allow this, apologise now," demanded Adam. After an awkward silence the Chief held out his hand and Ali shook it without hesitation.

"I'm sorry Captain; I love my daughter dearly and cannot imagine anything happening to her."

"I understand," replied Ali, "I never meant to disrespect you or your family; I will no longer train your daughter without your permission." Amina was upset by Ali's words, as Adam and Umar clearly saw.

"Amina," called Adam, "I have no doubt that your courage and desire to help your city is second to none but you must not disobey your father, this is not our way, understand?" Amina nodded silently with disappointment.

"Now that being said," said Adam turning to Ali, "how is she?" Ali looked back at the target and pointed towards it.
"To be honest Major, she is the best archer we have here. I've never seen anyone grasp it so naturally and quickly before,"
"Apart from you," said Umar with a smile on his face, Ali nodded in appreciation and embarrassment.
"The other women also, that Amina came with are amazing too," added Ali.
"What others?" questioned Adam.
"My cousins," said Amina, "we came together."
"That's right," said Ali, "eighteen in total, and all of them are a natural. Adam looked over at Chief Akbar, allowing a little time to pass before speaking.
"Chief Akbar, I would never come between a father and his children but these are extenuating circumstances."
"What are you getting at Major?" asked the Chief.
"We need every able hand in order to defeat them and the archers are the most crucial element to us winning."
"Are you ordering me to send my daughter into battle?" demanded the Chief.
"I am not ordering anything," replied Adam in a gentle tone, "but if we do not have our best archers on that platform then we may not have a city left. Ultimately the decision is yours and yours alone to make. "
The Chief looked at his daughter, the pain in his heart was clear to see by everyone.

17.
Battle of Abu Rashid

The light of the half-moon shone down on the calm lake, the ripples almost appeared like creases on a dark silk cloth. Najib and Umar sat quietly on the outskirts of the forest, with nothing but a large thorn bush to hide behind. For the past three days members of the Bani Hakeem and the Sultan's guard had watched the waterfall closely for any signs of movement.

Adam had ordered a lookout three days earlier in case they decided to strike Abu Rashid before the half-moon appeared. Najib looked on nervously, although the city had been preparing for the past two months his mind could not fully comprehend what was about to happen. For years they had been under the foot of this mysterious force, but now they would resist for the first time on a massive scale. He kept having thoughts about his family and the children of the city, would everyone be wiped out by the end of tonight or would they triumph? Umar saw the cogs turning in Najib's mind, for most of the day he had not engaged much in conversation.

"The mind can be a dangerous thing," said Umar, "often situations can be decided before they have begun, purely based on the person's thoughts." Najib looked over to Umar with a nervous smile.

"I hope that's not completely true, otherwise I won't be much good on the night of battle." Najib readjusted his position, becoming irritated at the stones and twigs that kept poking and pressing against him, Umar placed his hand on his shoulder.

"Relax, stop working yourself up Najib."

"I can't help it Umar."

"Just focus on your task, you keep thinking about everything, that's not your role. Let your father and Major Adam worry about that, stick to the plan and nothing else, ok?" Najib nodded.

Adam stood outside the southern fortress wall, just in front of the trench away from the wall. Ladders had been placed along the sides of the trench to allow quick access over them. Adam stared in the direction towards the forest, which was out of eye shot. He thought about Sheikh Yusuf and everything he had endured, patiently waiting for their arrival to help guide them to this moment. This battle was four generations in the making and now himself and the Bani Hakeem stood on the verge of victory or annihilation. Ali walked up to his side and patted him on the back.

"You've been out here a long time Major. Najib and Umar are not due to come back for a while yet."

"I know," replied Adam still staring ahead, "just making sure that I haven't left any stone unturned, one slip could mean the difference." Adam started walking round towards the western wall, checking everything outside as he did every night for the past week.

"Sir our success is with Allah, Most High, alone. You needn't add this burden onto yourself." Adam looked back at his Captain and smiled.

"Oh Ali, I thought I had taught you better than that." Adam climbed down to the trench and started walking along. "You think I'm not aware that everything rests in the Hands of Allah, Most High?"

"I never meant any offence Major," said Ali as he climbed down the ladder.

"I know you didn't Captain but just know, I constantly try to remind my heart of this but my body must do the opposite. My body must act that everything depends on my actions alone, that is the only way we can be sure that we do our best in every situation." Once Adam reached the other end of the trench he climbed up and made his way to the entrance of the fortress once again.

"I have seen many people fall into the trap of listening to the voice in their head, telling them over and over again 'Stop worrying, Allah, Most High, will take care of it. You are just a creation so just relax' before you know it you've sat yourself on your supposed 'throne' and expected everything to be done for you. This is not how servants behave; we don't behave this way when we serve people, so how can we get this complacent when we serve our Lord?"

"Understood Major," said Ali obediently.

Umar was doing silent zikr with his eyes locked on the waterfall, Najib felt his eyelids getting heavy and for the first time, since he began his watch, the nerves began to wither slightly.

"Najib," whispered Umar, forcefully. Najib looked over at the waterfall and saw the middle of water starting to part at the bottom. The dark bowstrip penetrated its way through the water, followed by the bow, as it slowly materialised from the mountain.

"It's time," said Umar as both men quickly got up and rushed back to the city.

Kamal stood on the platform just above the fortress entrance, for the past three nights himself and Orhan had took turns watching out for any signs from the lookouts. As Kamal prepared to change shifts he saw some movement in the distance, he held up his telescope to get a better look. He immediately saw Umar and Najib running with great urgency, Kamal climbed down the ladder while shouting the takbir. Adam and Ali quickly made their way to the entrance, as Najib and Umar made their way into the city.

"They're on their way!" shouted Najib.

Adam called for all of his senior soldiers, both from the Sultan's guard and the Bani Hakeem to meet with him so he could issue his orders.

"Ok this is what we have prepared for, Kamal and Ali, get all your archers into place and make sure every angle that we discussed is covered, remember nobody is to fire the first shot until I say. Chief Akbar, get your men and start evacuating all the children, elderly and those that can't fight to the mountain. Make sure the entrance is blocked using the sacks we made. Umar and Orhan with your group get all the ladders in and secure the doors with sacks. After this get everyone into their formations, is everybody clear." Once everyone confirmed they all set off to their tasks.

Adam stood on the platform above the front entrance staring ahead with his telescope. Gradually all the archers were in place, covering every platform across the three walls of the fortress. The last remaining sacks were placed behind the entrance before Umar made his way up to Adam.

"Locked up and in position Sir," said Umar. Eventually all the other leaders came back to confirm their tasks had been completed.

"Now we wait," said Adam, with his brothers behind him.

"They seem to be taking their time," said Kamal.

"Of course," said Chief Akbar, "for years they have taken with ease, why should today be any different for them?"

"Hopefully we can use that," said Ali. While the others made comments Adam stood completely silent and focused.

"Here they come," said Umar.

The first row of invaders appeared on the distant field, as they got closer the width of the army began to grow larger and larger. They appeared like disfigured shadows, with some sporting large horns on their helmets. The dark fur seemed to glisten in the moonlight, and their postures what like that of a wild animal close to pouncing on its pray. Once they saw the trenches the army came to a halt about one hundred meters from them. The tall figure, that they saw on the city square previously, walked out to the front. Adam looked through his telescope and saw he was speaking to a few of his men at the front; all of a sudden a third of the army started coming forward.

"Damn!" said Adam, "I'd hope he send more of them." As the group approached the trench Adam counted around five hundred of them, they looked down at the trench and then wondered round, looking for a way to cross. They appeared to be speaking with one another before several of them climbed down and tried to climb up the other end; they started climbing on each other's back in order to reach the top.

"Shall we fire Sir?" asked Ali.

"No, we need to get a large number of them in the first instance." Eventually one of the invaders was able to climb up and then more started to follow. Soon half of them had managed to climb over and were now making their way to the front entrance. As they started to push, the remaining invaders all climbed down into the trench to make their way across.

"Ok, tell the archers on the southern and eastern walls to take them out Ali," ordered Adam. Ali held up his sword.

"Archers!" he yelled, all the archers stood to attention and armed their bows, "South and east prepare to fire!" The invaders did not seem to react in the slightest at the orders being shouted.

"Stupid creatures!" shouted Orhan, "They don't even understand what we're saying!"

"Fire!" commanded Ali; the arrows flew into the invaders like rain falling to the ground. After five ways of firing all the invaders were lying dead either in the trenches or just outside. A huge roar could be heard in the distance from the remaining army, Adam saw the leader fall back into the crowd and disappear.

"What are you up to?" he whispered to himself, eventually half the army seemed to disappear back towards the forest.

"They're retreating!" said Orhan joyfully, some of the ground soldiers and the archers started to cheer.

"No they haven't!" yelled Adam angrily, "Everybody back to your positions and stay alert." Chief Akbar stood close to Adam and leaned in close.

"What is happening Major?" he asked in a concerned tone.

"They are stupid," said Orhan again, "they didn't even bother to react when Captain Ali was yelling his commands, this will be easy Chief Akbar." Chief Akbar had learnt enough from his new visitors not to assume anything anymore."

"What do you say Major?" asked the Chief.

"I think they did understand Ali's orders."

"Then why didn't they react?" asked Umar. Adam leaned over and looked back at the dead bodies that lay on the floor.

"Because they were just following their orders," said Adam, "that's what their leader ordered them to do, head for the entrance. Whatever else happened they just ignored."

"How can you be so sure?" asked Chief Akbar.

"Ali, Umar? Do you remember that night we were following them in the forest and they heard us? When they came back to inspect the noise I heard their breathing, it was relaxed and calm."

"Yes it was," confirmed Umar, Chief Akbar and his men looked on with confusion.

"What does that have to do with anything?" asked Kamal.

"They didn't react the way normal soldiers would. They were not worried or concerned; they were just going through the motions."

"Like cattle?" asked Ali.

"Exactly!" said Adam, "I think they've gone back to inform their leader of the situation, to get their orders."

"But I thought that tall figure was their leader," said Umar.

"So did I, but I guess there is someone else that he follows," replied Adam.

The remaining invading army stayed put, when Adam watched them through his telescope he noticed they weren't even moving. They appeared like dark statues in the middle of the field.

Adam saw light behind and realised that the rest of the army was returning.

"Here they come, no doubt they've sent their entire army this time, make sure everyone stays in position," ordered Adam.

As the army began coming forward they could see they were holding large shields.

"Ali take control of the archers, start attacking when they are in range," ordered Adam. Once in range arrows began flying at them from all three sides of the city. With each wave around forty of the archers were getting their mark. As the first row reached the trenches the city was able to see the entire army that was invading. There were at least four thousand soldiers that had come out; Adam knew they had to make a large dent in their numbers before any of them made it over the walls. The archers kept firing, picking off small numbers each time. The invading army did not go forward they just remained in the same spot in front of the trench, taking wave after wave of arrows.

Ali could see they were trying to deplete their arrows and then storm the city, he told the archers to hold their fire. The invaders did not react to the ceasefire; they still remained in their same position. All of a sudden Adam and the rest noticed something being passed down from the rows, when it got to the front they threw it down at certain parts of the trench. Adam looked and saw they had thrown large pieces of wood, ten meters apart from each other. Eventually there were large piles of wood scattered all around the fortress. A lit torch was passed to the invaders at the front, Adam and Ali knew what they were intending. Dense smoke from the burning of wet wood would make it almost impossible to see where they were.

"Don't allow them to light it, archers fire!" shouted Ali, the archers kept firing but eventually they were able to light all the piles. Soon the ground was covered in thick smoke, the archers kept firing randomly but they could not see if they were hitting their targets.

Arrows began coming up from below towards the Bani Hakeem, several archers were hit and some killed instantly. Many of the archers froze out of fear, but Ali and Kamal encouraged them to keep firing. The Bani Hakeem were firing through the smoke in a blind panic, not knowing where the invaders arrows were coming from. Eventually the invaders stopped firing and no sounds could be heard, apart from the cracking of the wood burning. The Bani Hakeem kept firing until Ali ordered them to cease. The entire city was listening quietly, trying not to be effected by the thick dark smoke. The eyes of the archers began to sting and their breathing became harder and harder.

All of a sudden one of the archers disappeared over the ledge with a large scream; the archers on that wall were still, not knowing if they should fire, as they could hit their own. Several more were pulled over, as well as large spears striking other archers. Ali knew that they couldn't defend in this situation; he ordered the group of woman, led by Amina, that were exceptional with a bow, to retreat to the roofs of buildings closest to the fortress platforms. The other archers were ordered to remain hidden behind the walls and strike if anyone climbed over. Amina's group were split into three, each group facing a fortress wall.

As the Bani Hakeem remained silent, several ladders appeared at the fortress walls. The archers hiding behind the walls quickly launched themselves at the ladders to push them back, some were successful but others got hit by arrows. Soon some of the invaders began making it to the tops of the ladders but Amina and her archers started taking them out one by one. Through their combination of efforts the archers were able to stop all invaders from climbing over the fortress walls.

"This won't hold them forever," said Adam "I'm sure they have a back-up plan."

At that moment a huge banging sound could be heard at the front entrance.

"They brought a battering ram!" shouted Umar, as he ran to the front doors, followed by a large number of soldiers. They pushed against the sacks that were blocking the entrance. With each ram the Bani Hakeem pushed forward but the door was beginning to feel the pressure and started to break.

"That door won't hold for long," said Chief Akbar, who was still standing by Adam on the front wall. The black smoke began to clear and Adam could see the invaders appearing on the ground, only around five hundred invaders had been killed. The front door shattered and the invaders started trying to push themselves through the sacks, armed with large swords, axes and shields. Their screaming could be heard once they started to push their way through, Ali ordered a large portion of his archers to fire at the front entrance. Amina's group tried to support them by taking out all the invaders that were still trying to climb the fortress walls, but soon they were unable to keep up with the many ladders that were now in use by the invaders. Around twenty invaders had climbed over and were now taking out the archers that were on the platforms. There brute strength and savagery enabled them to kill the Bani Hakeem with single blows.

Adam ordered a number of the ground soldiers to assist the archers on the platforms; soon fighting could be both seen and heard on the upper levels with the invaders screaming and growling and the Bani Hakeem chanting the takbir.

Amina's group tried their best to take out the invaders without hitting any of their own, but soon the number of invaders made it too difficult to fire safely. Adam led a group of soldiers to the upper levels to help the archers defend against the invaders, Ali directed Amina's group to the southern walls to push back the invaders trying to come through the main entrance.

"Do let up!" shouted Ali, "Keep them from coming in at all costs!" The women were brought extra arrows as they kept firing without pause; other archers came to support them also. Umar and his men were able to kill many invaders that tried to come through the barrier of sacks. With the support of the archers above, they seemed to be backing invaders away from the front entrance.

On the upper platforms Adam was able to take out a large number of invaders with his sword, as did Orhan and Chief Akbar.

An unusual sound could be heard further south behind the invading army, Adam quickly looked over the eastern wall to get a better look.

"Oh no," he said, "Umar! Get your people back!" before Umar could react to the orders the entire front entrance and large part of the wall surrounding it exploded. The catapult that Adam saw being dragged had quickly launched a large stone boulder, no doubt taken from the forest. Amina and her cousins had been flown back by the force of the rock and fell to the ground. Chief Akbar saw this and quickly ran with his men to the lower levels. They charged at the invaders head on, who now began to come into the city in large numbers. The Bani Hakeem was able to hold the invaders back long enough for the wounded to be moved away behind them. Eventually the invaders began killing their way through; Chief Akbar was one of the first to be struck by the invaders. A tall figure draped in brown fur and a bone face mask ran his sword straight through the Chief. Najib and Kamal tried to get to him but he fell dead to the ground as they arrived. The anger in the Bani Hakeem, at the sight of the leader being killed, enabled them to charge in one strong unit. The invaders were taken aback at this sudden surge of resistance, but Adam knew that this momentum would be short lived and quickly tried to make his way below to take charge of the ground troops.

As he ran along the platforms on the eastern wall a large axe came flying over the fortress wall, Adam was just able to dodge the blow by falling back. As Adam looked up he saw the familiar large figure climbing over the wall. "You," said Adam in a cold tone. It was the leader that he saw multiple times before, the leader quickly swung his axe down but Adam rolled right, missing the axe by inches. The red sparks as the axe struck the stone floor signalled for Adam to quickly launch his own attack. Unable to match his strength, Adam struck at the arms of the leader, in attempt to slow him down. The leader kicked Adam in the chest, sending him flying across the platform, as Adam tried to catch his breath he felt another large blow to his side as the leader kicked him again. The leader bent down and picked Adam up by the neck with a single hand, Adam heard him laughing under his helmet as he held up his axe over his head. In a quick manoeuvre, Adam pulled on the leader's wrist using it as leverage to launch his body over his arm. Once his full weight was on the leader's arm he was able to pull him down to the ground and bend it back until he heard his arm snap. The leader screamed in pain, Adam quickly jumped on top of him and finished him off with his dagger. As the dagger went in a large scream was heard from the invaders that were on the eastern wall, followed immediately by the same scream from all the invaders in the city. Finally another scream came from the invaders, but by all of them. The invaders stopped attacking and started retreating immediately. There was no attempt by any of them to attack, some of the Bani Hakeem tried to attack them as they retreated but Umar forbade them from doing so.

As the last of the invaders left the city and carried on south, Adam slowly made his way down, clutching his injured ribs with his hands. The number of dead from both sides was high, but he was glad to see that the invaders had suffered more losses than the Bani Hakeem. As Adam made his way to the broken front wall he saw a large number of people standing in a circle formation. Adam walked through the people and saw an injured Amina and her brother, Najib, holding on to their father's hands, who lay dead on the floor. Adam walked away to give the Bani Hakeem space to mourn the loss of their Chief and father.

Adam looked down the pathway that was full of the fallen from both sides, he saw Umar crouching down on the floor. Adam quickly hurried towards him and saw in his arms the body of Ali. He had several deep stab wounds on his chest, Adam knelt down beside Umar. Both men wept silently at the loss of their brother.

As time passed the city began collecting the bodies of their dead. Adam led the funeral prayer for all of the Bani Hakeem that died in battle. On the western side of the city an area of land had been used as a cemetery, once the burial had been completed Adam ordered that the city should spend the next three days taking care of their family and not worrying about any other matters. He also sent a large group of men to draw water from the well in the forest, as Chief Akbar was no longer around to object. Adam hoped that the fresh clean water would aid the people, especially during these difficult times.

Later that night Adam travelled alone to the outskirts of the forest. He saw the trail of the abandoned catapult come from the southern side of the forest, where the invaders had kept it hidden for emergencies. He built a small fire and sat down beside it. He watched the glow of the fire as the small particles floated up to the night sky. He cleared his mind and thought about his actions since arriving to Abu Rashid. Was he obeying Allah, Most High, the way He was supposed to be obeyed. In all this carnage and mayhem it is always easy to lose sight of your main objective, to please Allah, Most High.

He heard someone approaching; Adam looked back and saw Najib and Amina. Adam signalled for them to take a seat, which they did. Amina had injured her back during the fall and found it hard to move her upper body. Aside from a sprained ankle, Najib had managed to get through the battle relatively unscathed.

"How are you both holding up?" asked Adam.

"Very conflicted," replied Najib, he looked over at his sister who stared at the fire, "for the first time we have defended ourselves, we have protected our land and our people."

Najib's face began to become paler; he looked up at the stars in an attempt to stop himself becoming emotional.

"How do you do it?" asked Amina to Adam.

"You mean fight?" returned Adam, Amina nodded silently. "War is never a joyous thing, it is ugly and painful, but at times it is necessary. You are hurting of course, but your actions will help your future generations. Look forward, not back; at least that's how I try to deal with it. It's never a good feeling to take a life, even when you have to."

"What about Captain Ali?" asked Najib, "Surely you must feel pain and loss?" Adam looked at the fire, he was reminded of the first time he met Ali with Hasan around a camp fire.

"Of course," replied Adam, "he was my brother but he left this world as a martyr, protecting people from invading forces. We are unable to comprehend the reward he is receiving right now, as well as your father." Amina and Najib smiled at the comment.

"Your father died protecting his people and their land under the banner of Islam, there is no better way for a Muslim leader to leave this world, so be grateful to your Lord that he took him at that time."

"Ameen," replied Najib and Amina.

"Ameen," said Adam.

The three of them remained there in silence for a while, watching the stars.

"So what happens now?" asked Amina, "Is it over?" Adam thought about her question, the same question had been going through his mind since they won the battle.

"No," replied Adam, "we have to find out who their leader is, because while they have a leader they will always be a threat.

"How do we find the leader?" asked Najib. Adam looked over at the two of them and smiled.

"Let's forget about the invaders for tonight and talk about something lighter. Tomorrow we will deal with this issue."

The two of them agreed and spent the night talking about simple events and stories, making each other laugh and smile, for the first time in many years.

18.
Attack

At the table of the Chief sat six people Adam, Umar, Kamal,
Orhan and the children of the departed Chief, Najib and
Amina. Umar sat beside Adam with Najib and Amina seated
on the opposite side. Behind the siblings stood Orhan and
Kamal, like tall towers guarding them as they had guarded
their father.
"It has been three days since the battle," said Adam, "the
Bani Hakeem have already cleaned away the debris and are
currently rebuilding the city to the days of your forefathers."
"Yes," replied Najib, "thanks to your help we are free to
rebuild to the standards of our elders, how can we repay you
both?" Umar smiled and looked over at Adam.
"I'm sure that the Major will agree with me when I say that
reward is not the reason for us helping. We are here under the
order of the Sultan, as Muslims it is your right to be protected

by him and whoever follows him." Adam nodded in appreciation of his brother's words.

"I couldn't have uttered better words myself," added Adam, "now then, the first order of business that must be addressed is the choosing of leadership." The four members of the Bani Hakeem looked at each other in confusion, Orhan and Kamal exchanged comments in a quiet tone.

"Is there something wrong?" asked Adam.

"Forgive us Major Adam," replied Amina, "but we assumed that you had taken the role, especially since we still have the issue of the invaders striking again, as well as the danger that lurks in the forest." Adam and Umar could see the worry on the faces of their friends, the mention of leadership made them assume they would be departing and leaving them to their problems.

"Please forgive me," said Adam, "I haven't expressed myself clearly. Taking the role of leadership is an important one and must be done quickly. A city without a chief is like a lost child in the wild. I will remain here as long as you need me," the Bani Hakeem were relieved to hear those words, "the complete defeat of the invaders as well as the beast that lurks in the forest will be addressed before we leave. But we are not able to officially take the role as chief, this can only happen with the order of the Sultan as we are not from the Bani Hakeem."

"So we must choose a leader from our own people?" asked Kamal.

"That is correct," answered Umar, "and we will gladly advise and support your new chief."

"Of course," added Adam, "did your father say who he wished to take his place?" Amina looked over to her brother.

"He always wanted you to follow in his footsteps," said Amina.

"I'm not him Amina; he always said that I was too weak." Amina placed her hand on her brother's shoulder.

"Father knew that you would follow him so he was trying his best to get you ready for the position."

"But I'm not ready Amina."

Adam smiled and placed his hand on Najib's hand.

"I'm glad to hear you say those words Najib," Najib looked at Adam in confusion.

"Why?" Najib asked.

"Because it means that you understand the magnitude of the role, instead of looking at the luxuries you are looking at the responsibility, the sign of a good leader." Najib was embarrassed at the compliment; Amina looked over at Kamal and Orhan.

"Call everyone to come to the city square, tell them they are to make the pledge to follow our new chief."

"Of course Mother Amina!" replied Kamal immediately, both men rushed off to notify the people of her orders.

"So what is our next call of action asked Najib?" Both Adam and Umar stood up and walked in front of Najib, Adam motioned for Najib to stand up. Once on his feet Adam took hold of Najib's hand pledged to follow and obey the new Chief, so long as he adhered to the rulings of the Sultan. After the pledge Adam kissed his hand, Umar followed the same procedure and kissed his hand also.

"Thank you for your support, but I am a new Muslim, how can I govern my people in accordance to a faith that I am new in.

"Not to worry Chief Najib," said Umar, "we will advise you on such matters."

"But what about when you leave?"

"If you are not ready the Sultan will appoint an advisory for you."

Gradually the city square filled with the Bani Hakeem, many of the elderly that witnessed the downfall of their people and city were eager to come and witness this joyous change. They were carried by their children and grandchildren to the front of the square, directly in front of Chief Najib and his sister. Chief Najib stated that our elders should be first to make the pledge as it is they who raised us and guided us.

As they approached one by one they took the hand of their new Chief, the women of the city made the pledge via Amina, holding her hand while Chief Najib placed his hand on her shoulder. Adam and Umar stood back and watched the city united in the belief and hope of their new leader, but the element of fear was still hovering above their heads. Once the pledges had been taken Adam suggested that the new chief make a speech, Chief Najib nervously stepped up on a small platform and addressed the people.

"Bismillahir Rahmanir Rahim," said the Chief, he voice seemed to transform to one of authority, "we have been through a dark period in the past generations. Some of our elders here have witnessed a lot of these events first hand. We have been blessed by our Lord, Allah, Most High, and given the opportunity to come back to the religion that our elders once practiced before. Through our faith we will, Inshallah, have those blessed times back again." The Bani Hakeem started to chant the takbir; Chief Najib allowed them to chant several times before gesturing them to remain silent.

"We must never forget our past, we must learn from it so we never turn our backs to our Lord ever again, under the authority of the Caliph, the Sultan, I am leading the Bani Hakeem, but if I stray from the authority of the Leader of the Believers then do not obey me. Major Adam and the newly appointed Captain Umar will remain with us and support us in defeating our enemies."

Chief Najib looked over to Adam and gestured for him to come up and say a few words. As Adam approached the platform he kissed the hand of the Chief but did not stand up with him, but rather stood just in front on the ground.

Adam had been taught by his elders to always respect those in authority, and to show this through his actions.

"Bismillahir Rahmanir Raheem, we are thankful and seeking forgiveness from our Lord, The Most Merciful, The Most Forgiving, The Just, The Guardian of Faith and The One True God, Allah, Most High. We also ask for peace and blessings on our beloved Prophet, PBUH, the master of creation and the Beloved of our Creator. It is because of Allah, Most High and His Messenger, PBUH, that we are able to know the true path and to rectify our ways. If we go to Allah, Most High, walking He comes to us with speed. How easy it would have been for Allah, Most High, to replace the Bani Hakeem with another but He didn't, as in times before our Lord is Merciful and gives chances to His creation again and again. Thank you Allah, Most High, we are undeserving of Your Blessings and Mercy." The Bani Hakeem were moved to tears by the end of Adam's speech, he looked over at Amina and Chief Najib who were also crying at his words.

Adam walked away from his spot, back to Umar. "My brothers and sisters in Islam," said Chief Najib, "we all know that we still have work to do, whether attacking our enemies, growing our city or educating our children, but whatever our task is, ensure to remember Allah, Most High, in your heart continuously." The Bani Hakeem chanted takbir three times before Chief Najib allowed them to leave.

Chief Najib walked outside the fortress walls followed by the Adam, Umar, Kamal and Orhan. The bodies of the invaders had been buried in unmarked graves on the eastern side of the city. Soon after the battle emotions ran high with the Bani Hakeem after the death of their Chief, but Adam ordered that none of the bodies should be desecrated.

Chief Najib walked in front and looked at the trench that still remained around the city.

"I wonder when we will be able to fill this back to what it was before?" he asked out loud. Adam patted the Chief on the back lightly.

"Soon Chief Najib," said Adam, "once we have defeated the enemy completely."

"And when would that be Major?" further asked the Chief. Adam stopped walking and faced the Chief with his whole body.

"Are you asking my advice as to what we should do next Sir?"

"More than that Major, I am asking you to tell me what to do. I am not in a place to lead the people in war and neither was my father, that role is yours. Command us and we will follow." Chief Najib turned round and looked to Kamal and Orhan.

"What say you two?" asked the Chief.

"We follow you and those you command us to follow Sir," said Kamal.

"I second that Sir," said Orhan. Chief Najib smiled and nodded in appreciation to their loyalty. Chief Najib looked back at Adam and gestured with open hands that the Bani Hakeem was his to command in this situation.

"Very well," said Adam, "my commands are that we attack the invaders immediately, at their lair." Chief Najib and his men were shocked at his words.

"Only around a thousand of them were killed Major Adam, we lost a third of our soldiers. At the most we would have fewer than six hundred able to fight. We can't defeat three thousand with that many soldiers, especially on their land."

"We don't need to defeat three thousand; we just need to defeat one," said Adam.

"But finding that one will be difficult Sir," said Umar.

"I know but this is our only chance of defeating them Captain." Chief Najib signalled with his hands for both of their attentions.

"I'm sorry but I have absolutely no idea what you are talking about," said Chief Najib with a frustrated tone, "what do you mean 'one'? How will one death defeat an army that large?" By the end of his questions the anger was becoming clearly visible on the Chief's face.

"I can see a lot of your father in you Sir," said Umar, both Kamal and Orhan had smiles on their faces and had to bite their lips to prevent them from laughing out loud. Chief Najib immediately understood and took a few deep breaths.

"I'm sorry Captain," said Chief Najib.

"That's perfectly alright," said Major Adam, "although I'm sure there are better ways to give advice or criticism," Adam said while looking at Umar firmly.

"Apologies Major and Chief Najib, I will ensure to speak more wisely and with better manners in future."

"Thank you Captain," said Chief Najib. The Chief looked back to Adam.

"Please explain your words Major."

"Very well, on the night of the battle we were overmatched in every way, the invaders could have annihilated us before the rest of the army even entered the city, did you see why they retreated?" Chief Najib thought for a moment.

"I never really thought about it, just before they retreated my father was killed. My mind was too preoccupied at that moment."

"Which is understandable Sir, they retreated when their leader was killed."

"By you," said Kamal, Adam nodded.

"That's right," replied Adam, "the whole army could only function if a leader is present. Without them they cannot function."

"They just fall apart," said Chief Najib.

"Precisely Sir, these people have been raised to obey authority without question, which at times produces a strong and efficient force."

"But if you remove the head the body will cease to function," added Chief Najib.

"Yes Sir," confirmed Adam. Chief Najib looked back at his city; he knew this would mean the death of more of his people.

"Is there any way we could ask the Sultan for help? I do not wish to see more of my people's blood spilled." Adam placed his hand on the Chief's shoulders.

"No Chief would," he replied "but there is a big chance that the invaders will launch another attack before help arrives. I am guessing their leader will come up with a plan to ensure they do not fail this time."

"I understand Major, so I guess we need to find some way of penetrating their defences and locating their leader. Do you have a plan as to how we do this Major?"

"I do Sir."

Chief Najib asked Orhan and Kamal to escort Adam and Umar to the old armoury in the north side of the city. By the pathway to the mountain stood a detached building, the roof was almost dome shape much like a mosque. On the sides were carved patterns of flowers and moons. The walls were severely cracked and the doors close to rotting away.

"This armoury needs refurbishing," said Adam.

"Yes, Chief Najib has asked us to begin work once we have accomplished our missions," replied Orhan.

As the broken doors were opened the smell of mould, damp and dust spewed onto the four men, inside was an array of old weapons and in the middle of the room was a square metal grid hatch. Orhan opened the unlocked hatched which led down to a stone staircase. Kamal lit a torch and led all three of them down to another small room which was full of old wooden barrels.

"What's down here?" asked Adam, Kamal walked to one of the barrels and took off the lid. He pulled out an old set of armour which was comprised of metal and leather.

"Why is the armour kept down here?" further asked Adam.

"Because of the mould and damp on the upper level, we didn't have enough cattle to make leather in the past. With each invasion our supplies grew less and less, so Chief Akbar ordered us to bring it down here." Adam looked at the worn armour closely.

"It's old, but still usable, how many sets do you have?"

"Last time we checked around four hundred," replied Kamal.

"Why so few for such a large city?"

"In the past many of our soldiers wore this armour when venturing into the forest."

"And they never returned," finished off Adam, both Kamal and Orhan's silence confirmed his answer.

"Well four hundred is more than enough, let's bring these up and start getting ready.

Adam retreated back to his quarters and began suiting up in his armour; Umar was also getting ready alongside him.

"How many will be coming with us Sir?" asked Umar, as he was putting on his chain-mail.

"About three hundred," replied Adam as he sheathed his sword.

"Why so few Major? We have at least four hundred soldiers ready now." Adam walked over to the door and opened it, outside was Kamal and Orhan waiting in their armour.

"Tell everyone to march outside and wait by the outskirts of the forest, myself and Umar will be joining them shortly."

"Yes Sir," they both replied. Adam closed the door and walked up to Umar.

"Because the plan doesn't call for it Captain. Enough blood has been spilt, on both sides; my aim is to take whoever is in charge out as swiftly as possible.

As Adam and Umar approached the main entrance they were greeted by Chief Najib and Amina. Both of them were attired in battle gear, with Amina holding on to her bow. "What's all this Sir?" asked Adam confused.

"I and my sister will be joining you in the attack."

"I'm sorry Chief Najib but you both need to stay in Abu Rashid," replied Adam in an awkward tone. Both Amina and Chief Najib were shocked at the Major's reply, as they were expecting a more positive reaction.

"Major it is important that we show the Bani Hakeem that we are united," said Amina in an irate voice. Adam, not wanting to exacerbate things placed his hand on the newly appointed Chief's shoulder.

"You are right, unity is important but so is the stability of leadership. For the first time in many generations your city and its people are now governed under Islam. It would cause massive disruption if anything happened to you on this expedition. Please, for your people, stay and lead this city. Whatever the outcome of today the Bani Hakeem still need a leader," both Chief Najib and Amina knew in their hearts that Adam was right, after a short goodbye Adam and Umar set off to the waiting army.

Once they reached the army Kamal and Orhan ordered them to stand to attention and address Adam.

"Oh Bani Hakeem, we are on the verge of finishing off this conflict. I'm sure, much like me; you don't want any more bloodshed. You have been given your orders, do not attack unless absolutely necessary, if anyone kills without just reasons they will be severely punished on our return to the city. Is that clear?

"Yes Sir!" yelled everyone. Adam led the soldiers through the forest, as they approached the bank of the lake they were ordered to spread across in a single file. Once in place each soldier armed their bow, both Adam and Umar took of their armour and placed it and their weapons in a sack each. Kamal and Orhan tied the sack on to them using a medium length rope.

"Remember no killing unless absolutely necessary," reaffirmed Adam.

Umar and Adam both swam across the lake, with their sacks dragging behind them like heavy weights. When they finally swam though the waterfall they were greeted almost immediately by the bow of the ship. The ship was held in place by a large metal chain that went across the bow and was locked in place by a large wheel. Upon inspection they realised they could lower the chain if needed. As they quietly swam round the side of the ship they saw it was within a large lake inside the mountain, behind the stern the lake widened considerably allowing the ship to turn round when venturing out of the mountain. Outside the lake was a stone floor that was almost crescent shape, several meters across the floor was a large wall with an entrance in the middle. Adam found a rope ladder by the side of the vessel and climbed on board, followed by Umar. As they boarded the main deck Umar quickly opened his sack and took out a piece of flint. Adam broke a piece of wood from a side railing which Umar set alight using a metal dagger and the piece of flint. Umar used the fire to set alight the lowered sails and part of the upper decks, he then threw the lit piece of wood down a hatch to the lower decks.

Both Adam and Umar quickly jumped off the ship and swam back outside the mountain; they hid round the side of the water fall behind some large rocks on the side of the mountain. Upon seeing Adam and Umar hiding Kamal and Orhan signalled for the soldiers to begin their attack.

"Takbir!" shouted Kamal.

"Allahu Akbar!" yelled the entire army; this was repeated over and over again. Eventually Umar and Adam could just about hear some commotion coming from inside the mountain. Soon the invaders starting coming out from the mountain attired in their animal skins and armed with swords and spears. They tried to swim through the lake with their fur and heavy weapons, due to the burning vessel. This proved too much for them and so they quickly dropped their weapons and started taking off the skins before they sank into the lake.

Adam and Umar was surprised to see that the people hidden under the skins bore a remarkable resemblance to the Bani Hakeem and the Bani Khalid with regards to facial features and skin tone. Hundreds and hundreds of invaders came rushing out of the waterfall and with no weapons and drenched robes, they still swam towards the Bani Hakeem. They were yelling and screaming as they swam closer and closer, the Bani Hakeem were yelling at them to stop as they approached the bank, standing knee deep in the water. The invaders ignored their pleas and lunged at them, several of the archers unleashed their arrows which struck the invaders on the legs, they immediately fell to the floor clutching their wounds.

Adam and Umar swam back into the mountain once they realised that no more invaders were coming out. Through the intense smoke they both swam to the edge of the lake. They lifted themselves up onto the stone floor and quickly put on their armour and armed themselves.

The stairs in the entrance lead up the mountain through a narrow passage, as they travelled up they heard a muffled voice screaming. Once they reached the top of the stairs they came to the entrance of a large room, which was circle in shape. There were two levels, five meters above was a stone balcony that went round the entire room. On the ground was a bare floor with various symbols and words carved into the walls. As Adam walked up to the wall he realised that he recognised the words. Adam dragged his finger over the letters, reading them softly.

"'As our elders before us, so shall we'," read Adam quietly "most of the words have worn away, can you see anything Umar?" Umar walked round the bare room searching the walls for any information when he stopped suddenly.
"Major, come take a look at this," Adam rushed over to Umar's side.
"What is that?" asked Adam.
"Can't you see? It's a family tree and look at the top," Adam's eyes widened.
"We have to stop this quick Umar."
As they both turned around four arrows came flying down and struck the floor several feet away from them, clearly a warning short they both thought. They heard clapping up in the balcony, as they both looked up they saw four invaders dressed in their battle gear, each holding a bow that was armed. Between the four invaders stood a man and woman dressed in long black robes. Both of them had long hair, the man's to his shoulder and woman to her waist. Within their hair was red string tied amongst their hair strands, their eyes seemed black and their skin light brown.
"You are not men of fear, unlike those that you keep company with," said the man in a very deep tone.
"You insult yourselves supporting such pathetic creatures," added the woman in a scornful voice. Adam lowered his sword but kept his shield close to his chest.
"Who are you?" asked Adam, they both laughed at him.
"You know who we are; you have read our secret texts which our elders and master have blessed this mountain with. But you will never tell anyone of what you know. The order and balance must be kept, that is the way of our elders and my master."
"Tell us who your master is?!" demanded Umar.
"You dare demand his presence!" yelled the woman,
"Nobody can demand such a thing, it is he that demands.

Know your place worms!" Adam took a step forward and was met with an arrow, which he quickly blocked with his shield. "My name is Adam ibn Mustafa, Major of the Sultan's armour, the Caliph of the Islamic Empire. We demand your immediate surrender."

"And if we decline?" asked the man sarcastically, Adam smiled at his response.

"If you decline? Then the Sultan will send an army so large that when the beginning of his forces reaches the banks of this lake the end of the army will still not have left the empire's capital." The mysterious couple no longer found their presence amusing, as they knew Adam's threat was real. "Well I guess we better make sure that you never reach the Sultan," said the man coldly.

Over two thousand invaders stood on the banks of the lake, angry and spewing venomous words at the Bani Hakeem in their strange language. Kamal and Orhan knew that even with their weapons they could not hold all of them off, it was only a matter of time before they attacked them in full force and overcame them.

"Kamal, what do we do?" asked Orhan.

"We wait and pray to Allah, Most High, for support."

Adam and Umar ran forward, holding their shields above their head as the arrows came flying down. They ran up a narrow passage which led up to the balcony, half way up two invaders blocked the entrance by firing arrows. Umar hid behind Adam as he ran quickly up with his shield in front of him. Adam knocked over both of the invaders with his shield, the two invaders on the left side fired arrows at Adam which Umar blocked with his shield. Umar quickly threw his sword at one of the invader archers, which penetrated his stomach. Before the other invader could fire a second shot Umar threw his dagger which lodged in his neck. Adam used his sword to take out the invader on the floor but was quickly tackled by the last remaining invader, which sent both of them flying down the stairs.

"You look familiar," said the man.

"My name is Umar ibn Idris and I am a descendant from the Bani Khalid." Both of them were angered at his words and quickly picked up the weapons on the floor, as Umar charged at them with his shield he was able to block the arrows fired by the woman. Umar knocked her down to the ground with his shield but the man quickly swung his sword at Umar and cut his side deeply, as he fell to the floor the man held the sword over Umar's head.

"Never will we be brought down by a dog from the Bani Khalid," the words fuelled the anger inside Umar and as the man lifted his sword slightly Umar grabbed the blade with his hands stopping him from lowering it. As the man pushed down he could see the blade cutting Umar's palms, but Umar didn't scream or let go. He stood up, still holding the blade; the man was shocked at Umar's will and strength. Umar lifted the blade higher and kicked the man in the chest, as he fell back he quickly pulled out the dagger from the dead invader's neck and threw into the man's forehead, killing him instantly. With the anger gone he felt the intense pain in his hands and fell to his knees. He heard screaming from behind him and saw the woman running towards him with an arrow in her hand; Umar held out his arm to block the arrow. When the woman was only inches away an arrow came shooting past and pierced her through her back. As she lay dead on the floor Umar saw Adam standing by the stair entrance, with a bow, Adam had several cuts on his face and red knuckles.

"Did you take care of the last one?" asked Umar, Adam let out a long sigh.

"Just about," he replied, "quickly get their bodies!"

The invaders anger began to overflow and soon several of them charged at the Bani Hakeem, with no choice they had to fire at them. Soon most of the invaders started to attack and began overpowering the Bani Hakeem. With death eminent Kamal knew they had to retreat, when all of a sudden the burning vessel began to come through the waterfall.

The hissing sound of the water landing on the ship made the invaders look back; they immediately stopped their attack and stared at their burning vessel. Soon after a small boat came from behind with Adam and Umar rowing forward, once the invaders saw them they began to charge towards them. Kamal and Orhan ordered the Bani Hakeem to quickly fire at the invaders to save the Major and Captain but before they could Umar held up the dead bodies of their leaders. The invaders froze; they looked at each other like scared children and began to scream and cry. As Adam and Umar made their way through the distraught invaders without being attacked, they were helped onto the banks my Kamal and Orhan.

"What do we do now Major?" asked Kamal, "Shall we leave them?"

"No," replied Adam, "we are going to take them back to Abu Rashid."

"What!" replied Orhan in anger, "These savages have murdered our people for years we can now destroy them!"

"I said no!" yelled Adam angrily, "There is much you don't know, now obey my orders and help them onto land."

19.
Secrets on the wall

For three days the invaders had settled within the walls of
Abu Rashid, to Adam and Umar's pleasant surprise Chief
Najib showed no resistance when they were brought to the
southern fortress wall. Despite the cries of anger and concern
of a vast number of his people, he refused his guards to watch
over them with weapons but rather to show kindness and
compassion.

On the first day Adam spoke with Chief Najib alone
in his quarters and wanted to know why he accepted his past
attackers with no qualms or suspicion.
"To be honest Major I don't know why, upon seeing them in
their sorry state I was compelled to help them. Even now
when I see them within my city my mind reminds me of the
past pains yet my heart is pleased that they are here." Adam
looked at the Chief with a level of respect and admiration
similar to that of the Sultan.
"Your honesty and actions overwhelm me Sir," replied the
Major, "the heart finds tremendous content in two things, in

the remembrance of his Lord and love for His Prophet, PBUH. These noble actions you have performed acknowledge both. The Prophet, PBUH, acted in the same with his enemies and we only imitate those that we love and of course to love the Messenger, PBUH, is to remember the Creator who he represents." The Chief's tears flowed from his eyes greatly, for he did not feel worthy of such a feeling.

Adam and Umar, with several members of the Bani Hakeem visited the lair of the invaders several times to gain more information of their new guests.

Even though they could communicate basic words that the Bani Hakeem understood, it still proved difficult to obtain information from them. Soon Adam and Umar gained enough information from the texts that were carved onto the walls. Adam and Umar requested a private meeting with Chief Najib and Amina for both parties to update on recent events.

Under the starry night sky with the full moon reflecting its bright glow below on the city square sat Adam, Umar, Chief Najib and Amina at the chief's table. Adam put a piece of flat wood onto the table, on the wood were carvings that they had compiled from their numerous visits to the mountain by the lake.

"Apologies Chief Najib for hardly being in the city whilst you welcomed your new guests," said Adam.

"No apologies required Major," replied Chief Najib, "we know the nature for you absent and are both eager to learn what you have uncovered." Adam placed his hand over the wooden tablet and leaned closer to the Chief.

"We have uncovered quite a lot Sir, more than we ever hoped for. I feel it would be best for Umar to tell you what we uncovered." Adam slid the tablet in front of Umar; he cleared his throat as he picked it up.

249

"Do you know much about the history of the Bani Hakeem, Chief Najib?" asked Umar, "Such as where they originated from and the reason for the names of their people and their city?" Chief Najib let out a deep breath and looked over at his sister briefly.

"We were often kept in the dark on such topics, I'm not even sure if my father knew. I guess the shortest answer would be no Captain." Umar nodded, showing mild disappointment on his face."

"Was that not the answer you were expecting Captain?" asked Amina, Umar smiled.

"Actually it was Mother Amina; I just still find it sad when a people do not know their history." Umar looked over at the tablet before continuing.

"Abu Rashid and Bani Hakeem, two names that are missing pieces to a bigger puzzle. The history has been split into three different pathways and it has taken the contribution of all three to find the answers. It will probably be best to start from the beginning. Many years ago there was a Kingdom called Macuria, based in southern Egypt. This Kingdom, like most, became divided. Because of this three brothers, from the royal family, were banished by their father to the White Mountains. The names of those brothers were Khalid, Hakeem and Junaid."

"Hakeem?" blurted out Chief Najib, "So it is he who our people are descended from?" Umar smiled and nodded.

"You see Chief Najib; I am descended from the Bani Khalid who live on the other side of the White Mountains."

"So we are family?" asked Amina.

"That is correct," answered Umar, Chief Najib got out of his chair and walked over to Umar. He held him in a tight embrace for a long period before letting go.

"I wish my father had known that we were brothers, he certainly would've looked upon you as a son," said Chief Najib while shaking his head in pleasant disbelief.

"Thank you for your kind words Chief Najib but there is much else I need to say," once Chief Najib took his seat again Umar continued to disclose all that he knew.

"Once all the brothers and their families settled by the mountains they tried to recreate some of the same success they had in their old Kingdom. Through trade and ingenuity they were able to grow into a powerhouse, but once again fighting occurred and both Hakeem and Junaid left and went their separate ways.

"Where did you obtain the names of the brothers from?" asked Amina.

"From a family tree carved into the walls of the Bani Junaid's lair. We also found out that after many generations the chief of the Bani Khalid sent some of his people to reconcile with the two other tribes and once again join together to form a Kingdom."

"What was the name of the chief?" enquired Chief Najib, who was desperate to know.

"His name was not mentioned on the carvings, but it stated that the Bani Hakeem accepted his offer and for a brief time both tribes worked together, the Bani Hakeem and Bani Khalid." Amina looked over at her brother and grabbed his arm tightly.

"Don't you see brother it was Abu Rashid, that was his name." Chief Najib thought for a moment and then his eyes widened upon the realisation.

"It all makes sense; the name of our city is the name of the chief that brought unity to our people."

"That's what I and the Major deduced too, for the Bani Khalid had spoken of an Abu Rashid that had accepted Islam on behalf of their tribe and pledged allegiance to Hazrat Umar ibn Khattab, May Allah Be Pleased with him. We also assume that he was the one that brought Islam to the Bani Hakeem also."

"So what happened to our people, why did they turn away from Islam?" asked Amina. Umar looked over to Adam and gestured with his hand that he should carry on with the discussion.

"No Umar," replied Adam shaking his head-, "these are your people it is best that you tell them."

"Very well Major," replied Umar, "it seems at some point in history a man came to the Bani Junaid, just before Abu Rashid's representative did. This man was able to infiltrate through the ranks of the Bani Junaid and gather followers, secretly, until he eventually took charge. Through brainwashing and limiting their education he and his followers were able to take complete control of the Bani Junaid. Soon after they started to try and infiltrate the Bani Hakeem also but fortunately Abu Rashid's representative had arrived and accepted the pledge of the Bani Hakeem just in time. Abu Rashid was able to work out the intentions of Bani Junaid spies and cast them out, threatening to destroy them entirely."

"So was no further attempts made by Abu Rashid to win the hearts of the Bani Junaid?" asked Chief Najib.

"We couldn't find any records that suggest he did."

"Then what happened?" enquired Amina.

"The records say that efforts made by the Bani Junaid to attack the Bani Hakeem were quickly given up, as once the tribes were united under Abu Rashid they became too powerful. Instead they focused on creating an army based on savagery and blind loyalty; this was done by limiting their education and changing their language so the Bani Junaid could not learn anything from outside their tribe. Eventually with each generation dependence of the leaders grew and grew until they could no longer function without the orders from their leaders."

Both Amina and Chief Najib began to grow uneasy at the information that was being given to them; never would they have thought that this enemy had been so close to them for so many generations.

"Who was this man that started all this?" asked Amina angrily. Adam looked over to Umar and signalled he wanted to respond to the question.

"Mother Amina, for days we have gone through every piece of writing and drawing that has been placed on their walls. We don't know why they have recorded everything; maybe they see it as their historical library for their future leaders. But the one piece of information they have not written is who started all this. We don't know who they follow or what their sole intention was.

"Why do you think they have kept this hidden Major?" asked Chief Najib.

"My theory is that they are still working on their goal and recording their objectives may jeopardise everything."

"But all this doesn't matter now as they're dead," said Chief Najib, both Adam and Umar looked at each other briefly, "what is it?" asked Chief Najib.

"It appears the leaders of the Bani Junaid were also following orders from someone above them," said Umar, "someone they referred to as 'master' but we never found out who or where he is."

Both Chief Najib and Amina stared at Umar for a moment in silence; Chief Najib got up and started pacing around the table. Amina could see the look of worry on her brother's face as he tried to think what the best course of action was. As he walked behind Amina she leaned back and grabbed his hand.

"Najib please sit down, you don't have to carry this burden alone."

"But I am the chief Amina; I am the one who is supposed to carry it." Adam got up from his chair and walked up to chief Najib.

"Yes you are the chief Sir, but you now have the support of the Sultan and his empire, so allow this burden to be shared as we are altogether in this, ok?" Chief Najib felt some relief by hearing these words, they both sat back down.

"I'm still puzzled as to why our elders turned away from Islam, if it wasn't the leaders of the Bani Junaid than who else could it have been?" asked Amina.

"There was only one sentence that we found regarding this," said Umar, "it read *'destruction is from their own hand'* but we couldn't find anything else. We assume that once the Bani Hakeem turned away from Islam they then broke away from the Bani Khalid, which led to them being vulnerable to attack."

"I believe that the reason the Bani Junaid kept attacking again and again was simply to keep you weak, so you could never be what you once were," said Adam, "and that's why they started attacking the Bani Khalid so they could expand their army.

"Is that everything?" asked Amina.

"No," replied Adam, he reached into his pocket and pulled out a small piece of beige cloth that he handed to Chief Najib.

"What is this?" asked Chief Najib.

"We found an occurring symbol on the wall, I know I have seen it somewhere before but I can't remember where." Both Chief Najib and Amina looked at the drawing of the symbol; it was three triangle tips connected together with the middle triangle being taller than the other two. Above the triangle was a single line that was at an angle; at the bottom of the line were two other smaller lines that were connected to it. The smaller lines opened up outwards and appeared like a triangle but without a base line.

Chief Najib and Amina studied the symbol carefully. "Have you seen it before Najib?" asked Amina; Chief Najib studied the symbol further before looking at his sister and shaking his head.

"No, nothing like that at all." Chief Najib handed the cloth back to Adam.

"Was there anything on the walls about the forest and the beast or curse?" asked Amina.

"No Mother Amina, not even the forest itself was mentioned," replied Adam.

Chief Najib walked with Adam alone in the fields outside the fortress walls; they both looked at the trench that still surrounded the city.

"Kamal has informed that you do not wish to fill the trench yet Major?"

"No Sir, while we have stopped the attacks by the Bani Junaid will still have the matter of the beast in the forest, the trench may come in useful."

"I see, have you thought about the possibility of not doing anything Major? The situation has improved and we have access to clean water, as well as more people to help with farming. We have the increase of protection with the Bani Junaid now living in Abu Rashid; perhaps we could leave that part of the forest to whatever lurks there." Adam thought about his words carefully, the confliction he had in his heart stopped him from speaking at that moment.

"I can see that you have something on your mind Major, please speak."

"Chief Najib, as your city grows so will your need for expanding the city, raw materials and land will become a necessity. This forest is the only one that is in close proximity, if we were to think for the next five to ten generations there will come a time when that area will be needed." Chief Najib thought about Adam's words carefully.

"Are you saying that we must rid the forest of the beast Major?"

"No Sir, I am simply looking at the situation, there are two factors that I feel you must look at. First, as I mentioned

255

before as your city and its people expand the usage of more land and materials is essential. Secondly, and I feel this is the important of the two, can we both be absolutely sure that whatever does lurk in those woods will always remain there. With the women and children living in Abu Rashid, so close to the woods are you content to take that chance?" Chief Najib knew after hearing the second point that he could not be idle, of course there was no guarantee they would be safe he thought.

As Chief Najib remained silent on the words of Adam, he looked back at his city.

"It is true Major that the threat of that beast will always been on my mind as will it be for whoever that follows me after. Never will parents and elders feel completely content with their children running around these fields, knowing that danger lurks so close. It seems we have traded one prison for another."

"Chief Najib, there is something that I have not told you yet, something that I disclosed to your father." Chief Najib became curious and partly annoyed about the withheld information.

"Is there a reason you are withholding it?"

"Yes Sir, at the time we had more pressing matters with the passing of your father and the invading of the Bani Junaid. I believed that this information would have distracted us if brought up then."

"Seems reasonable, can you please disclose it to me now?"

"Very well, a while ago I and my men searched the forest to find out what was lurking in there. During our search we came across a mine."

"A mine?"

"Yes Sir, a gold mine," Chief Najib's face changed in the same manner as his father did when he found out, "the gold within that mine is vast, it would be enough gold for everyone in this city for the next ten generations." Chief

Najib kept silent; he looked back at his city, thinking of the peace and happiness of his people that had long been missing.

"The beast, does it prevent us from getting to the mine?"

"I believe the beast actually lives in the mine, when we followed the path there didn't seem to be anywhere else it can inhabit."

"I see, in your honest opinion Major do you think with the Bani Junaid on our side we can defeat this creature without too many casualties?"

"It's hard to say Sir without seeing it; perhaps we could do another search of the area for better intelligence."

"Very well Major, if the beast does appear too powerful for us to contend with what would you suggest then?"

"The Sultan has tasked me with helping this city; at the moment my task is only half complete. If I am unable to complete my mission then myself and Umar will return back to the Sultan and seek his advice, perhaps he will send a large army to help with the situation." The Chief nodded in agreement, Adam's suggestions seemed the best way forward he thought.

Adam met with Umar in their quarters and explained what had been agreed. Umar was happy to go back to the capital, if needed, as he would be able to see if any members of the Bani Khalid survived. Later on that night Chief Najib led the people in prayer for Isha, Adam had advised him that the leader of the people should be the one to lead the prayers.

After the prayer Adam was invited to meet with the Chief at his table, alone. Once seated Chief Najib smiled and handed Adam a few dates, as they ate they both discussed the situation of the Bani Junaid and how they seemed to be progressing well with the Bani Hakeem.

"Major there is something else that I wish to speak to you about, it's about Umar?"

"What about him Sir?"

"My sister Amina wanted me to enquire about him regarding marriage; she has been looking to marry and asked my advice. I said that I thought you or Umar would be a good choice, what are your thoughts on this?"

"Umar is an exceptional person Chief Najib; there are few people that the Sultan loves as much as Umar. My initial answer would be that you would find fewer people of his character. However Umar would not accept any proposal without first seeking advice and permission from the Sultan."

"Very well, we can ask Umar to seek the Sultan's advice when he next journeys there."

"Yes Sir, I will speak with Umar about it when we return to our quarters."

"Well unless there is anything else Major we should retire for night," the Chief began to get up from his chair, Adam leaned forward and tapped him on the forearm.

"Actually there is one last thing Sir, if I can have your attention for just a moment longer?"

"Of course," replied Chief Najib as he sat back down, "what is it Adam?"

"There was something else that I discovered when searching the woods. I found a large cemetery."

"A cemetery, how many graves did you see?"

"Almost a thousand Chief Najib," the Chief was shocked at the figure. He knew that many of his people had never returned from the forest, but he never imagined that the figure was that high."

"One thousand," replied the Chief, "how long has this thing been killing us, this has to stop Major."

"I know Sir." Chief Najib got up from his seat and looked over at the mountain to the north.

"No longer will we be prisoners in our home again," Chief Najib looked back at Adam with strong conviction in his face, "when you go back to the forest you will take an army with you Major."

"But Chief Najib it's difficult to go in undetected and investigate quietly with a large number of people."

"Major, in the history of my people I have never known us to have sent a large army to fight whatever is lurking there. We now have the might of two tribes plus the Major of the Sultan's army; if we are not ready now then we will never be ready."

"What are you asking me to do Sir?" Chief Najib placed his hand on Adam's shoulder.

"I am ordering you to march into the forest with the Bani Junaid and the Bani Hakeem, that's nearly four thousand men. Armed and ready to fight whatever is in front of them, will you do this for me Major?" Adam knew that this was a risk; he never marched into battle without knowing what was in front of him. But he could not imagine any creature being able to defeat such a large army by itself.

Adam agreed to lead both tribes but not until the Bani Junaid had learned better communication skills, as it was imperative to the mission. Chief Najib ordered both Kamal and Orhan to arrange lessons to be given to the Bani Junaid by members of his tribe, to assist them with their speaking. A deadline of two weeks was set before Adam would lead them to meet the beast.

20.
Alsam

Adam looked ahead and saw the city of Abu Rashid; he was standing on the ledge of the mountain that looked down on the entire city. Above the city he saw a huge round object floating above it.

"The Sultan's dream," he whispered, he looked up and was waiting for the floating city to fall down on top of the one below, as he was told by the Sultan. As expected he saw a gold coloured object travelling at speed crash into the city above, Adam knew this was the time that the city would fall, but it didn't. Adam looked upon the city and wondered why the events had changed, all of a sudden he saw people on the upper city falling off. Their bodies plummeting to the empty city below, Adam looked on in horror and then realised that they were being pushed off by other people in the city.

"They're killing each other!" shouted Adam, the pain, anger, disgust and powerlessness engulfed him completely. Adam looked closer and realised that the people falling were both the Bani Hakeem and Bani Junaid.

"This is now, they're still facing the same destruction but from who!" Adam could not understand what he was seeing; he had not prevented anything, the city of Abu Rashid was still heading for destruction. Adam felt a hand on his shoulder and saw it was the Sultan, dressed in a white and gold robe and turban. The Sultan remained silent, Adam noticed that he had his right hand closed and was clearly holding something. The Sultan opened up his hand and in the middle of his palm was a small gold nugget.

Adam woke up from his bed covered in a cold sweat, as he sat up he looked over and saw that Umar's bed was empty. Adam walked over to the bucket full of water and began to perform wudu, as he was washing the adhan began to be called.

The deadline of two weeks had arrived and he was due to lead the people out to the forest after Fajr prayer today. Adam walked through up the pathway towards the city square; Chief Najib had ordered the building of a mosque just outside the western wall after Adam returned from his mission with the Bani Junaid and Bani Hakeem.

The four thousand men lined up in prayer, with their armour on, following Chief Najib as he completed the two rakaats. After the prayer he suggested to Adam that it would be best if he gave his speech by the forest to the men, rather than in the city square. As the men prepared to arm themselves, Adam noticed Umar speaking with Amina and Chief Najib. Once the conversation finished Umar quickly made his way to Adam's side.

"Everything ok Umar?" asked Adam, Umar seemed slightly embarrassed at the question.

"You already know, don't you Sir?" replied Umar, Adam smiled and patted Umar on the back.

"Yes, Inshallah, it will be a blissful marriage, the first time in generations the Bani Khalid and Bani Hakeem joined together through marriage and blood."

"Not without the Sultan's permission," replied Umar.

"Of course Umar but for now keep your mind empty, let's make sure we complete this mission and then on to happier times."

The four thousand strong army marched through the entrance of the fortress lead by Adam, Umar, Kamal and Orhan. Adam ordered his men to recite the Oneness of Allah, Most High, as they marched; the Bani Junaid had embraced Islam after one week of living in Abu Rashid. The treatment and behaviour of the Bani Hakeem had shocked them in a pleasant way and won their hearts to the faith.

The words 'La Ilaha Ilallah' were heard across the land; over and over again the words were repeated. At the outskirts of the forest Adam ordered the soldiers to form into four infantries, each to be led by one of the four senior officers.

"Bismillahir Rahmanir Raheem, I testify that there is One God and Muhammad, PBUH, is His Messenger. We are here today on the commands of the Sultan, the Leader of the Believers and Allah's representative on earth. We must hold fast to that intention at all times, straying from the correct intention is the difference between success and failure, in this world and the next." Adam looked over at the soldiers and then to his senior officers.

"We are one today; under Islam we have no more divisions. We will march together, we will fight together, we will bleed together and Inshallah we will be victorious together."

"Takbir!" shouted Umar.

"Allahu Akbar!" shouted both the Bani Hakeem and Bani Junaid; this was chanted three times before Adam turned round and started marching towards the beast.

They marched slowly forward, Adam did not want to walk them through the graveyard, as it would affect the moral of the soldiers as well as cause disrespect to the graves by having four thousand soldiers trampling on them. Once they walked along the outskirts of the cemetery, which added a longer amount of time, Adam led them back on course in the direction of the mine.

As the trees began to be fewer and the signs of destruction became apparent with uprooted trees and large craters in the ground, Adam immediately ordered them to stop. With only one hundred meters separating them from the entrance of the mine, Adam knew that the beast would not be far away.

He organised the infantries to form into two-by-two formations, himself and Umar leading the front two and Kamal and Orhan leading the rear. As Adam stared ahead with a four thousand strong army behind him, he waited for a sign from the creature. He would not march out into the open in case of an ambush of some kind.

"Major," whispered Umar, "on your right," Adam looked over and saw a darkness spread across a vast number of trees, had the beast snuck up around them as they marched, he thought. The shadow appeared to grow larger and then appeared in front, as well as on the side. With each passing moment the darkness appeared to spread further until it completely engulfed them from all sides. Adam looked around and saw that they were imprisoned in some kind of dark circle, the ground began to shake violently and the trees swayed. The soldiers began to become fearful and some shouted out, Adam knew that he was not dealing with a creature or some kind of enemy, this was something different. Adam looked at his sword and then at the weapons of the soldiers, he remembered the words of Sheikh Yusuf, what he kept missing each time.

"Drop your weapons!" shouted Adam, Umar heard the order also and shouted out the same, gradually the soldiers heard and started to drop their weapons. Slowly the tremors grew less and the darkness decreased, once every soldier dropped his weapon the tremors ceased completely and the shadow disappeared, except for the front which remained. Adam and his men looked at the darkness ahead; the soldiers were both confused and relieved.

"What just happened?" asked Kamal, Adam turned round to face everyone.

"We need to leave now, nobody pick up anything," ordered Adam.

"Leave?" questioned Orhan, "But our mission…"

"Is over," Adam interrupted, "I am in command and I order everyone to retreat back to Abu Rashid, now." Umar ran up to the front with Kamal and Orhan, as they marched out Adam remained staring at the darkness ahead.

"What is it you want?" whispered Adam, before a flash of light appeared ahead. Adam opened his eyes and rubbed them, his blurred vision slowly came back into focus. On the ground he noticed shiny specks on the floor, as he bent down he saw the same small pieces of gold as before. He took it in his hand and headed back to the city.

As Adam made his way back to the soldiers he kept going over the dream he had last night, also he reminded himself of the teachings of Sheikh Yusuf and the line that he had read on the walls in the mountain '*destruction is from their own hand*'. Adam knew that all the pieces were linked but he did not know how.

"You left all our weapons!" shouted Chief Najib at Adam, who was surrounded by Kamal, Umar and Orhan by the Chief's table.

"Yes Sir I did," replied Adam, not reacting to the anger being showered on him.

"Major, that was almost our entire supply of weaponry, it will take months to replace them," said Chief Najib. Adam looked at the Chief sternly and then to Kamal and Orhan.

"Did you tell the Chief what happened out there?" they both nodded, Adam then turned his attention to Umar.

"Go to our quarters and get our things ready, we're heading back to the Sultan immediately," Umar went to rush off but was stopped by the hand of Chief Najib.

"Wait a moment, what is going on, you're leaving?"

"Yes Sir," replied Adam, "the situation is too big for us to deal with, had we not have dropped our weapons then and there we would've been killed." Chief Najib looked over at his men to see if they confirmed the same account, both of them just remained silent.

"How can you be so sure Major?" asked the Chief.

"Because I didn't understand the instructions of Sheikh Yusuf until now. He told me several times not to take anything with me when going to that part of the forest, but I picked up a weapon off the floor when I went there the first time, that's what set off the attack," Umar walked over to Adam and stood by his side.

"So what is it Sir and why is it protecting the gold?" asked Umar, Adam bit his lip as he pondered over the question.

"I don't know, I don't know why it's there and I don't know why so many have been killed." At that moment a noise could be heard coming up the path, as they all turned round a young man in armour came running up yelling.

"Calm down," ordered the Chief, the young man stopped running and crouched down to get his breath.

"Sir…they're outside."

"Who is outside?" asked Chief Najib."

"An army, a big army Sir," Adam and Umar looked at each other.

"How big is this army soldier?!" Chief Najib shouted.

"Ten thousand Sir!" Everybody was silent and shocked; they kept exchanging glances to one another.

"Sir shall we evacuate to the mountain before they arrive? We don't have enough weapons to fight them, if we don't evacuate now we'll be destroyed with ease," said Kamal.

"They're already outside the southern wall waiting for someone to come out," said the young man.

"Wait a minute," said Adam, "ten thousand soldiers came to the city walls without making a sound, and they're simply waiting for someone to come and speak with them?" the young boy nodded nervously, Adam looked over at Umar, who was already smiling.

"Chief Najib," called Adam, "come with me, there is someone I need to introduce you to."

"But the army…"

"They're no threat Chief Najib," said Adam, interrupting the Chief.

As Chief Najib walked out the main entrance, with Adam and Umar by his side, he was greeted by ten thousand soldiers, all on horseback. There sharp and crisp blue uniforms stood like an ocean wave, there brass buttons glistened in the sunlight. In the front of the army stood a man dressed in a long black robe with a white turban and cloak on top, beside him was a beautiful black horse that he held the red reigns of. On top of the horse sat an elderly man in a light grey suit and white turban.

"Chief Najib, I would like you to meet the Sultan," said Adam. Chief Najib immediately ran to the elderly man on the horse, he reached out and held his hand.

"Salam Alaikum my Sultan, May Allah reward you for coming in our hour of need," Sheikh Abdullah smiled at the Chief and gestured with his head to the man standing next to him.

"Walaikum Salam young man, apologies but you have me mistaken; the Leader of the Believers is he." Chief Najib immediately looked at the Sultan, who was smiling at the mistake.

"I'm so sorry your majesty please forgive me…"

"Come now it is perfectly fine," said the Sultan, "I cannot think of a better person to be mistaken for, I only wish I were half the man Sheikh Abdullah is." Chief Najib took the Sultan's hand and kissed it, the Sultan embraced the Chief tightly. Adam and Umar walked over to the Sultan.

"Salam Alaikum Leader of the Believers," said both of them, the Sultan returned the greeting and embraced them both

"I have longed to meet you again, thank Allah, Most High, that you made it to the city. Where is Ali?"

The look on Adam and Umar's face told everything.

"I see," replied the Sultan sadly, "to Allah we belong and to Him we return, how did it happen?"

"There is so much to tell you Sir, perhaps it would be best to go inside so we can catch up on things," replied Adam.

At the Chief's table sat the Sultan, Adam, Chief Najib, Umar and Sheikh Abdullah. Adam informed the Sultan of all that had happened since they left the dock in the capital. The Sultan remained silent the whole time not even moving as Adam revealed the entire journey.

"Subhan Allah," said the Sultan once Adam finished his account, "well done Major and you also Captain," the Sultan looked over at Chief Najib and then back to Umar.

"Najib, would it be possible for Amina to come and join us?" asked the Sultan. The Chief called for his sister immediately who came and sat by her brother nervously, the Sultan smiled as he looked at Umar and Amina.

"I have been informed that the two of you wish to be married, is that correct?" Amina nodded shyly as did Umar.

"Captain Umar did not want to accept the proposal without your permission Sultan," added Adam. The Sultan nodded in appreciation and looked over at the Chief.

"I am happy to allow it on one condition."

"What would that be Sultan?" asked a nervous Chief Najib. The Sultan placed his hand on Umar's shoulder.

"This is very painful for me Umar as I have enjoyed your company so," said the Sultan, "my condition is that Umar become Chief of Abu Rashid, through your children's bloodline you will unite the Bani Khalid and Bani Hakeem and now that the Bani Junaid are also living within the city a strong Kingdom can be restored again." The Sultan looked over at the Chief to see his reaction.

"Of course Sultan, it would be an honour to serve under Captain Umar, my brother." Sheikh Abdullah signalled for the takbir to be chanted, which it was, three times.

"My Sultan, why did you come here and how did you find your way through the mountains?" asked Adam, the Sultan smiled and looked over at Sheikh Abdullah to respond.

"We can thank the Bani Khalid for that," said the Sheikh.

"Are they safe?!" asked Umar, the Sheikh smiled and nodded, "Alhamdullilah," said Umar.

"Yes, they managed to avoid the landslide; once they couldn't find you they went back to their tribe and then ventured back to Benghazi," said Sheikh Abdullah.

"Once the news reached me I immediately journeyed over with an army," added the Sultan.

"But how did you manage to make your way through the mountains with such a large army?" asked Umar.

"Again we can thank the Bani Khalid for that also; they know every part of that mountain including hidden pathways. Through their advice we were able to make it through within two weeks," replied Sheikh Abdullah. The Sultan stood up and looked at the heavily populated square, he pointed at Adam, who quickly got to his feet.

"Yes Sultan," said Adam.

"We have three tasks that need addressing, firstly the creature in the woods, secondly the mystery figure called 'master' and lastly the repeating symbol." Sheikh Abdullah slowly got to his feet with the aid of Umar and Najib."

"Major Adam has informed me of his dream in detail; do you require my interpretation Sultan?"

"Of course Sheikh Abdullah, I would never do anything without your consultation first." The Sheikh gestured for the Sultan and Adam to be seated.

"In order for me to tell you about the dream I will need to fill in a few blanks during your time here Major Adam."

"Thank you Sheikh, we are all desperate to know," replied Adam eagerly.

"Very well," said the Sheikh as he cleared his throat, "Bismillahir Rahman Raheem, many generations ago the Bani Hakeem and Bani Khalid were united as one. Soon after that they were blessed with incredible wealth…"

"The gold," said Chief Najib, interrupting the Sheikh, Adam placed his hand on Chief Najib's forearm to stop him from interrupting."

"Yes Chief Najib," answered the Sheikh, "you see the gold was used for the construction of these great walls, plus the technology you see within this city would not have been possible without the wealth they obtained. But slowly the gold corrupted the hearts of the people and soon killing began to incur. The graves you saw in the forest are people killed by their own tribe; this gold brought a curse out in the people themselves." Sheikh Abdullah placed his hand on the table, with his finger opened outward.

"There is no creature or curse killing the Bani Hakeem, whatever is in there is a mercy, it has protected the Bani Hakeem from becoming corrupted murderers again."

"We were destroyed by our own hand," said Amina, the Sheikh regrettably nodded in confirmation.

"That was why our elders left Islam, because of the gold and killing that followed it," said Chief Najib.

"The hearts of people have always been weak when it comes to wealth," said the Sultan.

"Not all people," added the Sheikh, the Sultan looked to his teacher with curiosity, "you see Sultan, the one who goes to the gold needs to have a heart that is unfazed by its beauty. Someone whose heart cannot be captured by this world and its gifts," the Sultan looked at everyone sitting around the table.

"Can you please give Sheikh Abdullah and myself a moment alone?" everyone quickly got up and left the two of them sitting at the table.

"You know what you have to do Sultan," said the Sheikh with a serious expression on his face. The Sultan looked up at the clouds in the sky before leaning closer towards his Sheikh.

"Yes my Sheikh, it seems this whole journey has been about this treasure. Tribes and kingdoms have been destroyed throughout time because of this yellow rock," Sheikh Abdullah nodded gently in agreement; he placed his hand over the Sultan's hand.

"You must break this chain of pain and misery. Mend this broken kingdom with the authority and strength that your Creator has given to you in this world.

The Sultan, Adam and Umar looked down at the ground at the many weapons that lay on the floor. Ahead of them the dark mist slowly appeared ten meters away. As the Sultan took a few steps forward the ground trembled silently. "Enough!" shouted the Sultan in a stern voice, the trembling immediately stopped. The Sultan walked up closer to the dark mist until he was only several meters away from the darkness.

"I am the Leader of the Believers and Allah's representative on earth, my heart finds no comfort in any of the gifts of this world. I know that I will face my Lord with the whole of my people standing on the other side as witnesses of my judgement. Whether gold or whether coal it makes no difference to me, so allow me to take it so I may help those in need!" the mist parted in the middle and the Sultan walked through in the direction of the mine. Adam and Umar walked forward several paces but the mist began to close up the parting before they could get through.

The Sultan entered the mine and looked at the gold submerged into the walls. He reached forward and pulled out a small piece of gold with his hand. At that moment with a large flash the darkness vanished instantly, Adam and Umar looked ahead and saw that the mine was now visible from a far.

"It was meant for him," said Umar, "that mine was not to be approached by anyone except the Leader of the Believers." The Sultan turned round and gestured for both Adam and Umar to come stand beside him in the mine.

"Both of you have done well, you have completed the mission that I gave you. Now a once broken kingdom can be what it once was."

With a loud thud the large gold block landed on the floor by the entrance of Abu Rashid. Chief Najib and Amina stared at it in awe.

"This is what caused the near destruction of my people?" asked Chief Najib. The Sultan nodded and placed his hand on Chief Najib's shoulder.

"Had you have gotten to the gold it would have destroyed you also."

"So what happens to the gold now?" asked Amina.

"My soldiers are in the mine now, they will dig out all the gold and we'll distribute it to those who need it. I will make sure that this city is restored to what it once was."

"Thank you Sultan," said Chief Najib.

Adam and Umar were speaking with some of the other soldiers in the field when Sheikh Abdullah tapped them both on the back with his stick.

"Well I guess we can start preparing for the wedding of the soon-to-be Chief," said the Sheikh with a smile on his face.

Umar blushed and pretended he had tasks to attend to before becoming too embarrassed, both Adam and Sheikh Abdullah laughed as Umar quickly scampered away.

"That symbol Adam," said Sheikh Abdullah, "please show it to me again," Adam took out the cloth and handed it to the Sheikh. The Sheikh looked over at the symbol and ran his finger over the thin line.

"Alsam," said the Sheikh."

"Alsam?" asked Adam, the Sheikh turned the cloth so Adam could see the symbol.

"That arrow like line is Alsam, a constellation."

"Yes I know of it, we can see it from here on some nights. What does it mean Sheikh?"

"You must find the constellation over three mountain tips, just like this. That is where you will find your answers to your questions."

"What questions Sheikh?"

"Who is the master and what does he want?" Adam looked at the symbol again.

"Do you know where these mountains are Sheikh?" Adam felt a firm hand on his shoulder; he turned round to see the Sultan.

"Yes we do know," replied the Sultan, he took the cloth from his hand and pointed to the mountain tips, "we may have another mission for you Major, if you're interested?" Adam smiled.

"Yes my Sultan."